Beastly Bones

ALSO BY WILLIAM RITTER
Jackaby

Beastly Bones

A Jackaby Novel

WILLIAM RITTER

ALGONQUIN   2015

Published by
Algonquin Young Readers
an imprint of Algonquin Books of Chapel Hill
Post Office Box 2225
Chapel Hill, North Carolina 27515-2225

a division of
Workman Publishing
225 Varick Street
New York, New York 10014

LIBRARY OF CONGRESS CATALOGING-IN-PUBLICATION DATA
Ritter, William.
  Beastly bones : a Jackaby novel / by William Ritter.–First edition.
    pages cm
  Summary: When dinosaur bones from a recent dig mysteriously go missing,
  and an unidentifiable beast starts attacking animals and people, leaving their
  mangled bodies behind, Abigail and her eccentric employer R. F. Jackaby,
  investigators of the supernatural in 1892 New England, find themselves
  hunting for a thief, a monster, and a murderer.
  ISBN 978-1-61620-354-2
  [1. Mystery and detective stories. 2. Supernatural–Fiction. 3. Monsters–
  Fiction. 4. Imaginary creatures–Fiction. 5. New England–History–
  19th century–Fiction.] I. Title.
  PZ7.R516Be 2015
  [Fic]–dc23   2015010990

10 9 8 7 6 5 4 3 2 1
First Edition

For Russ,
who has taught me that the wood knows best
what shape it ought to be,

& for Eleanor,
who has always followed her own path
and paved it with precious words.

Beastly Bones

Chapter One

"Follow my lead, Miss Rook," Jackaby said, rapping on the ornately trimmed door to 1206 Campbell Street. Were my employer a standard private investigator, those might have been simple instructions, but in the time I've been his assistant, I've found very little about Jackaby to be standard. Following his lead tends to call for a somewhat flexible relationship with reality.

Tall and lanky, Jackaby swam in his long, brown coat. It looked like it might have once been an expensive garment, but it was now battered and affixed inside and out with myriad clinking, jingling pockets and pouches, each loaded with trinkets and tools he insisted were essential to his work. Around his neck he had wound a ludicrously long scarf, the ends of which brushed the cobblestones as he walked.

On his head, stuffed over a dark mess of wild hair, was the main offender. Jackaby's cap, the knit monstrosity, was a patternless composite of uneven stitches and colors. The threads clashed with his scarf. They clashed with his coat. They even clashed with one another. Alone on a hat rack, the thing would have looked mismatched.

Jackaby was not an ugly man. He kept himself clean-shaven, and always seemed to smell of cloves and cinnamon. In a fine suit and tie he might have been downright attractive to the right sort of girl, but in his preferred garb he looked like an eccentric lunatic. He was fond of reminding me that "appearances aren't everything," but I dare say they aren't *nothing*, either. My employer can be single-minded about some things. Most things, in fact.

The woman who answered the door appeared far too overwhelmed by her own concerns to bother about silly hats, anyway. Jackaby and I soon found ourselves ushered past the threshold and into an elegantly furnished sitting room. The house looked like so many of the regal English manors to which my mother had dragged me as a child. My father was a bit of an explorer—you may have read about the intrepid Daniel Rook—but my mother much preferred tradition and civility. Mother took full advantage of my father's notoriety to find her way into countless London garden parties, and she brought me along in the hopes that a little exposure would make me wish to be a proper lady as well. It generally made me wish instead that I could go outside and play in the dirt, like my father.

In some ways, there was really nothing *new* about New England. Our current hostess looked as though she would have fit very comfortably into my mother's social circles. She introduced herself as Florence Beaumont and offered to take our coats. Jackaby flatly declined for both of us. I would have preferred he hadn't, as the heat of the chamber was a sharp contrast to the breeze outside. The spring of 1892 had arrived in New Fiddleham, but it had not yet fully chased away the last of the winter winds.

Mrs. Beaumont led us to a small alcove at the rear of the room. Within the recess were a pile of blankets, a little pink collar with a bell on the front, and a set of silver bowls perched on white doilies. In one bowl was a bit of what looked to be leftover tuna, and in the other were water, a great deal of cat hair, and a live fish. The fish circled uncomfortably, being nearly as wide as the bowl itself.

Jackaby squatted, resting his forearms on his knees and staring into the water. He watched the fish take a few cramped laps, studying its movements, and then he plucked a bit of damp cat hair from the rim, sniffed it, tasted it, and tucked it into a pocket somewhere in the depths of his coat.

I whipped out the little black notepad Jackaby had given me upon the completion of our first case, trying not to let Mrs. Beaumont see that I was still on the very first page.

"Your message said something about a sick cat?" I prompted the woman while my employer poked at the sticky pile of leftovers in the other bowl. "I'm sure Mr. Jackaby will want to see the animal."

The woman's lip quivered. "Mrs. W-W-Wiggles."

"Yes, and where is Mrs. Wiggles now?"

Mrs. Beaumont tried to answer, but she managed only a sort of squeak I could not decipher and gestured toward the alcove.

Jackaby stood. "Mrs. Wiggles is right here, isn't she?"

The woman nodded.

"Mrs. Wiggles is the fish, isn't she?"

She nodded again. "Only since recently," she sniffed.

"I see," Jackaby said.

His matter-of-fact response seemed to burst a dam within the woman. "You must think me mad! I didn't know to whom I could turn, but your name has come up from time to time. I entertain, you see. Very prominent people come to my soirees. Mayor Spade had tea here, just last week. Some of the people I dine with tell me that you specialize in things that are . . . that are . . . *different.*"

"To put it mildly," I submitted.

"Nice to hear I've come so highly recommended, madam," Jackaby said, turning his attention back to the big fish in the little bowl.

"Oh, I wouldn't call them recommendations, exactly,"

she added. "More like anecdotes, some of them warnings, actually . . ."

"Yes, yes, very nice." Jackaby's attention had migrated back to his investigation. He dropped to his hands and knees, peeking at the pile of blankets.

"I've always taken such good care of Mrs. Wiggles," the woman continued. "I keep her brushed and washed, and I buy her the most expensive cat food. I even get her fresh fish from Chandler's Market from time to time. At first I thought she was just feeling a bit off due to her–well–her state. But then she began to sprout s-s-scales, and now . . . now . . ." Mrs. Beaumont broke down again, her voice wavering into uncomfortable octaves.

"Due to her state?" I asked, trying to press forward. "What state was Mrs. Wiggles in?"

"She was pregnant," Jackaby answered for Mrs. Beaumont. The woman nodded.

"How did you know that?" I asked.

Jackaby pulled up the corner of the blanket to reveal a pile of adorable, sleeping kittens. Here and there a patch of scales peeked through the fur. The smallest had fuzzy gills, which puffed up and down as it snored, but they were precious nonetheless.

"Do I deduce correctly that, until recently, Mrs. Wiggles has had significantly more freedom to roam about at night?" Jackaby asked.

The woman blinked back to self-control. "Yes, yes, that's true. I generally leave the window open at night, and Mrs. Wiggles likes to pop out, but she would always be back home in the morning. I decided it was best to keep her in this past month, at least until she had her litter. It's been freezing cold out, anyway. Didn't want the poor thing–"

"Yes, that's all very good," Jackaby interrupted. "You mentioned you purchase fish for her from the market, occasionally. Is it also correct to assume you have been treating her to such morsels more often of late?"

"I just wanted her to be happier, cooped up indoors like–"

"Always the same sort of fish?"

"Er . . . yes. Mackerel from Chandler's Market. Was that wrong?"

"On the contrary, Mrs. Belmont–"

"Beaumont," she corrected quietly.

"On the contrary, Mrs. Beaumont, it may have been just the thing. Don't worry. We will see to it the animals receive adequate care."

"You're taking the kittens, too?" She sniffled. Her eyes welled up, and her lip quivered.

Jackaby sighed. "Give me just a moment to confer with my esteemed colleague." He gestured me closer as Mrs. Beaumont wrung her hands.

Jackaby leaned in and adopted the sort of hushed, secretive tones that one nearby cannot help but overhear. "Miss

Rook, on a scale of one to pomegranate, how dangerous would you say this situation has become?"

"Dangerous?" I faltered.

"Yes, Miss Rook," prompted Jackaby, "in your *expert* opinion."

"On a scale of one to pomegranate?" I followed his lead, checking over the notes I had scribbled in my notepad and speaking in my most audible, serious whisper. "I should think . . . acorn? Possibly badger. Time alone will tell."

My employer nodded solemnly.

"What? What is it? Can you make them . . . better?" Mrs. Beaumont fidgeted, worrying the lace on her collar as Jackaby considered his response.

"Contamination, madam. Viral infection, no doubt. You've been thoroughly exposed, but don't worry, you're probably just a carrier. It is most unlikely you will display any symptoms yourself. What's important now is to be sure the litter does not further contaminate the neighborhood."

"Is it really as bad as all that?" she asked. "Sh-should we tell the police or . . . or the animal control officer?"

"If you like." Jackaby looked thoughtful. "Of course, it might be best if we simply take Mrs. Wiggles and her litter to our facility and keep the whole thing quiet. I'm no expert in entertaining, but I do not imagine one's social standing would weather well the news that one is a carrier to an exotic, viral plague. How is Mayor Spade, by the way?"

Mrs. Beaumont sniffed and digested the detective's

words for a moment. "Let me fetch you a bigger bowl," she squeaked. "I want Mrs. Wiggles to be comfortable, at least." With one last sniffle, she ducked away into the house.

Some girls work in shops or sell flowers. Some girls find husbands and play house. I assist a mad detective in investigating unexplained phenomena—like fish that ought to be cats but seem to have forgotten how. My name is Abigail Rook, and this is what I do.

Chapter Two

In a few short minutes, my employer and I found our-selves back on the cobbled road, now with one box of somewhat fishy felines and a bulky, crystal punch bowl full of fresh water and a slightly hairy mackerel. Jackaby nobly opted to carry the kittens. The cool New England breeze was picking up in sporadic bursts, whistling through the narrow alleyways and making me keenly aware of the small patch of damp developing on my shirtwaist where the bowl occasionally sloshed.

"What was that show about back there, sir?" I asked, straining not to completely soak my blouse with fishy water.

"Show?" Jackaby raised an eyebrow.

"One to pomegranate? And I'm an expert, now?"

"As I understand it, you are a bit of an expert, albeit in

the rather monotonous field of digging up and studying old rocks. I found the title convenient at the time."

"Paleontology, not geology. I was studying fossils before we met, not old rocks, thank you."

"Ah, yes, fossils. In other words, bones that, over a great deal of time, have mineralized and turned to . . . what?"

"To stone."

"Stone. As in . . . rocks?"

"Oh, fine. I don't know if a handful of classes and one failed expedition qualify me as an expert, but all the same, I'd prefer that you not use my scant few credentials to lie to old ladies."

"I'll keep that in mind when next I find it necessary."

"Thank you for that. Speaking of which, shouldn't she be quarantined or something?" I asked, glancing back at the stately old house.

"What on earth for?" Jackaby tickled a soft orange nose as it poked gingerly out of the box. "Oh, that whole plague business. No, no—there isn't any virus. Nothing to worry about. I simply felt it would be much less jarring to the poor woman than the truth."

"And what's the truth, then?"

"Pervasive, carnivorous shape-shifters. Oh, look. This one has a fluffy dorsal fin! Hello there, little fellow."

I stopped in the street. The water sloshed over the far edge of the punch bowl, and the mackerel circled, obliviously.

"Would you run that last bit by me again, sir?"

"Don't be so bothered," Jackaby said. "I'm happy to explain. The dorsal refers to the ridge along his back. I was merely observing that—"

"Not about the fin! They're carnivorous shape-shifters?"

"Oh yes! It's a somatic camouflage. Isn't it marvelous? These little beasties are aggressive mimics of an exceptional degree. They physically adapt to take on the appearance of a local food source, infiltrating their prey and allowing their unwitting hosts to provide them with comfort, protection, and supplemental nutrients. Then, when they have won their trust, they devour them. It seems Mrs. Wiggles was fond of snacking on cats, up until she got herself cooped up."

"But that's horrific!"

"Not at all. That's nature. Cuckoos are aggressive mimics as well—brood parasites—and those little scamps get immortalized on finely crafted clocks."

"I . . . suppose." I continued walking, eying the mackerel more closely as we crossed the street. "Still, rather disturbing to think of a cat out there cannibalizing other cats."

"It isn't cannibalism if it's only camouflage, Rook. In your hands is proof enough that the beast wasn't feline at all. As soon as she was forced to identify a new, regular food source, her body adapted."

"So these . . . *things* can just magically turn into whatever creature they eat?"

"It isn't magic, Rook. It's science. The abilities of certain creatures to adapt spontaneously to fit in to their surroundings are well documented. Aristotle himself wrote an account of the camouflage mechanism of octopuses. They can change color spontaneously."

"Like chameleons?"

"Precisely. The biological mechanism at work here is more complicated, obviously, but not unlike a chameleon changing its skin. In fact, Darwin dubbed these little creatures *chameleomorphs*, in reference to the little lizards with their colorful camouflage. A misnomer, of course, as the term *chameleon* refers not to the adaptation, but rather to the Latin for 'lion of the ground,' but such is the tradition of naming one beast after another."

"That can't possibly be right. Charles Darwin never discovered shape-changing animals. He'd have written about it."

"Oh?" We crested the hill at the top of Market Street, and Jackaby gave me a sly smile as we started back down. "Didn't he?"

There was something about Jackaby that made me want to impress him. It might have been his earnest arrogance, or the way he spoke frankly and didn't pander or talk down to me. True, Jackaby could be brash and outright insulting—but being treated with kid gloves always felt like a greater insult. I wanted nothing more than to prove myself, and Jackaby gave me that chance. I would like to say, therefore, that I countered my employer's smirk with a witty rebuttal, or at least that I carried my weight in the ensuing conversation. Unfortunately, one does not always get what one would like.

Instead, just as I opened my mouth to speak, my heel caught on a broken piece of brickwork, and I pitched forward in a graceless stumble, drenching myself in fishy water before launching the crystal punch bowl—and its unhappy inhabitant—down the slope of bustling Market Street.

The crystal miraculously withstood the jarring drop and bumpy ride for the better part of a block, bouncing down the cobbled road like a runaway sled. New Fiddleham streets are never empty, and half a dozen passersby stood watching until the road bent off to the right and the bowl slammed into the curb. Pedestrians jumped aside as the container exploded at their feet, spraying the storefront of a small leather shop with expensive shrapnel. The last glittering shards had not yet spun to a stop before I was back on my feet and after it.

The startled mackerel flopped and waggled across the damp cobbles, and from half a block away I could see it balancing on the edge of the storm drain. I cursed under my breath and willed the fish to just hold still. Was it too much to ask that, just once, one of my failures be a simple little thing, instead of compounding itself into a big ordeal? Time slowed as the scaly little rascal flipped itself up in a clean arc directly over the grate.

The very moment it seemed that my failure was absolute, my salvation arrived in the form of a broad bear of a man. His thick fingers swept down with remarkable skill, snatching the fish up by its tail in midhop. He palmed the mackerel in one hand and helped steady me to a stop with the other. When my feet were firmly beneath me, the man laughed a deep, throaty laugh and patted me firmly on the shoulder.

"Hah! Gotcha!" His wide smile sat nestled in a thick, bristly, auburn beard.

"Catch of the day, Hudson," came my employer's voice from directly behind me.

"Bah. The mackerel's not bad—but I don't think this one's fully grown. I'll have to toss her back! Hah!" The man laughed again, loudly, and slapped me on the back so enthusiastically, I nearly toppled. "Figures that the fish start flying and yer the one behind it! Good to see ya, R. F. Oh, hey—speaking of which, let's get this fella a drink. Hold on."

The big mountain of a man lumbered back toward the leather shop and popped inside, still clutching the struggling fish. My shirt dripped, and crystal shards tinkled under my feet as I turned to face my employer. "Mr. Jackaby, I–"

He regarded me sternly.

"I am so sorry," I said.

His eyes remained fixed on mine, and his eyebrows rose a fraction.

"I am so, so, so sorry."

He sighed. "The number of *so*s in your apology is irrelevant. Miss Rook, what do you see when you look at these creatures?" He held the box toward me, and a little furry face peeped out, inquisitively.

"I see . . . a kitten."

"Would you like to know what I see?"

I nodded. Jackaby was not an ordinary detective. The cases he tracked were not the sort an ordinary investigator could unravel, but fantastic pursuits, delving ever beyond the pale. What made Jackaby so good at uncovering the perplexing and paranormal—more than his extensive library of the occult, more than his vast knowledge of the obscure—was that Jackaby was perplexing and paranormal himself. Where you or I could observe only the surface, Jackaby perceived a deeper reality. He said this made him "the Seer"—though not like any old tarot reader or charlatan with a crystal ball. Jackaby saw the truth behind every thing and every person.

"What do you see?" I asked.

"I see untempered chaotic potential—they're positively bubbling with it. It doesn't rest above their skin like an ordinary aura. It pops and fizzes and rolls. They are adorable at present, and relatively docile for now, but with the capacity for untold destruction. Darwin discovered the little chameleomorphs for the first time on the island of Mauritius. You won't find them in any grammar school textbook, but he did. There was a bird that used to live there as well—until something began to prey upon it. Dutch sailors dubbed them *walghvogels*, the 'loathsome birds.' According to a few very old accounts, including a secret dossier compiled by Darwin himself, they were witnessed devouring their own kind. Within half a century of their discovery, the birds had been eradicated. You may know them better by their more common name, the dodo."

"You think cats are going to go the way of the dodo if I accidentally let one of these chameleon-morph things escape?"

"They appear as cats today, but as you have seen, they could be anything tomorrow. My point is simply that the introduction of a foreign predator, particularly one with such intense latent potential as this, could be devastating to the local ecosystem."

The big hairy man emerged from the leather shop, and our discussion came to an end. "Heyo, Jackaby! You owe that fella inside a new mop bucket. Don't worry, I gave it a good rinse." He held out a dented tin bucket, and I stepped up and accepted it graciously. The fish spun within it, cramped again, but safe and unharmed. "And who would you be, then, little lady?"

"Abigail Rook, sir. I really can't thank you enough."

"Whoo—a Brit! Watch out, Jackaby. You might accidentally pick up a little class workin' with this one. The name's Hank Hudson, Miss Rook."

He offered a hand and I shook it. Clad in a thick brown duster with wide lapels and boots that looked fit to cross the continent, the man was a mountain of worn leather, and he smelled like horses and firewood. He was like the rugged, American mountain men I had read about as a little girl, only Davy Crockett had never looked so massive in the pages of my magazines.

"Mr. Hudson is a skilled trapper and a cherished associate of mine, Miss Rook. How long have you been back in New Fiddleham, my friend?" Jackaby braced the box of kittens on his hip and held out his own hand, but Hank Hudson pulled him into a quick hug, instead, giving Jackaby a hearty slap on the back while my employer awkwardly struggled not to drop the box.

"Only here on a quick stop. Spent a year out in Oklahoma Territory, tradin' with the Cherokee. There's good huntin' out there, but I got that cabin in Gad's Valley to tend to. Once I've unloaded some goods an' restocked, I'll be headed back down that way. I'm glad I caught ya. I picked up some good herbs from the traders you might be interested in. Oh—hey, and I also got me a Cherokee medicine wheel you might take a shine to. You gonna be in this evening?"

"Yes, indeed. I'm still up on Augur Lane. Do you remember the house?"

"Sure enough—hard to forget a haunt like that." Mr. Hudson gave Jackaby a wink, which made me wonder if he knew the full details of the odd house on Augur Lane. "See you folks later, then. A pleasure meetin' ya, little lady."

He tipped his fur cap and tromped off down the sidewalk in the opposite direction. Jackaby and I resumed our trek back to Augur Lane. I took great care to watch my step and keep the bucket level. I hoped Jackaby might explain how he had come to know the trapper, but my employer said nothing. I found it hard to read from his expression if he was still miffed at me for my bungling, or if this was just his usual lack of social tact.

There was a lot about Jackaby I found difficult to read. He was so blunt and direct all the time that it became easy to lose sight of the fact that I knew almost nothing about my employer. I had noticed, for instance, that Mr. Hudson had referred to him by his initials, when virtually every other person we'd met called him only "Jackaby."

"What does 'R. F.' stand for?" I asked as we crossed through the business district, nearing Augur Lane.

He turned his head and regarded me for a few seconds before responding. "In my line of work, investigating eldritch events and all manner of magical matters, it behooves one to maintain certain safeguards of a supernatural nature."

"You mean, like the garlic and lavender you put all around the property line?"

"It isn't lavender; it's Irish white heather—but yes, like that," he replied. "Names have power. To purveyors of certain very old, very dark arts, a name, willingly surrendered, is tantamount to strings on a marionette. I choose to keep my own name closely guarded."

"I promise not to turn you into an evil puppet," I said. "I don't know any dark arts, anyhow. I don't even know any card tricks."

"Reassuring though that is, I think I'll keep it to myself all the same. It isn't you I'm worried about, Miss Rook," he added, "but you will find my resolve on the matter absolute. I've not even shared my full name with Jenny, and she is not only exceptionally reliable but also dead."

Jenny Cavanaugh was one of those peculiar details about the house on Augur Lane. The property had once been hers—and she had stayed on even after her untimely and mysterious demise. My employer raised no complaint, and the ghostly Jenny had simply become a regular member of the household. In spite of her grim history, Jenny was the most pleasant specter a person could ever hope to meet. She had turned out to be a closer confidante and far less of a curiosity than my enigmatic employer.

"May I guess?" I said.

Jackaby rolled his eyes. "You may do whatever you like. It will have no bearing on my decision."

"Is it . . . Richard Frederic?"

"No, and I am not going to–"

"Russell Francis?"

"No. You're being–"

"Rumpelstiltskin Finnegan?"

Jackaby sighed. "Yes, Miss Rook. Rumpelstiltskin. You've found me out. I am the devious imp of the fairy tales."

"It wouldn't be the strangest thing you've told me since I started working for you."

Chapter Three

Upon our return to the house on Augur Lane, Jackaby sealed himself alone in his laboratory. I had offered to help him manage the furry little chameleomorphs, but he shooed me out with a waggle of his hand and kicked the door shut behind me. I shuffled down the crooked hallway and slumped to my desk in the foyer, resolving to throw myself back into my daily work. The piles of Jackaby's wrinkled receipts and old case files were still in sore need of organizing, but as the afternoon stretched on, my mind refused to focus.

I had only recently managed to convince my employer that I was not some porcelain vase that needed to be protected. I was not inclined, now, to accept a role as the bull in his china shop, either. Admittedly, the fish fiasco was not my finest moment, but I could handle myself in the field. I could. I stuffed another long-forgotten receipt into the dusty filing cabinet behind me and scowled. Nothing set my skin to itching quite like feeling useless.

It wasn't that I didn't understand my employer's concern. My post as assistant to the foremost and perhaps only detective of the supernatural was wondrous in so many ways—but I couldn't deny that it was also dangerous. Jackaby's mad laboratory looked as though it might be equipped to raise Frankenstein's creature, and the library housed menacing shadows that crept across the floor and reached for my heels if I trod too close to the Dangerous Documents section. All around me sat exotic animal skulls and angry statues of foreign gods. Even the innocuous-looking drab green frog in the terrarium beside me—Jackaby called him Ogden—had a habit of venting a noxious stench from his eyeballs when he felt threatened. Such was life with my employer, a medley of madness and menace, and all this within the walls of the house.

During my very first foray into actual fieldwork, I had nearly gotten myself killed, facing off against a murderous villain. Like a careless damsel from one of my storybooks, I had failed to heed the warnings and bumbled directly into mortal danger. I hated to admit it, but if it hadn't been for Jackaby's intervention, I would almost certainly be dead, and I wouldn't be the only one.

"Does it still hurt?" came a gentle voice, startling me back to the present.

Jenny Cavanaugh had drifted into the room, her silvery feet hovering just above the floorboards, and her translucent hair drifting gently behind her. My hand had risen unconsciously to brush the small scar on my chest, a memento of that nearly fatal night, and I quickly let it drop.

"No, I'm fine. Just thinking."

"Good thoughts or bad?" she asked. Her movements were fluid and graceful as she came to rest, leaning on the corner of the desk. Since my arrival in New Fiddleham, Jenny had become my closest and dearest friend. Immaterial though she was, her counsel had always been solid and sound.

"I botched an assignment today."

"Any casualties?"

"Just a crystal punch bowl—and very nearly a fish that isn't a fish."

She raised an opalescent eyebrow.

"It was a Jackaby case," I said, and slumped my head down on the cluttered desk.

Jenny nodded. "Sounds about right, then. Don't worry about Jackaby. He'll come around. That man has botched plenty of assignments without your help."

"I know. It isn't even really Jackaby—it's just . . ." I pushed my hair out of my face and slumped back on the chair. "It's everyone. It's the ones who said I couldn't or I shouldn't.

My parents. Myself, mostly. In a strange way, I'm glad that Jackaby is disappointed. Don't tell him I said so, but it's nice to have somebody actually expect something of you for once. Still, it makes it all the harder to let go of the regrets."

Jenny's eyes drifted down to her translucent hand. "I do understand," she said quietly. "It's refreshing to be treated as an equal. It's one of the reasons I said yes, all those years ago." The ghost's engagement ring was a slim band, a spectral hint of silver nearly lost in her own silvery complexion. I held my breath as she touched the metal delicately. Jenny so rarely spoke about the years before her death. "Hard as it may be to imagine," she said, looking up, "I have a few regrets of my own."

I swallowed. "Jenny . . ."

Her face lightened, and she smiled at me softly. "Let them go, Abigail. Leave the past to us ghosts and focus on where you're going next. Besides, Jackaby is great with spotting *paranormal* stuff, but you know he's positively lost when it comes to *normal*. If you want to impress him, don't think about your weak spots—think about his. What did *he* miss?"

I shrugged. "This was a pretty simple case—or as simple as his cases are. The whole thing only took a few minutes. He spotted the creature right away—and a whole brood of its kittens."

"I thought it was a fish."

"They're fishy kittens. Long story. You know Jackaby's

not the sort to bring home an ordinary pet." I paused. A timid thought peered from around a corner at the back of my mind. "But Mrs. Beaumont is precisely the sort," I said. "And she seemed to think that she had."

"Why, Abigail, are you being clever right here in front of me?" Jenny teased.

"Not clever—just wondering," I said. "Jackaby said they're rare and they're not indigenous. So, where did Mrs. Wiggles come from?"

"Oh, look at you, all inquisitive and focused." She smiled affectionately. "I'm beginning to think you and Jackaby are cut from two ends of the same cloth."

Before I could respond, three loud knocks issued from the front door, and I found myself suddenly alone in the room. I said a quiet thank-you to the space where Jenny had been, and I rose to receive our visitor.

Chapter Four

I glanced out the window as I crossed the room. Parked on the street outside was a sturdy-looking coach with two muscular horses yoked at the front. Unlike the sleek black carriages and hansom cabs one normally saw about town, this wooden cart was somewhere between a modern mail coach and the sort of covered wagon the pioneers all rode in my magazines of the Wild West. It looked delightfully rugged and out of place against the gray buildings of the business district.

It was no surprise, then, that Hank Hudson's bushy beard and broad grin greeted me when I opened the door. "Mr. Hudson! How lovely to see you again."

"Aw, Hank will do just fine, little lady."

"Do come in. I'll let Jackaby know you've arrived."

I hung Hudson's coat beside the door, and tried not to notice the sharp hatchet hanging from one side of his belt or the long bowie knife strapped to the other. He had picked up a paper from a newsboy on the way over, and he waggled it as I escorted him down the winding hallway.

"Electric streetlights, here in New Fiddleham! Can you believe it? Within the year—at least accordin' to the papers. You can tell that mayor fella's up for reelection. They've got 'em up in Seeley's Square already. Hah! I can still remember when they were puttin' in the gas lines!"

I nodded. "Commissioner Marlowe's got them talking about running telephone wires out to the surrounding cities as well."

Hank shook his head in astonishment and whistled. "It's a helluva world. Still, I'll take stars in the sky and the dirt beneath my feet any day. I'm glad Gad's Valley's a little behind the times. I'm a little behind the times, myself, I guess."

We reached the end of the hallway, and I knocked gently on the laboratory door. "Just to caution you," I whispered. "Mr. Jackaby is in slightly bad humor—"

The door burst open and my employer stood before us, holding a long rod with a half-molten nub of metal at the tip. A pair of brass goggles had been pushed up on his head, forcing his already unruly hair upward in uneven tufts. He smiled broadly and threw his hands in the air enthusiastically, catching the door frame with a glancing blow from the metal rod. "Hudson! Auspicious timing. Come in, come in!"

The usual madness of the chamber was in full force, with racks of beakers and test tubes filled with liquids of various hues, a pinging copper boiler with its pipes reaching out like spider's legs, and an odd, lingering aroma of strawberries and sulfur. Strewn across every available surface were panels of thick glass and strips of metal. Jackaby had popped one side off a stout terrarium and had extended the glass box by adding a few new walls. In a corner sat the dented bucket and the box from this morning, and a soft mewling told me the kittens were still inside.

Jackaby crossed the room and flicked off the hot blue flame on a Bunsen burner, dropping the metal rod beside it. "You've put together more animal enclosures than I have," he said. "Do you think you could assist me in constructing a somewhat larger vivarium? I could certainly use another pair of hands on the soldering."

Mr. Hudson dropped his newspaper on the table and strode happily over to the project, inspecting the freshly tacked joints.

"You could have called me in, sir," I said. "I am here to assist—and I'm good for a lot more than sorting papers. As a matter of fact, I've been thinking about an angle on our latest case."

"It isn't personal, Miss Rook. Hudson and I have simply worked together on similar projects in the past. We all have our areas of expertise, and penning animals happens to be one of his. The beasts *he* hunts are generally still alive."

Mr. Hudson looked up from the glass box. "Not really sportin' to hunt the dead ones, is it?"

"I believe my employer is referring to hunting fossils— which is actually quite a challenge. The paleontologist's prey might not be up and running, but they do have a tendency to scatter themselves about the landscape and lodge bits of themselves in solid rock."

"Dinosaurs, huh? Bet you're just as excited as a badger in a beehive about that find down in the valley, then."

"What find? They've found fossils?" I asked.

Hudson jabbed a finger at the newspaper on the table. "Yup. Gad's Valley. Farmer dug 'em up when he was cuttin' into the hillside. The place ain't but a mile or two from my cabin. I've known Hugo Brisbee since way back. A decent rancher, but that place seems like it's always one bad crop away from broke. He's the one who found the bones. Apparently he's got to keep a closer eye on 'em, though. Here, have a look fer yourself."

I leafed through the paper until I found the article. The story was just as the trapper said. Written by one Nellie Fuller, it read as follows:

Phenomenal Find Leads to Farmland Fiasco.

Gad's Valley may be known for its simple rustic charms, but for one local farmstead, this past week has been more sensational by far. Death, dinosaur bones, and daylight robbery have shaken up the residents of the quiet countryside.

Ground was broken last Wednesday in the foothills behind the Brisbee family farm, unearthing a massive prehistoric fossil. The discovery quickly gained the attention of local enthusiasts and international experts alike.

The excavation has already been marred by some sad and unsettling developments. First and foremost, Madeleine Brisbee, 64, was found deceased yesterday morning near the site of the find. Having taken ill several weeks earlier, she is believed to have collapsed from exertion. Foul play is not suspected.

In the midst of this tragic loss, progress on the discovery has been further hampered by another troubling development. The deceased's husband, Hugo Brisbee, 67, had scarcely returned from making funeral arrangements, when he received word that an invaluable artifact had been stolen from the site. Investigation into the theft is ongoing.

Brisbee has been in correspondence with the renowned American paleontologist Lewis Lamb since the earliest stages of the discovery. Lamb, head of Glanville University's Geological Survey, is expected to arrive within the week to take charge of the excavation.

One thing is certain: in spite of trouble and trag-
edy, a great deal more will be coming out of the Brisbee soil this season than carrots and cabbages.

"Jackaby, read this! We absolutely must look into it!"

Jackaby took the paper with a scowl and glanced over it
for a few moments. "Hmm. Now this *is* interesting."

"More than interesting, it's spectacular. I mean—very sad
about the poor woman, of course—but this is precisely our
sort of case! A brazen robbery in which the stolen property
is a priceless scientific relic! Do you suppose that if we track
down the missing bone, they might let me assist with the
dig as well?"

"What's that?" Jackaby looked up from the page. "You
already have a job, Rook—and I wasn't talking about that
dinosaur business. Here, notice anything peculiar?"

The page opposite the excavation article was littered
with half a dozen local happenings, minor accounts of van-
dalism, petty theft, and missing persons. "The absent professor?" I guessed. "Unusual for an instructor to be truant,
I suppose."

"Falderal! Cordovan's Shoes. There." He pointed to an
article of only two sentences.

The entry briefly explained that an unidentified miscreant had broken into a shoemaker's shop three times in the
past week.

"Please tell me you're kidding, sir. It says the cobbler couldn't even find anything stolen. That's annoying, but it's not a case."

"You mean cordwainer," Jackaby corrected. "Cobblers only make repairs. Do you know who else is known for slipping into shoemakers' shops and not taking anything?"

"Please, sir. Don't say elves."

"Elves!"

"It doesn't say they made a nice pair of shoes for him—they just broke in. It's probably some poor vagrant looking to keep dry for the night. It's not elves."

"It *could* be elves."

"It *could* be elephants—what it is *not* is a case. Honestly, sir, how often will we have a chance to track down genuine dinosaur fossils?"

Hank leaned against the counter to watch our exchange.

"I really don't see why you find old bones so interesting, Rook," said Jackaby.

"You told me yourself that you're a man of science. Paleontology is a science, and a thrilling one! Surely you're a bit intrigued."

"Anything can be studied scientifically. Pedology is a valid science as well, but I have no interest in staring at dirt. I much prefer to devote my time to the study of pertinent, urgent matters, and to preparation for legitimate potential encounters. The likelihood that I will find myself face-to-face with a dinosaur at any point in my life? Very slim. The likelihood that a secretive little scamp will breach Cordovan's Shoes again this very night?" He brandished the page at me again. "Nearly absolute."

Hank laughed heartily and clapped a hand on Jackaby's shoulder. "Hah! You haven't changed a bit, my friend. Aw, let the girl have her fun. What d'ya say, Miss Rook? I'm headin' out to Gadston first thing tomorrow. I got some business in town before I get down to the valley, but I could meet you down there an' introduce ya to Brisbee. That is ... if yer grumpy ol' boss will give ya the time off." He nudged Jackaby, who rolled his eyes. I liked Hank Hudson even more than I had before.

"That is out of the question," Jackaby said. "The last time I permitted an assistant to pursue an investigation alone, he came back as waterfowl. I need someone in this house to maintain her opposable digits, or I shall have to do everything myself."

"Yer gonna be doin' that anyway if you drive her away." Hudson gave Jackaby a nudge. "You've got those special eyes—take a good look at the kid. Tell me the truth. Is she the type to let go of an adventure when she's sunk her teeth into it? Ain't a bad quality in yer line of work."

I felt my employer's piercing gaze for several seconds and resisted the urge to shuffle my feet. Jackaby took a deep breath. "Be that as it may, she has yet to finish chewing on our current morsel. As a matter of fact, weren't you just saying something about another angle on the case, Miss Rook?"

I silently cursed his selective attention. "Right. That. I'm sure it's nothing."

"You're better at sorting papers than you are at lying." Jackaby raised an eyebrow at me.

"I was just having a bit of a think earlier," I admitted, "and I realized we never asked Mrs. Beaumont where she bought her cat. There might be something in it—but it could just as well be nothing."

"Or it could be everything." Jackaby's eyes narrowed. "It definitely merits further investigation. We will call on her first thing in the morning. I'm sorry, Miss Rook, but we must finish properly insulating New Fiddleham from wild, insidious predators before gallivanting off after a bit of dry bone."

Hank's smile remained, but his eyes took on a focused glint. "There somethin' you forgot to tell me?"

Jackaby turned back to the trapper with a sly smile. "Why do you think we're building the box?"

Jackaby was rarely forthright with the public about the nature of his cases—possibly owing to the public's tendency to laugh, jeer, or throw things at him when he did speak his mind—but he held nothing back as he explained the chameleomorphs to Hudson. The trapper's eyes shone with excitement as he listened. "Wait—that mackerel I snagged for ya was one of yer camel-morphy things? Didn't look like nothin'—you swear you ain't just messin' with me? You know how much I love me a rare breed."

"Would you like to see her kittens?" Jackaby asked.

"The fish had *kittens*?"

Three of the little fur balls fit in the palm of Hank's big hand, and he stroked their ears and fuzzy fins with remarkable gentleness.

"Can I keep one of 'em?" He looked like an enormous toddler, coddling the little things as they played in his arms. "You know me, Jackaby—I'd take real good care."

"I'm afraid that is out of the question," Jackaby replied. "As I have been explaining to Miss Rook, they are far too dangerous. I much prefer to manage their handling myself."

"You ain't gonna kill 'em, are you?"

"No, as it happens, I am not—but if you find the thought of killing an adorable kitten distasteful, then keep in mind that is precisely what *these* creatures are currently disguised to do."

Hank carefully deposited the litter back into the box. "Well, I can't say I ain't a little disappointed, but I do appreciate you lettin' me have a look at 'em. We're gonna need us a much bigger box."

"The vivarium will not be housing them in their current form for long—that's the point of the endeavor. I would like them to fit comfortably, but they will be far less dangerous if I can force them into a smaller form as soon as possible and introduce a more plentiful food source. The Gerridae are just maturing, and in our little pond, alone, we're likely to see more than our fish can consume."

"Gerridae? That some kinda bug?"

"Indeed. More commonly, I believe they are called water striders or pond skaters."

"Skeeters? Yer gonna turn these sweet little kittens into skeeters?"

"They are not kittens, and yes. Providing them a small, manageable form will allow me to keep them more easily contained, and it will allow them to live out their lives without continuing to ravage the actual feline population."

Hank looked a little sad, but nodded. "Yer probably right. Durn shame, though. I woulda called the little one Peanut." He gave the kitten a last scratch between its ears and returned to assembling the big glass terrarium. I caught Jackaby's arm before he could start up the burner and get back to soldering.

"I do hope you'll reconsider Gad's Valley, sir," I said. "You know I would be an excellent paleontologist."

"Of course you would. Don't be thick. By the same token, you would make a fine dishwasher or a street sweeper—that doesn't change the fact that you have more important work to do here. You matter, Miss Rook. What we do matters. You may be eager to see this case tucked away, but like it or not, you've stumbled upon a pertinent point. Population data in the field of transmutational cryptozoology is hazy at best, but chameleomorphs are rare. Very rare. That Mrs. Wiggles ended up in our proverbial backyard is staggeringly suspicious, statistically speaking. We will speak to Mrs. Beaumont in the morning," Jackaby declared. "And that's the end of it."

We would see Mrs. Beaumont in the morning—Jackaby was right about that much—but it was far from the end of it. Neither of us knew it at the time, but we were only at the start of something much, much bigger.

Chapter Five

The following morning I dressed early and descended the spiral staircase to find Jackaby puttering in his laboratory. The daylight streamed through myriad glass tubes and bottles arranged along the windowsill, casting the room in a medley of warm, vibrant tones. The kittens were tumbling about in the finished enclosure in the corner, unperturbed by their captivity. Over his usual attire, my employer had draped a leather apron that might have looked more at home on a blacksmith. He was examining the uneven surface of a thick disc of amber glass, just a little wider across than a dinner plate. From behind it, his face bulged and rippled in golden waves.

"Good morning, sir," I said. "Sleep well?"

"Not generally. Help yourself to a bit of fruit. It's oranges this week." He dropped the heavy glass on the table with a clunk, and waved a hand in the general direction of the cauldron. The cauldron was perpetually brimming with food, powered by some impossible enchantment. Admittedly it only ever produced fruit, and rarely of exceptional quality, but it was miraculous nonetheless.

I selected an orange off the top and sat down, looking more closely at the lumpy glass on the table. The slightly raised nub to one end looked like a slender handle. "I would offer you juice, but I underestimated the efficacy of my catalyzing agent this morning," said Jackaby.

"Come again?" I asked.

"Breakfast science. The thermochemical reactions involved proved more intense than I anticipated." He tapped the amber glass with his knuckle. "Jenny was not thrilled about her pitcher, either."

"How did you melt—"

A firm rapping issued suddenly from the front door, and Jackaby pulled off his apron. "Who do you suppose that is at this hour?" he said, heading out into the hallway. I abandoned my orange and followed close behind.

The man on the front step was dressed in a stiff blue coat, as he had been when we first met—but in place of twin silver bars, his lapel now bore a silver eagle and a badge declaring him commissioner of the New Fiddleham Police.

"Marlowe," said Jackaby.

"Jackaby," said Marlowe.

"Good morning, Commissioner," I said. "You're looking well. How is the new appointment treating you?"

Marlowe sighed. "It's just *acting commissioner*, Miss Rook. And *acting* is a stretch. The only *actions* I've made in the past month have been to wade through bureaucracy and argue with politicians."

"Well, there are no bureaucrats nor any politicians on the premises," I assured him. "Jackaby puts up wards against that sort of thing. Salt and fresh sage, I think. Would you care to come in? I'll put the kettle on."

The commissioner shook his head. "Thanks, but I've come on police business."

"What sort of business would merit a personal visit from the *acting* commissioner of the New Fiddleham Police?" Jackaby asked.

"Bad business, I'm afraid. It's about a personal friend of the mayor. I understand you've met Florence Beaumont?"

"Is that what this is about?" said Jackaby. "You can assure the woman that Mrs. Wiggles and her kittens are being treated with the utmost care. Better yet, we will tell her ourselves. We'll be returning to Campbell Street presently. We have some other matters to discuss with Mrs. Beaumont, as it turns out."

"Is that so?" Marlowe grunted. The commissioner's eyelids looked heavy, but I could see that he was watching my employer intently. "Then you're going to need to bring a medium—unless communing with the dead is something you do now."

My breath caught in my throat.

"All too often, in fact," Jackaby replied, missing the implications entirely. "I had one nattering at me all morning about her glassware. I never have bothered with the trappings of spiritualism, though, if that's what you mean. I don't go in for hand-holding and flickering candlelight and all that falderal."

"Mr. Jackaby," I said.

"Although I was once told that I look quite fetching in a loose headscarf."

"Mr. Jackaby!" I said. "He means that Mrs. Beaumont is . . ." I swallowed.

Marlowe nodded. "Dead."

Jackaby straightened, his brows furrowed. A somber focus finally crept into his cloud-gray eyes. "Murder?"

Marlowe nodded.

Jackaby took a deep breath. "I see. And your sources have obviously informed you that we paid the lady a visit only yesterday. I assume you've slid me into the top of your suspects list, as usual, then?"

"Don't flatter yourself. I'd love to know what you were doing at the scene, but maids have reported seeing the woman alive well after you two left to make a mess of Market Street." I cringed slightly. "I'm not here to arrest you this time. I'm here to . . ." Marlowe took a deep breath and closed his eyes. "I'm here to enlist your services."

Jackaby raised an eyebrow. "What did you say was the manner of Mrs. Beaumont's death?"

"Call it *unnatural causes*," said Marlowe. The corners of my employer's mouth twitched upward. Marlowe rolled his eyes and nodded obliquely toward the street. "Just hurry up. I've got a driver waiting." He stamped off down the front step, not bothering to ask if we would be right behind.

Chapter Six

O ur ride through the early-morning streets was a cold one, and so was the body at the end of it. Mrs. Beaumont lay on her back at the feet of a plush divan when we arrived, the intricate swirls and rosettes of a Persian carpet splaying out beneath her. At a glance, she could have been sleeping. I found myself watching her chest, waiting for some sign of breath—but as the seconds ticked by, I began to feel a knot of queasiness rising in my stomach, and I looked away.

"Maybe it's best if you wait outside, young lady," said Marlowe.

I shook my head. "If you've enlisted Mr. Jackaby, then you've enlisted me as well, Commissioner." I plucked up my nerve and my notepad, and began to record the scene before me. Marlowe turned his attention to my employer, who was already bent over the body.

"First impressions?"

Jackaby stood beside the corpse. His hands hovered over the body, stirring the air. "There has been an abomination in this house." He pulled back with a grimace, rubbing invisible particles from his fingers with distaste.

"You mean like a murder?" Marlowe suggested flatly.

"Worse," said Jackaby. He stepped to the woman's head and knelt. He drew a magnifying glass from his pocket, but rather than gazing through it, he held it by the glass and used its stem to gently nudge the lace collar away from the woman's neck.

"I was wondering how long it would take for you to find that." Marlowe paced around the body and stood across from Jackaby. "What do you make of it?"

I inched closer and peered over my employer's shoulder. On the woman's right side, just beneath her jaw, was an oblong blemish the length of my forefinger—a violet bruise, dappled with dark plum spots. Within the mottled oval was a pea-sized circle of deep red where the woman's skin had been pierced.

"Peculiar," said Jackaby. "There ought to be two."

"There's no exit wound," Marlowe informed him. "It's the only mark we've found on the body. Doesn't look like a typical gunshot, but I've asked the coroner to look for bullet fragments, all the same."

"He won't find any," said Jackaby without looking up. "It's not a projectile; it's a puncture. The assailant struck the jugular directly. Exsanguination is almost certainly the cause of death. The lack of blood about the body and the burst capillaries around the injury indicate suction . . ."

"A vampire," I said.

Jackaby tucked the magnifying glass back into his coat. "A touch too glaring for my taste, Miss Rook, but that would be the most obvious conclusion."

Marlowe groaned and rubbed the bridge of his nose with one hand.

"You disagree?" Jackaby said, rising.

"Of course I disagree. The 'most obvious conclusion' is a lunatic with an ice pick or a jealous lover with a letter opener . . ." He took a deep breath. "But the most obvious conclusion keeps falling short—which is why you're here. So, that's your first guess, then? You're opening with *vampire*?"

"I'm not ruling out the Russian strigoi or Chinese jiang-shi. This is a country of immigrants, after all. There are also countless numbers of demons and ghouls known for bleeding their victims dry, but vampires certainly make the list."

The commissioner's eye twitched, and he sighed. "Not a word of this leaves this room. I mean that, and stay away from the press, both of you. Reporters haven't stopped hounding me for details from our last case—and they would have a field day with a vampire in New Fiddleham. This town is still reeling from one supernatural serial killer. The last thing we need is to spread panic about a second."

"So you've brought us here just to shut us up?" said Jackaby. "You know very well you can't make this go away by not believing in it."

Marlowe stared at the corpse on the carpet for several seconds. "Yeah, I know," he grunted. "I didn't believe in redcaps or werewolves a month ago–but apparently they didn't much care what I believed. I think it's fair to say I'm a little more open to the existence of monsters today."

"Charlie isn't a werewolf," I said defensively. "And he's not a monster." Charlie Cane was the junior police officer– the only police officer–willing to listen to us during our last case. He was paranormal, it was true–possessed of the ability to assume the form of a great hound–but he was still every bit a gentleman. Charlie had sacrificed his greatest se-cret to protect the city–to protect me–and yet he had been rewarded for his courage with exile into the countryside.

"You're right about that. He's a sharp officer who knows the value of discretion, which is one of the reasons he kept *this* strictly confidential." Marlowe pulled a slim envelope from his pocket. It bore Charlie's pseudonym, *C. Barker*, and I recognized his handwriting at once. I reached for the envelope, but Marlowe withdrew it. "Strictly confidential."

"Understood, sir," I assured him. "Not a word outside this room." Jackaby nodded, and Marlowe relinquished the secret report.

"'Madeleine Brisbee' . . . ," Jackaby read over my shoulder. "Why is that name familiar?"

"My word! She's the woman from the article," I said. "The one who passed away out by the excavation site! But, they said foul play was not suspected. She was ill . . ."

"Don't believe everything you read in the papers. She was found on the rocks—banged up from a short fall. No broken bones, though, no blood, nothing that should've been fatal. Local doc called it overexertion. Local cop disagreed."

"I take it the local cop was Charlie?" I said.

"Cigar for the lady," Marlowe said flatly. "Our boy hasn't lost his edge just because he's living outside the city limits. He kept his suspicions quiet—but he made a sketch to include in his report. It's there on the second page."

Flipping to the next paper, I found a rough pencil sketch of a woman's head and neck, complete with a shaded oval just beneath her jawline, one dark spot inscribed within it.

"Commander Bell told him it was nothing, just an indentation from the rocks, but Charlie wasn't convinced. The sketch arrived in yesterday's post, so you can imagine my surprise when my men brought in an identical report about Mrs. Beaumont this morning."

I folded the paper and returned it to the commissioner. "People are dying in my city, and I've got nothing but children's stories to tell their families," Marlowe said. "I need to know exactly what we're dealing with. I've got my men on alert here in New Fiddleham, but even if he had the manpower, Commander Bell has no idea how to handle something like this, and I'm not even sure he would believe us if we involved him."

"Yes. Nothing more frustrating than a bullheaded lawman." Jackaby raised his eyebrows meaningfully at Marlowe, but the commissioner ignored him.

"Charlie is lucky enough the press didn't recognize him the first time they came to the valley. He's already put his neck out farther than he should. What we need is a thorough, discreet report from somebody accustomed to working outside the usual parameters of the law."

"What a coincidence," Jackaby said. "I've been thinking of putting that very thing on my business cards. So you're sending us on assignment?"

"I'm not sending you anywhere. The valley is out of my jurisdiction. He doesn't know it yet, but I have a strong feeling your old friend Officer Barker will be forwarding you an official request for a consultation by this afternoon. For all Bell need know, you'll just be looking into a related petty theft. That should provide you ample excuse to explore the scene of the murder. Whatever did this, it started in Gad's Valley, and if it left behind so much as a boot print, I want you to find it."

Chapter Seven

As the morbid atmosphere of the crime scene slid away behind us, I began to process the turn of events the morning had taken. My heart thudded as I considered the reality of a second bloodthirsty killer roaming the streets, but I couldn't help but also consider the prospects blooming before me. We would be visiting the valley after all. Even if the burglary was only a pretext, I had my ticket onto the dig site—and the fact that we would be working closely with Charlie Barker only made the notion more appealing.

Marlowe's driver deposited us in front of Jackaby's building, and I hurried up the walk and through the bright red door. I would have to pack, of course, and I couldn't wait to tell Jenny the news. I bounded up the stairs toward my room, but before I could step out onto the second-floor landing, a quiet sound from above caught my ears. Something about it made the hair on the back of my neck stand on end. I strained to listen and tiptoed up one more flight of the spiral staircase.

Jackaby's house was an eclectic assortment of architectural styles and engineering oddities, full of abstract additions and mystifying modifications. My favorite of these was the third-floor pond. The space opened before me as I stepped off the staircase, the simple wooden landing stretching out a dozen feet before melting into lush green grass and budding clover. There were no interior walls on this floor, only the occasional column supporting a high ceiling above a rolling, living landscape. Sunlight poured in through broad windows on either side, casting a golden glow over moss-carpeted cabinets and desks draped with ivy. A narrow path of floorboards cut through the green, coming to an end near the edge of a broad pond, the waters of which bounced the sunlight up to the ceiling in rippling, ethereal waves. The pond stretched across most of the floor, both wider and deeper than it should have been given the dimensions of the house; the laws of physics were more flexible in the hands of the sort of craftsmen Jackaby contracted for his remodeling. There was something mildly unsettling and yet profoundly comforting about the slight lack of reality in this space.

The wildflowers had begun to blossom, and the air was

rich with a blend of sweet perfumes, but there was something else in the atmosphere that I couldn't quite identify. As I stepped along the walkway, a cold chill swept through my dress and I shivered. Something was wrong. Even during the coldest days of winter, the third floor acted as its own greenhouse, keeping the peaceful pond and sweeping green field warmer than the surrounding New England streets, and yet goose bumps were creeping up my arms. I was beginning to see my own breath in wispy clouds. The quiet sound crept over the water, chilling me even more deeply than the cold. Whether male or female I could not tell at first, but a voice across the pond was weeping.

I swallowed hard and considered going back downstairs to fetch Jackaby, but I shook the thought from my head. I did not need him to hold my hand through every little thing. Stepping off the path, I wound my way around the pond. The grass was tall and wet, and it did nothing to help the shivers running over my skin as it tickled my legs. A thick veil of ivy draped from the rafters on this side of the room, and as I pushed it aside, I was met with an explosion of movement.

I flew backward, landing on my backside as a flurry of brown and green and white flapped into the air above my head. The startled drake, nestled inconspicuously in the foliage until I nearly trod on it, now soared over the rippling water and away, beating its wings in a mad dash to the opposite side of the building. I caught my breath. Douglas was the pond's foremost resident, and nothing to be afraid of. The stately waterfowl had once been human, and Jackaby's assistant, until he had been caught off guard on a creepy caper and fell victim to a curse. Jackaby had never turned his back on the stalwart fellow, so Douglas stayed on, tending the archives with remarkable aptitude for a mallard. What my fine-feathered coworker could *not* do was weep in a mournful human voice. The cries continued.

Douglas, typically so composed, had fled the scene in such panic, I was left wary of what might have put him on edge. I steeled my nerves and pulled myself to my feet, inching forward to push the curtain of leafy vines aside. Coming through the ivy was like stepping into an ice chest. The moist air condensed into a thick fog, and the bushes on this side of the pond formed a secluded, shadowy glade. It took me a moment to make out the source of the moaning cries. Veiled in the heart of the fog, in the darkest of the shadows, was Jenny Cavanaugh.

Jenny had only ever appeared to me as a spectral beauty, possessed of a mercurial laugh and effortless grace—the spirit of mirth and elegance. The morbid figure now before me was something else entirely. She sat, crouching in the shadows with her head cupped in her hands, and sobs rippled through her shoulders like steam bubbling from a pot. Her hair was draped in damp, matted strands, clinging to her slate-gray arms like algae to a wet rock. Her dress was decrepit and decayed, torn at the collar and hanging lopsided and loose around her neck.

The invasive cold thudded into my chest, and I froze. Jenny's body faded in and out of clarity with the curls and drifts of mist. Focusing on specific features began to hurt my eyes, like trying to pick out details in a poorly exposed photograph. The dirt and leaves beneath her slipped in and out of view, becoming distorted like the horizon on a hot day as the figure solidified and faded with each heaving breath. All around her the air churned and roiled, ominously volcanic in spite of the icy cold.

The breath I had not taken for several long seconds rushed suddenly into my lungs in a quavering gasp, and Jenny looked up. Her face was like a grim reflection in dark, turbulent waters. She showed no sign of recognition as she rose with shuddering fury to her full height, her expression slipping from misery to wrath. The specter's eyes, peering from beneath the angry shadows of her brow, held none of the cheer and compassion that had come to define the spirit I knew. They were lit instead with a wild, inhuman frenzy. "You shouldn't be here," she said, her voice raw and hushed. Mist boiled around her, and, like a demon from the pit, she burst across the glade toward me.

"J-J-Jenny?" I stammered at last, my voice barely a whisper.

She was not two feet away, barreling at me like a cannon,

when a flicker of familiarity blinked across her eyes. In an instant her face became a wash of pitiful confusion, and just as quickly she was simply gone. Momentum carried the wave of cold fog into me, but without its source, it was nothing more than mist. No sooner had it engulfed me than it began to dissipate, slipping into the mossy floor as it faded.

The returning warmth of the third-floor oasis was slow to chase the shivers out of my bones. I trod unsteadily back around the pond and staggered to a stop on the lush green. Douglas flapped over beside me, and we sat together quietly, looking over the pond's bank for several minutes.

"That was unexpected," I said at last.

Douglas bobbed his head from side to side in a noncommittal sort of way.

"Has that happened before?" I asked. "I mean—does she get like that often?"

Douglas ruffled his feathers and looked up at me. His eyes glistened like beads of ebony. He was a marvelous listener, but still frustratingly avian.

I sighed. "Well, I don't like it." As the raw terror of the experience ebbed, my insides were left with the subtler ache of seeing my friend in such torment. Jenny was always effortlessly confident and self-possessed, not at all like that frenzied ghoul. "We should talk to her," I said.

Douglas cocked his head to one side.

"You know what I mean. *I* should talk to her. She looks as though she might need a friend just now. Come with me?"

The prim little mallard shook out his wings and flapped into a rapid launch, gliding away across the pond to the little island in the center, settling onto a plum-colored arm-chair in the middle of the shrubbery.

"A simple *no* would have sufficed." I pushed myself up. I couldn't blame the cowardly duck. A vision of the phantom's eyes, ice-cold and mad with primal intensity, swelled in my mind. I swallowed hard and willed the image away. Jenny was not that feral creature. She was my friend, and—girl or ghoul—she needed me to be hers.

Chapter Eight

Before descending the spiral staircase, I glanced back over the field of wildflowers. "The smallest gestures can have the biggest impact," Mother always used to say. I retrieved a porcelain vase from a cabinet on the far wall and looked for the right flowers to fill it, trying to remember which ones were Jenny's favorites. There were so many varieties, from common daisies to rare exotic blooms. Jenny could name every bulb and blossom. On quieter days, she had walked me up and down the slope, telling me what each plant was good for and its special meaning. All I could seem to remember was that a remarkable number of pretty little herbs had names that ended in *wort*.

I paused at an elegant plant. Its long stem stretched past a cluster of drooping leaves to burst at the top into a broad cone of bright white blossoms. It reminded me of Jenny, pale and pretty, but also fragile. I picked a few, arranging them in the vase. The collection looked lonely, so I added a cluster of purple, star-shaped flowers that hung in a shady corner from creeping vines.

I carried the vase down the stairs and onto the second-floor landing. My own room stood open to the left, still cluttered with the excess bric-a-brac from the days when it served as Jackaby's storage closet. Across the hall lay Jenny's bedroom. I hastened to her closed door and knocked lightly.

"Jenny?" I called. "Jenny, it's me, Abigail. Are you in there?" There came no response. Timidly I tried the handle, and the door opened a crack. "Jenny? I brought you some flowers—I just wanted to . . ."

The door swung suddenly inward, and I had to catch myself from dropping the vase. Jenny stood in the doorway, her hair sweeping along her soft cheekbones in elegant silvery curls. Her dress was pristine, and her expression bright and sweet, without a trace of distress. "Abigail, are those for me? You're an absolute sweetheart!"

"I . . . I just . . ." I blinked and started again. "Are you . . . all right?"

"Of course, dear. I'm always all right."

I stood in the hallway feeling thoroughly discombobulated and increasingly awkward. "I just . . . I thought you might like . . . these," I said, "for your bedside table."

Jenny glanced behind her, her smile faltering for just a moment.

"It's okay," I said, remembering too late. "I know you don't like anyone in your room. You can just take them from here." The entire house had once been Jenny's. She seemed largely unperturbed by Jackaby's inhabiting every other corner of it, but her room was her room. Why she needed one at all, I didn't know—to the best of my knowledge she never slept—but I had never pressed the matter and had no intention of doing so today. I kept to my side of the threshold and held out the vase.

"No. I'm afraid I can't." She sighed softly, holding up her translucent hands. "My gloves have gone missing."

Since her mortal demise, Jenny could only directly interact with things that had once been hers—and even then, only with great focus and concentration. To skirt this limitation of her afterlife, she frequently wore a pair of her old, lace gloves to gain a little traction on the material world. She was so rarely without them, I had nearly forgotten that she needed them at all.

"Haven't you got a spare set?" I asked.

"Several. All of them gone."

"Jackaby?" I asked.

"I assume so. The two of you were out all morning, though, so I haven't had a chance to ask him. It has been tremendously frustrating, but what day isn't with that man?" She tossed her head in a show of exasperation, but the wretched turmoil I had seen overwhelming her had completely vanished. "Well, you needn't stand out in the hallway, dear," she said. "Go ahead and set that bouquet on the nightstand and tell me all about your latest escapades."

She drifted gracefully back into the room, drawing back the curtain to let in the sunlight. I stepped inside hesitantly. The twists and turns of life on Augur Lane were enough to give a girl whiplash. Jenny's room was always pristine, the bed neatly tucked and the floor polished. Dust did not dare settle atop the wide rosewood armoire, although its contents had rested untouched for the better part of the decade. Had Jenny not begun lending me her things with ever-increasing enthusiasm, her impressive wardrobe might have been left to its fate forever.

I set the vase on the little table and adjusted the flowers.

"Asphodels and bittersweets." Jenny's voice was just over my shoulder as I straightened up. "They make for an interesting arrangement. Of course, in any other garden they would never grow together—they need completely different climates. Jackaby calls it something big and impressive. *Transtemporal seasonal augmentation* or something like that. I think it makes him feel better to explain impossible things as though they're science, even when the explanations don't really explain anything at all. Asphodel doesn't belong up this far north at all—but then again"—she gave me a wink—"neither do I."

I smiled, the knot in my chest finally starting to relax. It was a great relief to see that she seemed to have returned to her usual cheeky self.

"The white ones reminded me of you," I said, "and I guess I just liked the little purple ones."

"A nice choice for an aspiring young investigator. Bittersweets stand for truth. Fitting, I suppose. The truth is often bittersweet."

"What do the white ones mean?"

"Asphodels?" Jenny reached a tender finger toward the drooping white buds, pulling back her hand before it could pass through the flowers. "Oh, never mind about that. I'm sure you don't want to listen to me drone on about silly flowers, anyway. Tell me about your adventures, Abigail. Any diabolical new cases to investigate?"

"Yes, as a matter of fact—bones and bodies and everything. We'll be leaving for Gad's Valley tomorrow."

"Isn't that where that handsome young policeman of yours got stationed? What's his name?"

I felt my cheeks flush, which made Jenny smile impishly. "Charlie is hardly *my* anything," I said. "But yes, he'll be involved. Not that there are enough flowers in the world to make that romance a reality."

"You don't need flowers, dear. You need confidence. Next time you see him, you should just go right up to him and plant a kiss on that boy's pretty face."

"Jenny!"

"Fortune favors the bold, Abigail!"

"Sure it does. The last time I was bold, I nearly got the man killed, and then he changed his name and moved a hundred miles away. That's not exactly a strong start to a relationship."

"You silly girl. Of course it is—he risked his life for you!"

"Oh, never mind about it, anyway. I'm not going to the valley looking for romance—there are more important matters at stake. I'm looking for a murderer."

"You should definitely have kissed him right after the big fight." Jenny smiled, willfully ignoring my protests. She let her gaze drift to the window. "My fiancé got in a fight over me, once. He lost terribly, the poor man—he never was much of a pugilist. He looked like an absolute mess afterward, with gauze wadded up in each nostril and one eye all swollen, but it was still just the sweetest thing. And the stupidest. I told him as much . . . right before *I kissed him.*" She turned her eyes meaningfully back to me. "Because *that's what you do.*"

"What was he like?" I asked. "Your fiancé. You never talk about him."

Jenny's brow furrowed for a moment, and her eyes looked very far away—but then she rallied, giving me a sly grin and shaking her finger. "Oh no you don't, Abigail. We were talking about you."

"There's nothing to talk about! I'm going on an assignment. Dirt. Bones. Corpses. Villains. I doubt very much Charlie is thinking of anything else, either. If he had wanted a kiss when we last said good-bye, then I might have been happy to surrender it. Now he's . . . and I'm . . . It's complicated." I was getting flustered, and I could feel my cheeks burning red. I wished we could talk about anything else.

"It couldn't hurt to try. You can't live your life without taking any chances."

"Well, that's easy for you to say. It may not matter to you, but I still have a life to ruin, you know."

Jenny was quiet. The brightness drained from her eyes, and I knew at once I had crossed a line.

"Jenny, I didn't . . . ," I said, but the spectral lady was already fading. In a moment she had vanished. "I'm sorry," I said to her empty room.

Chapter Nine

Jackaby was in his office when I plodded back down the stairs. His coat was draped over the back of his armchair, and he had plucked off his shirt collar. It was the heavily starched sort meant for fancy dress, although it had become a bit crinkled along the top, and one lapel had a permanent bend to it, reaching up as if it were in the middle of a dramatic soliloquy from *Hamlet*. It lay on the desk in front of him as he fidgeted with a needle and a spool of coarse metallic thread.

"Mr. Jackaby?" I said.

"We've had a telegram from Barker," he said, not looking up from his efforts. At least he didn't seem to be annoyed with me any longer. "We'll be on the first train to meet him tomorrow morning. It departs at half past six, so best to prepare everything you need tonight." The end of his thread finally found its way into the eye of the needle, and he unwound a long stretch before snapping it off.

"I'll be ready first thing," I promised. "What are you doing there?"

Jackaby had begun working the thread through the collar's stiff fabric. "Lining my neck with silver. I've already taken the liberty of sprinkling your traveling hat with mustard seed. No need to thank me."

"Very kind of you, sir. May I ask why?"

"Apotropaic preparations. I felt it prudent to employ a broad range of protective wards in advance. I'm out of garlic, however. I'll need to make a run to the market this afternoon."

"It's vampires for certain, then?" Saying the word out loud felt both absurd and dreadful in equal measure.

"Of course it isn't certain. We could be up against a South American Chonchon or an Aswang from the Philippines. There's a cheeky cricket demon in Malaysia known to burrow holes in its victims' heads, inexplicably causing them to hallucinate about cats. I'd be more concerned about that one if I didn't know that Mrs. Beaumont had legitimate cat problems, but I've copied down the charm to neutralize those little parasites as well, just in case. Can't be too careful." He finished stitching a crooked line along the inner circumference of his collar and tied off the thread. "There. Now, what was it you wanted?"

"Well—I was just hoping to talk to you about Jenny before we left. She seemed . . . distraught earlier. I'm sorry to say I don't think I improved matters much."

"She's just miffed about her gloves, I imagine," Jackaby said casually, stuffing the spool away in a drawer.

"Yes, she did mention that they had gone missing. You wouldn't happen to know where they are, would you?"

"I would, as a matter of fact. I've taken them."

"Why on earth would you do that? You know how much she needs them."

"I am proving a point."

"Well, can you prove it some other way? She's quite upset about them . . . and perhaps also about some things that I may have said accidentally. I'll take them up for you if you like. It would be nice to be able to improve things a bit. I tried with flowers, but I think I'll need more than asphodels to make amends."

Jackaby winced and breathed in through his teeth. "Rather somber choice of foliage for a cheering up, don't you think?"

"Somber? Why?"

"Asphodels?" He looked at me and then shook his head. "Honestly, what do they teach in those schools of yours? Asphodel is for mourning, loss, and most of all, death. The fields of asphodel were the afterlife for the ancient Greeks. The wicked went to Tartarus, and great heroes went to Elysium—but for everyone else, there were the just the fields of asphodel. Unexceptional spirits were left for all eternity to flit about like shadows among the flowers. I suppose they are rather pretty in their own way, but given Miss Cavanaugh's current state, perhaps not the most helpful."

I sighed. It was a sign of just how badly the day was going that Jackaby was giving me good advice about tact.

"Just give her some time," Jackaby said, slipping the collar back on and fastening it clumsily beneath his chin. "Jenny's a stronger spirit than you might think. She survived her own death, for heaven's sake—I think she can weather a social faux pas. Help me with the back, would you?"

Jackaby tossed me a little metal stud, and I attached his collar to the back of his shirt.

"Right, then. I'm off to the market," he said, pulling his bulky coat off the chair. "I have a few specialty items to procure, so I may be out late. Try not to go offending any more members of the household in my absence, would you? Douglas puts up a stalwart front, but he's all soft underneath."

After Jackaby had left, I climbed up the stairs to Jenny's bedroom, but Jenny was nowhere to be found. The pond was abandoned as well; even Douglas had flapped off to do whatever ducks do in the afternoon. I slouched back behind my desk in the foyer with a sigh. A throaty croak issued from the bookshelf, and I turned to face the drab green frog. "Well, Ogden," I said, "at least you've warmed up to me."

My batrachian companion replied by puffing up his throat and venting a sudden burst of noxious gas in my general direction.

"Oh good Lord!" I gasped, stumbling to open a window. "Was that really necessary?"

I quickly deserted the first floor, surrendering what was left of my evening and resigning myself to an early night. Tomorrow, I vowed, was going to be a much better day.

Chapter Ten

A sudden, deafening clacking inside my room hauled my mind unceremoniously to wakefulness. I clapped my hands over my ears and sat up in bed, bleary eyed and disoriented.

"Oh good. You're awake," said Jackaby. The noise clicked to a stop.

"What . . . ?" I pushed my hair out of my face and willed the room into focus. Jackaby had lit the lamp on my dresser, and by its soft glow I could see that he was holding a simple wooden ratchet contraption with a stubby handle.

"Five o'clock," he announced. "We should be at the station in an hour. Bright new day, Miss Rook! Well, technically a dark one for the moment, but sunrise is coming."

"Right," I said. My ears were still ringing slightly. "Did you just wake me with a policeman's rattle? You can hear those things from two blocks away."

"A what? No, this is a grogger—it's an old Judaic instrument. It's used during Purim to make a deafening racket during special readings. Charming, isn't it? Marvelously raucous custom."

"Knocking gently also works."

"You have no appreciation for culture. Hurry up. We have a lot to do." Jackaby swept out of the room, and I heard his footsteps tripping blithely down the spiral staircase.

Breathing in deeply, I stood and drew back the curtains to look out onto the city. The stars were just visible, but the sky had already taken on the eager purple flush that precedes the dawn. Quiet though the morning was, it was an anxious quiet, as though the city of New Fiddleham were excited to begin its day. Already I could see a pair of newsboys hauling paper bundles toward Market Street, and an old doorman was unlocking the big financial building across the lane. At the corner of the crossroads, just up the way, a short, stout man stood waiting for someone.

A tingle wriggled up my spine, and my scanning eyes doubled back to the figure. He wore a dark coat and hat, and his skin was pale, but there was something else disquieting about him. It may have been my imagination—he was difficult to make out from all the way down the block—

but he looked as though he were staring directly up at me. My breath had fogged the glass, and when I wiped it clear to get a better look, the stranger had vanished.

I blinked and glanced up and down the road, but there was no sign of the pale man. Between the murder on Campbell Street and Jackaby's talk of bloodsucking ghouls, I suddenly felt a lot more thankful to be standing in the only house in town with more superstitious safeguards and holy relics than the Vatican—although they did not erase the eeriness of being watched. I would have to tell Jackaby about the figure before we left.

Jenny, I discovered, had laid out a handful of her old clothes across the oak chest at the foot of my bed. She had become in many ways like the older sister I had never had, and she was still looking out for me in spite of my thoughtlessness. I was relieved to be past the unsettling events of the previous day, but I felt all the more guilty about my lack of tact in the face of her kindness. I resolved to make amends before leaving. I picked out a simple dress with a nice high hem that looked fit for traveling, and tucked the rest into my suitcase.

Jenny's bedroom door hung open just a crack, and it swung inward as I knocked. "Jenny?" The chamber was dim and silent. "If you're in here, I just wanted to say thank you—and that I'm still very sorry about yesterday."

I stood in the doorway, feeling stupid and foolish. I could see that the flowers I had picked were all slumped to one side of the vase, and the asphodels were drooping mournfully. I took a deep breath and tiptoed into the room. As silently as I could, I adjusted the stalks, trying to bring the bright little clusters of bittersweets to the front. It was a meaningless gesture, but my lessons in etiquette had somehow failed to cover what to do when one had been unintentionally unkind to the undead. Perhaps I ought to have simply removed the whole unhappy arrangement before Jenny returned.

"You shouldn't be here."

The voice from behind me was forceful but frightened, accompanied by a sudden chill. It was as startling as if someone had poured ice water down my collar. I started and spun, knocking the bouquet off the table as I did. The vase did a quick pirouette in the air, and then shattered against the ground, splashing water and flowers across the floorboards. Jenny's slate-gray eyes looked lost and confused, fixating on the lopsided pool that was darkening the floor.

"Oh bother! I'm so sorry!" I dropped to the floor, mortified, and began picking up the shards of porcelain as quickly as I could. "I'm so, so sorry. I'll have it tidied up in a moment."

"No!" Jenny's voice was urgent and somehow distant. I stopped and looked up. She was staring at me and at the broken vase, visibly agitated, but somehow at the same time she was also facing away, toward the doorway. I blinked as my mind tried to process the double image. "No!" she repeated. "You shouldn't be here."

"Jenny?" I set down the broken pieces and stood up slowly. "Jenny, it's all right."

"I know who you are." Jenny's voice was cold and quavering, and it hurt my eyes to try to focus on both of her.

"That's right, it's me . . . ," I began, but Jenny continued as though she hadn't heard me.

"You work with my fiancé."

"I—what? No I don't. I work here with . . ."

"You shouldn't be here."

The little puddle of water at my feet began to crystalize as the room grew colder, and a stalk of asphodel slid along the floor as an icy gust of wind whipped through the small room.

"Jenny, you're frightening me," I said.

"You shouldn't be here!"

The gust became a torrent, and the curtains began to flap madly in the rapidly building maelstrom. The duvet flipped off Jenny's always impeccably made bed, and the doors to the armoire rattled and then whipped open and closed with a violent slap. The sound snapped something primal inside of me, and I found myself out of the room and in the hallway before I realized I was moving. When I turned back, the bedroom had fallen completely still and silent, and Jenny had sunk to the floor. Some part of her was looking up in terrible distress, and another part was crouching over the broken vase, her delicate fingers reaching toward a fallen sprig of bittersweets. Her silvery hand passed through the little purple buds like vapor, and at the same moment she screamed, "No!" once more, and the door slammed shut like a gunshot.

Chapter Eleven

I knocked and called out, but Jenny's room was as silent as the grave, and her door would not budge. I felt like I had just been punched in the gut, and I wanted to cry. With a deep breath, I plucked up my suitcase and what little fortitude I had left, and trod wretchedly down the spiral staircase.

I heard the sound of movement and found Jackaby in his office. He was unloading a basket of odds and ends, tucking the occasional object into his traveling satchel and leaving the rest in a heap on his desk. The wooden noisemaker lay beside the pile, and the scent of fresh garlic hung in the air.

"Nearly ready," he said. "Just reorganizing a few items I picked up yesterday."

"Sir," I began, not entirely sure how to proceed. "Jenny

is—that is, I think that she . . ." I took a breath. "Sir, there's something very wrong."

"Is there, now?" He pulled a gnarled root and a gold-rimmed teacup from the basket, setting them on his desk. There was a tea service on the end table already, and the new cup clashed with the soft pastels of the original set.

"Yes, sir. I don't know if it was the gloves or the flowers or what I said." I sighed. "Or just everything. She's getting worse."

Jackaby tossed the root into his satchel and turned toward me. "It isn't you, Miss Rook," he said. "Our immaterial associate has trapped herself in a sort of purgatory here. She cannot leave the house because she can only exist where she feels she belongs, just as she can only physically touch items that she feels belong to her. It is for this reason that progress on her own case stalled. She could not accompany me in my investigations."

"Her own case? You mean her death?"

Jackaby nodded. "Her murder, yes—and a bit more than that."

"Do you need her alongside you to solve it?"

"I could certainly pursue it on my own—and I have, to a degree. Douglas helped me compile an extensive file of relevant information." He rummaged in a drawer for a moment and produced a file. He set it on the desk, and I could see Jenny's name printed neatly on the front. "It is incomplete, but this is everything we know about Miss Cavanaugh and

her fiancé–newspaper clippings, evidence, persons of interest. Deep down, our dear Jenny does not believe the truth
is hers to find. Until she does, I do not know if providing it
to her would be a kindness. Perhaps she fears the answers
might be more painful than the questions, and I cannot say
that they will not be. When she is ready, though, I think
she will find herself able to go wherever she must."

"You *think* . . ." Jenny's voice came from behind the desk,
and gradually the gentle lines of the specter's face coalesced.
She looked bitter and annoyed, but at least the confusion
and panic had vanished, and she appeared to be in control
of herself. "But you don't *know*. You could simply *believe* me
when I say that I want to know, instead of talking about me
in secret and stuffing me away in your desk like an abandoned project."

"It's your file," Jackaby said. "It has your name on it and
everything. Just open it."

Jenny scowled darkly at the detective. "Where are my
gloves?"

"I've told you before, you don't need them. In fact, I
think I can prove it." He picked up the new gold-rimmed
teacup from the desk and plucked another one from the
tray. "Here, this is from your heirloom tea set." He tossed
the pastel blue cup, and Jenny's eyes widened as she swept
out her hands and caught the fine china projectile. "And
this one I picked up at the market this morning while I
was out." Without giving her time to think, he pitched the

new gold-rimmed cup toward her. Instinctively, Jenny held out a hand, but the new one passed directly through it and smashed against the bookcase.

She cradled the first cup in her hands and frowned at Jackaby. "Stop trying to destroy my belongings. You haven't proven anything! We already know that I can only touch things that are mine to touch. You're just tormenting me, now—and will you stop smiling while I'm being cross with you!"

Jackaby shook his head but kept smiling. "You can only touch things you *believe* you have a right to touch. After all, that isn't your teacup you're holding. Don't you recognize the set Mrs. Simmons gave me for that gnome business I cleared up last year?"

Jenny stared down at it, and the little blue cup started to sink through her fingers. She fumbled frantically to save it, but it clattered to the floor in half a dozen pastel pieces.

"Similar colors, of course, but *believing* was all it took. State of mind, Miss Cavanaugh. It's all in your head." He slid the file across the desk toward Jenny, who looked up from the broken shards. "It's your case. All you have to do is open it."

Jenny stared at the file. I watched breathlessly as she reached a hand toward the desk. Her fingers paused on the folder, and for an instant I was certain the papers beneath bent to her touch—but then her hand sank to the wrist through the file, past the blotter, and into the desk itself.

She recoiled as though bitten and held her hand to her chest, her expression addled and uncertain.

"Try again." Jackaby's voice was surprisingly gentle.

Jenny looked up at the detective, and then at me, and then back to the file. She shook her head and backed away uneasily, melting into the bookcase as she withdrew.

"Jenny, wait!" I said, but she had gone again.

"I think that went rather well, don't you?" Jackaby stuffed the empty basket on a cluttered bookshelf. "I wasn't entirely certain that my theory would hold ground in practice, but I would say the experiment was a resounding success."

"Mr. Jackaby, really! Jenny isn't some scientific oddity—she's your friend!"

Jackaby raised an eyebrow. "In point of fact, Miss Rook, she's both, and that's nothing to be ashamed of. All exceptional people are, by definition, exceptions to the norm. If we insist on being ordinary, we can never be truly extraordinary."

"That is a very well-rehearsed and eloquent excuse for being an absolute brute to a sad, sweet woman."

"She's fine. I assure you, you'll know when she's been pushed too far. It's not a pretty sight. When I was having her old kitchen renovated into the laboratory, she even began to echo."

"Echo?"

"Many spirits can do nothing else. Many spirits *are* nothing else. When a spirit echoes, she is nothing but the shadow of her last living moments—a clumsy, overlapping mess of emotion and pain—caught, like an echo in a canyon, reliving her final thoughts."

"You mean things like, 'You shouldn't be here'?" I asked.

Jackaby's confident expression faltered.

"And something about working with her fiancé?" I added.

"Did the temperature drop noticeably?"

"There was ice. And a sort of a whirlwind."

He blanched.

"Do you think I should try talking to her again?" I said.

Jackaby swallowed and glanced up at the ceiling. Jenny's bedroom sat directly above his office. "No—no, our little expedition may have come at just the right time. I think it's best we give our dear Miss Cavanaugh a wide berth—for a few days, anyway. You know—to allow her some peace and quiet and all that." The temperature in the room began to drop, and my arms prickled with goose bumps.

I nodded. "I think you might be right, sir."

Chapter Twelve

By half past five, Jackaby had finished making various arrangements and tending to the terrarium of chameleomorphs. He explained their care and keeping to Douglas while I watched the little kittens through the glass. One of them batted playfully at a water strider with its big fluffy paw, and then pounced and polished the thing off. It might have been my imagination in the dimness of the gaslights, but already they looked a little smaller and skinnier. I would be happy to miss watching their transformation from felines into insects. Fins on fur had been disturbing enough—I did not like to imagine the process they had ahead of them. It was still hard to fathom that the mackerel circling lazily in the pool toward the back was the same species as the wide-eyed little fur balls tumbling around in front.

Jackaby pulled on his coat, which clinked and tinkled as the contents of its myriad pockets rattled into place. He slung his satchel over one shoulder. "Well, Miss Rook, shall we?"

I nodded and followed my employer, casting a glance up the stairs as we stepped into the hallway.

"Do you think she'll be all right?" I asked.

"Of course not," said Jackaby. "I think she will be dead. Generally speaking that falls outside the realm of *all right*. I do not, however, think she will be any worse for our absence." He stepped into the front room and pulled on his multicolored knit cap.

"I still feel dreadful," I said. "I wish I could do something. Jenny had been giving me some good advice about . . ." I looked at Jackaby, swimming in his bulky coat with the ridiculous hat stuffed over his messy hair, and decided not to go into the details of our conversation. "Well, anyway, she was being rather kind, and reminding me that fortune favors the bold."

"That's nonsense," said Jackaby. "Fortune favors the prepared. Unless you're talking about the Fates, in which case fortune generally favors Zeus. Were you talking about the Fates?"

"No. We weren't talking about the Fates. Never mind. I went and botched it, that's all—not that you helped anything this morning with that teacup business. I know you might think it pointless, but I just wish I could fix it. It's bad enough to bungle things professionally and . . . well . . . romantically. It would be nice if I could at least get a friendship right."

"I don't think it's pointless," said Jackaby. "I don't think it's pointless at all. I think it's a marvelous sentiment."

"Really?"

"Absolutely. Atonement and reconciliation after an argument demonstrate strength of character and bolster the atmosphere of the workplace."

"Oh. Well, yes. Mostly I just wanted her to feel better."

"And mostly *I* just want to be sure you don't come to me to discuss your romantic entanglements. I much prefer that you remain on comfortable terms with Miss Cavanaugh. Although, should she ever be unavailable," Jackaby said earnestly, "I want you to know"–he put a hand gently on my shoulder–"that Douglas is an excellent listener."

"Thank you, sir. I'll bear that in mind."

"Please do. In the meantime, try not to dwell on Miss Cavanaugh. She has more going through her metaphysical mind than you or I could ever fully comprehend, and in the end she must cross certain mental bridges alone. She needs time more than she needs flowers or kind words right now. When we return, you can regale her with glamorous accounts of tracking a bloodsucking murderer, maybe even tuck in a few rousing tales about digging up rocks, and I'm sure everything will go back to–well not *normal*, but whatever it was before."

Jackaby might have had the social graces of a brick, but I did feel fractionally better. The least I could do was take Jenny's advice, and try to be bold on my little adventure. Today was about investigating my very own mystery, about helping unearth historic discoveries, and, admittedly, just a little bit about seeing a really sweet boy who made me feel sort of wobbly inside. I picked up my valise and pulled open the bright red door.

The train station was not more than a dozen blocks from Augur Lane, although accounting for distances precisely was never an easy task along New Fiddleham's unorthodox roadways, and no less complicated in the dim predawn light. I would never fully come to understand the logic behind the city planning. Some streets ended abruptly after only a few blocks, while others mysteriously changed names and ambled off. Roads meandered and intersected at odd angles, necessitating creative mosaics of masonry where conflicting cobblestones converged. Gradually growing familiar with at least a few of the city's quirks felt like becoming privy to an inside joke, and I had started to feel the subtle pride of being in on it.

We made good time, and although the sky was aglow in anticipation, the sun still had yet to make an appearance when the thick marble pillars of the station house rose before us. I took a seat on a bench inside and watched the milling crowd while Jackaby went to purchase tickets. The station opened onto two broad platforms framed by heavy roman columns. The main building had a high roof with an ornate tin ceiling, which helped the space feel open in spite of the growing crowd of waiting passengers.

A group of well-dressed businessmen shuffled along, arguing about something or other, and as they passed, my eyes locked on a figure beyond them. Standing just outside the doorway to the first platform was a stout man dressed in a black coat with a dark waistcoat and a wooly scarf. His skin was sickly pale, and his chin had the bluish stubble of a day-old shave. There was no mistaking it; he was the man I had seen from my window, and he was staring right at me. Between the Jenny situation and our leaving for the valley, I had completely forgotten to tell Jackaby about him. The man caught me looking but did not drop his gaze. He only turned up the corner of his lips in a slow smirk that made my skin crawl. A family with six or seven noisy children cut between us, and when they had passed, the pale man was gone.

Curiosity burned through my chest, and before the man could get far this time, I hopped up from my seat and rushed to the door. The platform ran along the length of the building, and I caught sight of a dark coat rounding the far corner as I emerged. I glanced back, but Jackaby was still waiting in line at the counter, his back to me. Scowling, I rocked back and forth on the balls of my feet for just a moment, and then took off out the door and down the platform.

Passersby gave me affronted looks as I wove between and around them to hurry down the length of the building. I came skidding to a stop as I reached the end of the station house and rounded the corner, narrowly avoiding plowing into a little old lady in ragged clothes who was rummaging through the refuse bins. I stood, panting and peering from building to building, but the pale man was nowhere in sight. The sun was just creeping above the line of the horizon, and its reflection bounced blindingly off the nearby windows.

"Abigail Rook!" The ragged woman smiled up at me like a pleased old auntie.

I caught my breath. "Oh goodness—Hatun. How nice to see you again." Hatun was one of Jackaby's occasional contacts on the streets of New Fiddleham. "Did you happen to see a man run through here?"

She thought hard for a few seconds. Her face crinkled up in concentration.

"Just now?" I prompted. "Did you see someone run through here just now?"

Her face brightened "That's what it is!" She clapped her hands happily. "You're alive! That's what's different about you."

I blinked. "Yes. Erm. I was alive the last time you saw me, too."

Hatun waved her hand dismissively. "Right, right.

Sometimes I see things a little out of order is all. All the same, I'm glad you're not dead just yet."

"Well, thank you for that, I suppose."

"You're leaving town?" she asked.

"Yes. For Gadston, on the next train. You didn't see anyone?"

"Well thank goodness. Hate to see you go, but it's for the best. I am fond of the fellow, but remember what I told you about following Mr. Jackaby. I've seen it." She leaned in and whispered loudly, "Death."

Hatun did not look like much, but she was exceptional in her own right. While Jackaby had a unique vision of the world, Hatun saw the world through a sort of kaleidoscope of angles, some of which were more helpful than others. Her premonitions were generally on the less-reliable side, ranging from talking teakettles to an apocalypse of eggplants, but they were on the right track often enough to generally merit a listen. She had once told me that I would follow Jackaby to my demise, a prophecy that turned out—very fortunately—to be exaggerated. I had only *nearly* died, although I had the scar above my heart to remember it by.

"Oh—right, that. No, I'm not *leaving* leaving. I am still working for Jackaby. That business you were worried about, though—I came out of it only a little worse for wear. That's all over."

"Is it, now?" The way Hatun looked straight at me—as

though she were looking much, much farther than my eyes—made me more uncomfortable than I care to admit.

"Rook!" Jackaby called from the doorway. The train had begun to rattle loudly into the station, and he had to yell over the sound of the hissing steam. "Rook! What on earth are you up to?"

I waved him over. "Just saying hello to an old friend."

He marched along the platform toward us, a pair of tickets clutched in his hand. Along the way he seemed to catch sight of something in the air. He slowed and reached one hand out to gently feel ahead of him, as one might reach over the side of a boat to brush the waves. A puff of steam engulfed him. He waved it away and continued on to the end of the platform.

"Jackaby. You're looking well," Hatun said.

"Good day, Hatun. I don't suppose either of you noticed something peculiar hanging about in the air around here? Sort of a purplish, ashen color? Vaguely funereal? No?"

"Yes!" I said. "Well, no. I saw a man. He was terribly creepy, and I've seen him before, Mr. Jackaby. He was outside the house this morning."

"Hmm." Jackaby's expression darkened. "I've seen that aura before as well."

I swallowed. "Campbell Street?"

He nodded solemnly.

"Fire," said Hatun, barely above a whisper.

"Come again?" Jackaby asked.

The little old woman stepped toward Jackaby. Her eyes were closed to slits and she breathed in deeply through her nose. "So much fire."

Jackaby and I exchanged concerned glances.

"Or possibly fireflies," Hatun amended, blinking. "Or flint. Feathers? Something with an *F*. What were we talking about?"

"We were just leaving. Always a pleasure, though, Hatun." Jackaby handed me my ticket.

Hatun bid good-bye to Jackaby but then shot me a concerned glance.

"Don't worry—in a way, he's technically following me on this one," I assured her. "No death this time, I promise."

She nodded and gave me an unconvinced smile as we parted. Looking back, I can't blame her—it was a promise I was in no position to keep. In retrospect, there would be quite a lot of death.

Chapter Thirteen

*By request of my employer, the contents of chapter thirteen
have not only been omitted; they have been pulled directly from
my typewriter, shredded, and used as terrarium liner
for a particularly pungent frog.*

—ABIGAIL ROOK

Chapter Fourteen

Through the window in our train car I watched the streetlamps and brick buildings give way to trees and hilly horizons. "How far is it to Gadston?" I asked.

"About three hours until we reach town," answered Jackaby. As soon as we had slid into the cabin, Jackaby had set to work packing a little leather pouch with a string of rosary beads, a handful of dried herbs, and a fat blue bauble that looked like an eye. He stood on his seat to hang the lumpy bag above the door with a pin, dropping back down to the cushion with a *whump* when the task was managed. "Gadston is only the mouth of the valley, so it will be another hour or two by carriage before we've properly reached our destination."

The city was truly behind us, and we were now rattling

through the natural, rolling New England landscape. Signs of spring crept up on all sides, with bright fields of flowers and fresh green hillsides. Free of the looming buildings and shady alleyways of New Fiddleham, I could let the uneasiness that had begun to settle over me give way to a tingle of excitement. Ahead lay not only the thrill of a new, important case, but also the prehistoric discovery I had been chasing since the day I left the shores of England.

Gadston was not a large town. A few houses dotted our approach, each situated on a wide stretch of mostly wild landscape. As we grew nearer, the properties pulled themselves together to form something more closely resembling a neighborhood, but even the smallest lots still looked as though they covered at least a healthy half acre. Gradually the buildings shuffled closer and closer until, by the time the train was hissing and slowing down for the modest station house, something resembling a town center had appeared, although none of the buildings was more than two or three stories tall. We rolled past a cheery red schoolhouse and a weathered grange hall, and as we lurched to a final stop, I could just see a white church steeple peeking over the nearest rooftops.

We collected our things and disembarked. I was met by the smell of dust and horses as I stepped out of the station house, along with something sweeter drifting on the breeze from a bakery across the street. It was a cozy, pleasant little town. I don't know precisely what I had suspected—dimly lit saloons, I suppose, and gritty cowboys having pistol duels at high noon. A local couple passed by, startling me out of my thoughts with friendly greetings and a hearty welcome. I smiled and nodded cordially. Their cheery goodwill only made me more keenly aware that I had left the big city, where sidewalk courtesy rarely extended beyond avoiding eye contact and not intentionally pushing fellow pedestrians from the curb.

"It looks as though we're not the only ones who still have a trip into the valley to make." Jackaby stepped up beside me, motioning down the road to the trapper's sturdy cart. The rugged timbers and heavy burlap looked a little more at home here, but it was still an easy vehicle to pick out. Hudson had parked it just outside a shop with a wooden sign that read simply COYOTE BILL'S. The muscular horses shifted their hooves absently as they waited for their master to return.

As we neared the door, Jackaby slowed. His hand rose to feel the air ahead of him, as it had outside the train station.

"Sir?" I asked.

Jackaby ignored me and stepped up toward Coyote Bill's, his brows knit in a scowl and his eyes lost in concentration. He knelt just outside the entrance, his fingers delicately tracing along the door frame. The door burst open, and Hank Hudson emerged, nearly toppling over Jackaby. The trapper had a couple of boxes under one arm, and in his fist was a thin bundle wrapped in brown paper.

"Whoa! 'Scuse me, there, buddy."

"Hudson!"

"Jackaby?"

"Hudson, you must tell me—this shop, is there something peculiar about it?"

"Yup. That's why I like it. All kindsa stuff they don't stock anywhere else."

"No—no, something more malevolent than eclectic wares. It's very strong here, lingering about the door. Please. Use all your senses."

Hudson blinked, but then he leaned down tentatively and gave the doorknob an obliging sniff. "It smells like . . . metal?" he said.

"Not—I don't know—a bit saturnine?" asked Jackaby, "with a hint of stygian exigency?"

"You know what any of those words mean?" Hudson asked, looking to me for help.

"I think one of them might be a sort of cheese."

Hudson let the door close behind him. "Smells like an old brass doorknob, Jackaby, and maybe a bit like sweaty man hands."

My employer nodded and straightened up. "Chasing shadows, I suppose, but I have the most troubling suspicion that some unsavory element has frequented this establishment."

"Hah!" Hudson laughed and slapped Jackaby on the shoulder. "You ain't never met Bill, have you? Unsavory elements are sorta his clientele. He's real good at getting hold of whatever a fella might need. Not exactly a hundred percent clean, but real good at the trade. Me an' Bill go way back. I always save him a few of my best hides, and he's gotten me some . . . some hard-to-find items when I needed 'em most. He always keeps shells in stock for my best rifle, too, so I make a point of stocking up when I come through." He nodded to the boxes under his arm. "They're the big ones."

"This wouldn't be the same Bill you told me about from the war, would it?" Jackaby asked, his eyes narrowing. "The one who sold Southern pistols to the North and Northern rifles to the South?"

Hudson chuckled and strode over to the cart. "In his defense, neither batch of 'em worked. Bill's as crooked as a bag of snakes, but he ain't one for blood, if he can avoid it. He's just a fence."

"A fence," I said, "who deals in rare artifacts?"

Hudson nodded approvingly. "I do like this one, Jackaby—she's a razor, ain't she? You and I had the same idea, little lady, but no such luck. If somebody is looking to unload a stolen fossil, they didn't go through Coyote Bill. He doesn't know nothin' about it." Hudson pulled back the burlap flap and stashed the rifle shells in the back of his cart. He tucked the paper parcel in his belt. "Y'all headed down to the valley? Happy to give you a lift—I'm all done up here."

"That would be wonderful," I said.

"Actually, if you don't mind, I'd rather meet Coyote Bill for myself, first," said Jackaby.

Hudson shrugged. "Go ahead and say hello, then. It'll take me a sec to clear some space in the back, anyway."

"Hold this, would you, Miss Rook." Jackaby handed me his heavy satchel, which nearly threw me off balance as he slung it over my shoulder. "I'll only be a moment."

Hudson relieved me of the luggage as my employer vanished into the little shop. "Lemme give you a hand with that." For all his rough and rugged appearance, the burly mountain man proved to be every bit the gentleman. Something squawked loudly as he nestled my suitcase into the back of his cart, and I jumped at the noise.

"Don't pay Rosie no mind," he called over his shoulder. "She's an ornery thing, but she won't be able to reach ya."

I peered into the carriage at a bulky shape, draped in a heavy cloth. Only a small corner toward the bottom revealed the bars of what might have been a massive birdcage sitting atop a simple wooden crate. It was easily as tall as I was.

"Fair warning, though," Hudson added, pulling the canvas closed. "If she does her business on the way, you're gonna want the windows wide-open back there." He made a funny face and fanned his nose in pantomime.

"I think I'll be all right," I said. "I've had to develop a certain tolerance for unexpected aromas working for Jackaby. Has he shown you his frog?"

"Who do you think caught the lil' stinker for him? Hah!" The cart rocked as Hank pulled himself up into the main compartment. "Had to throw away a nice moleskin coat after I bagged that critter." He chuckled at the memory, shuffling the contents of the cabin to make room on the bench. He was clearly not accustomed to carrying passengers—the cabin was crowded with boxes, furs, and jars of dried goods, and it was hung with rifles, ropes, and antlers along the interior. He cleared a space and draped a hide of soft, lush fur over the bench for us.

The door opened, and my employer emerged just as the trapper was finishing up. Hudson helped us both into the carriage and climbed up into the driver's box. With a click of the reins we were on our way. The tools and traps hanging all around us jangled ominously as we began rolling, but the hide beneath us was impossibly soft and comfortable.

"Find out anything interesting?" Hudson asked from the front.

"Nothing especially," Jackaby replied, fidgeting with a slim metal tube I hadn't noticed before. "There have indeed been all manner of individuals in that shop, and recently, too—but no one aura I could single out. You never mentioned that your friend was of goblin blood."

Hudson's head appeared through a little flap in the front of the cabin. "Come again? Known Bill for years. He ain't no goblin."

"Half blood, almost certainly. I would guess goblins are

on his mother's side, based on the ears. For some reason they tend to be more pronounced down paternal lines. Notorious brigands, their lot. Not the least bit trustworthy, but it stands to reason that he has a propensity for peddling pilfered goods. A useful associate to have on your side, all things considered, so long as you're not counting on loyalty."

The trapper looked about to object, but then nodded. "Huh. Actually explains a few things."

"He does indeed deal in rare goods," said Jackaby, "but he told me the same thing he told you. Bones he can do—sheep, salamanders, even a few human reliquaries—but there are no dinosaurs in the bunch. He does have quite a few curious items tucked in with the ordinary goods on his shelves, though."

"Is that one of them?" I pointed to the small metal tube in his hands.

Jackaby held it up a bit sheepishly. "Oh, this?" I saw that it was a little penny whistle. It looked like the sort you could buy from any dime store. "Not exactly. No."

"Then why on earth did you buy a—"

"He is a remarkably talented salesman."

Hudson chortled and pulled the bundle of brown paper from his belt, waggling it through the flap in the canvas. "Tell me about it! Ain't ever left that shop without somethin' I didn't need." He passed the parcel back, and I unfolded it to find several strips of dried meat. "Deer jerky. Help yerselves."

Through the window I could see that we had already left the little town behind. Gadston was nestled just outside the mouth of Gad's Valley, twin bluffs bordering the natural gateway into the broad valley like marble pillars. As the cart rolled through the pass, we were briefly draped in shadow, and then the splendor of the landscape opened to us like a theater curtain. Light poured over the carriage, and vast acres of woody hills and waving grasses lay before us. The path wound past burbling streams and fields of wildflowers, with only the occasional barnyard or cottage adding a human touch to the scenery.

The wheels began to bounce against a stretch of washboard bumps in the rough road, and the whole carriage shook. The boxes of ammunition beneath our seat rattled, and a bear trap, its steel jaws fortunately closed, swung free from its peg above us, whipping back and forth like a grisly pendulum. Jackaby dropped his whistle to grab at the trap, but on the third swing, the chain holding it slipped as well, whipping over his shoulder and rattling into the back of the cart.

There came a loud squawk from behind us, and I looked back to find that the cloth shrouding Rosie had been knocked away. The bear trap had clattered to the floor, its long metal chain drooping over and into the poor bird's enclosure. Every bar of the massive cage had been lined with what looked like corks from wine bottles. It had a round base about three feet in diameter, and as the creature within flapped to steady itself, I could see that its wingspan must have been twice as wide. The bird's plumage was dark amber and rust red, with wings of brilliant gold. It was built like a large crane, with less neck and more beak—and what a beak! It was slightly curved and as glossy as polished brass. Rosie squawked again and shifted her weight from foot to foot as she eyed the intrusive chain with annoyance.

I reached back to pull the jangling chain off her. "I wouldn't do that if I were you," Jackaby said. "You don't want any part of you too near that bird."

Hank's head appeared through the flap again. "She's a softie, these days, but he's right. Best to keep yer fingers clear of–"

Rosie let out a shrill screech, and I turned back in time to see her rear up and lash at the chain with her sharp beak. Two halves of a cleanly split link fell to the bottom of Rosie's cage, and the ends of the chain slid away to either side. The light streaming through the flaps caught Rosie's beak and danced along its razor edge, and she preened briefly before settling back down.

"Don't worry. She's a grumpy old thing, but she's basically harmless," said Hudson. "Besides, she doesn't go for the bars anymore. Haven't found a metal she can't cleave clean through, but she gets stuck in the cork."

"W-what?" I stammered. "What kind of bird is she?"

"One of a kind!" Hank smiled. "Used to be whole flocks of 'em, once upon a time. I did some trade with a funny little Greek fella out of Arcadia a few years back. One day his ship comes in—he's lost half his cargo, three crewmen are gettin' hauled off to the hospital, and he tells me this pretty thing got loose in the hold. She carved her way through to the mess hall like it was a tin can and put a breach in the hull before they managed to get her secured. Poor girl was so trussed up in leather straps, she could hardly move. Well, the Greek is more than happy to let her go for a decent price, but he knows she's worth more'n I can pony up—plus he's got all them ruined goods to make up for—so, I brought your boss here out to the docks with me to see her for himself."

Jackaby nodded, confirming the story. "Seemed a shame to let such a remarkable creature be sold off to the highest bidder, and worse yet to see her fall into the wrong hands—besides which, Hudson had already proven himself a capable handler."

"So," continued Hudson, "he drops enough for a whole new boat, which makes the Greek happy as a fish in whiskey, and he gives Rosie to me, along with a little history lesson to make sure I knew what I had bought."

"And what was that?" I asked.

Hudson winked. "Stymphalian bird."

"Have you ever heard of them, Miss Rook?" Jackaby asked.

"Isn't that one of the labors of Hercules?"

"Hah!" Hudson looked very pleased. "No wonder Jackaby

hired you. Yup, the very same. Beaks like bronze, only sharper and stronger. Feathers like daggers. If she has enough room, Rosie can whip one of them suckers faster'n I can pull a trigger." He leaned in with a grin, "An' that's purdy darn fast. Apparently old Hercules had to scare 'em off with some sorta magic chimes. The cork was Jackaby's idea."

"Not entirely," said Jackaby. "I did find a few relevant passages that suggested it had worked before. Soldiers in Arcadia made armor out of cork, because the birds carved right through iron. With the cork, however, their beaks would catch and become stuck.

"Better than birdlime!" Hudson added.

"I can't imagine an entire flock of them," I said.

"That woulda been somethin' to see." Hudson sounded a little wistful. "I like ta think there might be one or two out there, maybe a few in captivity like my Rosie, but the rest are all gone. I do like a rare breed."

"I can see why you're fond of Jackaby."

"Hah! He's as rare a breed as they come—that's the truth!"

Jackaby rolled his eyes.

"I'm real glad you two came out." Hudson turned back to the road. "You'll like Gad's. It's purdy out here in the valley. Only, best you don't go explorin' too much on yer own. Word is something big's come to the valley. Bill says a couple local hunters found some paw prints a few weeks back like nothin' they'd ever seen. I'm right keen to get a crack at it, whatever it is."

I nodded and absently gnawed a bite off the strip of deer jerky in my hands. I tried to imagine what sort of lumbering beasts might lurk in these hills. The last time I'd gotten lost in the woods, I really had been attacked by a vicious creature– and it would've done me through if not for Charlie coming to my aid. Even at his best he had barely been able to stand his ground. I blanched and nearly choked on the chunk of gamy meat.

Had local hunters already stumbled across Charlie Barker's secret? Charlie–properly Charlie Cane, as I had known him in New Fiddleham–was part of a nomadic family, the House of Caine, all of whom were born with the ability to change from men to dogs and back again. It was the exposure of his inhuman heritage that had forced Charlie out of New Fiddleham, and it was his most closely guarded secret. I took its keeping very seriously. I would not know it myself, had he not risked everything to protect his town. But Charlie could not endlessly deny his full na-ture; he had to occasionally change, and in his canine form, he would certainly leave footprints unlike anything a local had ever seen.

Jackaby and I exchanged glances. I could tell that the thought had occurred to my employer as well. "What sort of prints did Bill say that they had found?" Jackaby asked. I eyed the heavy rifles and sharp skinning knives tethered to the walls of the carriage. "Mountain lions, perhaps?"

"Naw," Hudson called back. "Said it was like a fox or a wolf's, but big—bigger'n a bear. He's been trading with hunters in these parts longer'n I can reckon—so if there's something in these woods he ain't seen before"—the big, bushy-bearded face popped back into the carriage with a wide grin—"then I wanna hunt it." He pulled himself back out and hummed happily as the carriage bumped along the rocky pass.

The soft hide I was resting on suddenly felt a little less pleasant, and the sharp trapper's tools looked a lot more dangerous. I swallowed hard, and the lump of deer jerky slid uncomfortably down my throat. Charlie Barker and Hank Hudson had been two of the most pleasant acquaintances I had made since my arrival in the States—but now it seemed I would be spending my trip worrying about whether one of the bullets Hudson had just purchased had Charlie's name on it. The ammunition boxes beneath my seat clinked as the carriage bumped along. They were the big ones.

Chapter Fifteen

After a long, winding ride, a farmhouse inched into view ahead of us, the details crystalizing slowly as we approached. It was a two-story house near the base of a rocky, sloping hill, which rolled and bumped its way up into the bordering mountains. Beside the building sat a barn with a slightly sagging roof, and beyond that, a half-dozen goats were grazing in a wide field bordered by a simple wooden fence. I spied a figure in the sunlight, and then a second and third. They seemed to spot us as well, and three men came to greet the carriage as we drew to a halt.

The first was an older gentleman in faded coveralls and a battered, wide-brimmed hat. He gave Hank a friendly wave as we approached. The second was a young man in sturdy slacks and a tailored vest, though he had rolled up his sleeves, and his trousers were caked with dirt. A fine layer of dust seemed to have settled all over the fellow. The third was dressed in a policeman's blues, and I recognized his face at once. Charlie caught my eye through the window and smiled as we drew near.

"Hank?" called the man in coveralls when the horses had stopped. "Hank Hudson, it is you! It's been forever since you were out this way."

The carriage rocked as Hank hopped to the ground. He greeted the man with a hearty handshake. "Hugo Brisbee. Good ta see ya, old man. Listen, I was real sorry to hear about Miss Madeleine. If you need anything at all . . ."

Brisbee forced a pained but appreciative smile. His eyes looked like they were welling up, but he blinked and shook his head. "That's very kind of you, Hank, but I'll make do. I've got to press on. My Maddie was never one to let me mope around when there was work to be done. She always . . ." His voice caught, and he took a deep breath. "Anyway, you should meet my new friend . . ."

Brisbee made a few introductions I couldn't quite hear, and Charlie stepped forward to assist Jackaby and me out of the carriage. "Thank you, Mr. Barker," I said, climbing down first.

"I wish I had known you would be here this early. I would have come to greet you at the station," he said. "Things run a little more slowly out here in the valley. My new cabin is up the road just a few miles, so I took the liberty of meeting you here, instead. I hope you don't mind?"

"Of course not. You're lovely–I mean, it's lovely!" My face instantly flushed. "To see you again. It's lovely to see you again."

"The pleasure is all mine, Miss Rook. You're the first visitors I've seen from my old life." A hint of melancholy flickered across his face. I couldn't imagine how he must have felt. It had been hard enough for me to choose to turn away from the life I had known, but in Charlie's case, it was his life that had turned on him. "Mr. Jackaby," he said, "I'm very happy to see you as well. I still owe you a great deal."

Jackaby waved him away as he stepped down. "Nonsense. New Fiddleham owes us all a great deal, but cities are notoriously unreliable debtors. You're better off dealing with goblins. How is banishment these days?"

"Not as wretched as you might imagine." Charlie's voice was soft, accented with a few gentle, Slavic undertones. "The valley is really quite serene, and I am getting to know my neighbors, few though they may be. There are good people here."

"One fewer of them than there ought to be," said Jackaby quietly.

Charlie nodded gravely and glanced back. The three men were chatting cordially behind him. "I haven't discussed the matter with Mr. Brisbee," he whispered. "I did not wish to cause him any further distress. The woman's death was already hard enough—and it might have been nothing . . ."

"It's never nothing, though, is it?" Jackaby gave me a meaningful glance. "Don't worry. We will endeavor to keep our investigation clandestine."

Charlie nodded.

Hudson laughed at something the dusty stranger had said, and then he turned his attention to us. "How about you, young man?" he called over to Charlie. "You ever go huntin' big game?"

My stomach lurched.

"Big game?" Charlie asked.

"There's somethin' big come to Gad's Valley." The trapper was grinning avidly. "And I aim to catch it. Ever been on a hunt yourself?"

If Charlie realized that he was the prey in question, he gave no indication. "I'm afraid not, sir," he answered. "I've only hunted criminals."

Hudson nodded. "Respectable line o' work," he said. "Yer like to get a bit restless out here in the hills, though. Gad's is mostly just quiet farm folk."

"I'm looking forward to a quiet post for a while," Charlie said. It might have been my imagination, but there seemed to be just a moment of uneasy silence as the two locked eyes. In my mind, the big trapper could look straight into Charlie and see the beast beneath the surface—but the moment passed.

"Where are my manners?" Hudson clapped his hands together. "Let me introduce my old buddy, Hugo Brisbee, and–oh sorry, what was yer name again?"

"Owen. Owen Horner." The young man flashed us a winning smile, complete with dimples and gleaming white teeth. "A pleasure."

Owen Horner. The name bounced around in my head for several moments before finding its place. Owen Horner was more than a farmhand. At home in England, I used to devour my father's scientific journals, and Owen Horner had made his way into several publications over the past few years as a rising star in the geological field. I tried to re-member what great accomplishment had gained him such notoriety, but the details had slipped off into the corners of my mind.

"Right." Hudson gestured back to us. "And this here's R. F. Jackaby and Miss Abigail Rook. They've come to help the coppers track down that big old bone they were talking about in the paper."

"Oh–you read that? Hmm. Heck of an article," said Hugo Brisbee, nodding. "That reporter came all the way out from New Fiddleham just to interview us. It was only supposed to be about the dig, of course–but then . . ." He rubbed his hands and swallowed hard. "She said it'll be running up in Crowley and Brahannasburg, too–maybe even national if she can get all the big papers to pick it up. Maddie would like that. She always wanted to get out of the valley. I've been getting all sorts of kind letters from names I haven't heard in years. It's real nice to see some folks in person, though, too. Mr. Horner's presence has been a gift this past week. He's been keeping me company, taking care of everything while I was in town making arrangements—and of course he's been working the site all by himself. He was just about to show me the latest find, as a matter of fact."

My heart skipped. "I don't suppose you would mind if Mr. Horner showed us his progress as well?" I ventured.

Brisbee shrugged. "As good a place to start as any—why don't you all come have a look?"

My mind was humming with anticipation, but Hudson held up a hand. "Mighty kind—and I'll be sure to take ya up on that offer soon enough, but I'd best be gettin' Rosie back to my place first. We been out in the world for a long stretch, and I reckon she's about done being cooped up in that wagon. Got a few other odds and ends I should see to while I still got daylight, too."

"It *has* been a long time," said Brisbee, "or else maybe I don't know you as well as I thought. Would've guessed you'd be the first one in line to get a look at our creature."

Hank chuckled. "Oh, I'll be back—you'd better believe it. Them bones have waited a long time, and they can wait a little longer. Show me somethin' that's still walkin' the earth, and you'll find me a little faster on the draw."

"Fair enough. Nice to see you again, Hank. Don't be a stranger!"

"Same, Brisbee. Good meetin' you fellas, too." He gave a nod to Charlie and Owen Horner, and then turned back to Jackaby and me. "You two gonna need a ride back into town later?"

I hadn't even thought about our accommodations for the evening. I noticed an inn on the way through town, but I had not realized the trip would take us so far into the valley.

"I'm sure that will not be necessary," Charlie interjected. "Mr. Jackaby and Miss Rook are dear friends, and they are welcome to stay with me. My cabin is a short ride from here." He looked to us. "If that's all right with you?"

"Splendid," said Jackaby. "Rook, you don't mind staying the night in a cozy little cabin with Mr. Barker, do you?"

I could feel a faint warmth rushing to my cheeks, but I answered quickly, before it had time to build to a proper flush. "No, sir. Not at all."

"Well then," said Jackaby, "that's settled. Thank you kindly, Mr. Barker."

Hudson pulled our luggage out of the carriage. "I can't thank you enough," I told him as he passed me my bag.

He waved me off casually. "Weren't nothin', little lady. I was mighty glad for the company. You take care of yerself, and that boss of yers, ya hear?" He plopped himself back into the coach box and gave the horses a nudge with the reins, throwing a final, friendly wave. As he locked eyes with Charlie, the expression beneath the trapper's bushy beard didn't really change, but something about his gaze hardened for a fraction of a second. A glance at Charlie's pleasant, reserved countenance would have had me believe it had all been in my head again, and by then Hudson had turned back to his horses.

"Well," said Owen Horner, clapping and rubbing his hands together as the carriage rattled away, "who wants to see a dinosaur?"

Chapter Sixteen

We left our luggage at Brisbee's and followed the farmer around the back of the farmhouse. The old man walked with a slow, steady gait, his eyes on the ground. He was a fine and pleasant host, but there was an incompleteness to him that made my heart ache.

"How did you come upon the fossils, Mr. Brisbee?" I asked him. "The article didn't say."

Brisbee blinked and looked up as if awoken from a distant dream. "Right, let me see now . . ." He smiled congenially and put one hand across Jackaby's shoulders and the other over mine, ushering us up into the bumpy foothills. "I found the first one, but it really wasn't anything. It was a week or so ago. I was just clearing ground for a new crop, hitting rocks every few feet. My plow ran into something big, so I hooked up a couple of horses, gave it a pull, and—*BAM!* There it was. I didn't know what I was looking at. Except that it was a single bone as long as one of my cows."

"A femur," Owen Horner said from just behind us. "And you've got a sharp eye, sir. It doesn't take a scientist to make history, just a keen and clever mind like yours." The shadows clouding Brisbee's eyes lifted just a little. Horner continued. "Don't think for a moment you haven't played the most important part in this excavation. The renowned Gideon Mantell started this whole dinosaur-discovery business, but it was his wife who found the first bones of the mighty Iguanadon."

"That is a lovely story," I said, "but it's not really true."

"I think you'll find that it is, miss. Over on your side of the pond, in fact. Essex, I think."

"Sussex," I corrected automatically. "Sorry. Mantell admitted the fib about thirty years later. As it happens, my father worked with his son, Walter—it was one of his first jobs, helping with the Moa remains in New Zealand."

I hazarded a glance backward, expecting the usual grimace of annoyance. My mother had often reminded me that men hated to be outdone by a lady.

But Owen Horner was grinning broadly, visibly impressed. "Your father, Miss Rook? Wait—Rook? You're not related to Daniel Rook, are you?"

"Who's that, now?" Brisbee asked.

"Only one of the finest minds in the field. I studied his paper on plesiosaurs when I was at university." Horner and Brisbee both looked to me to confirm or deny the relation.

"That's my father," I admitted. "You're no slouch yourself, though, Mr. Horner. I understand you made quite a name for yourself in . . . Colorado, was it? I know I've read something about you in the journals."

"South Dakota most recently," he said, "but neither site holds a candle to what we're digging up here."

"This is marvelous!" Hugo Brisbee tightened his grip around my shoulders, beginning to sound genuinely excited. "We've got Owen Horner, the up-and-coming prodigy, and now we've got the daughter of the famous Daniel Rook, and by tomorrow I'll be meeting Lamb, too! That settles it. I'm sending word to that reporter right away—I bet we could land a picture on the front page of the *Chronicle*. Maddie would be so proud."

"Wait a moment—Lamb, as in Lewis Lamb?" I asked.

"That's right," Brisbee confirmed happily. Horner nodded without enthusiasm.

"*Horner and Lamb . . . ,*" I said. "Now I remember what I read about you last! Oh good heavens. And you knew that Lamb was involved?"

Horner cringed but nodded again.

"Fantastic bit of luck, isn't it?" said Brisbee. "Lamb was the first one to get back to me about the bones. I promised him the site, so I guess he will technically be in charge when he gets here. I'm sure he'll be happy about the fine work Owen's been up to already, though."

"It's some kind of luck," I said, "but I wouldn't call it fantastic." I stopped in my tracks and faced Horner. Brisbee's hand slid off my shoulders, and Charlie and Jackaby turned to face us. *Now* the charming young scientist looked uncomfortable. "Owen Horner and Lewis Lamb have been at each other's throats for years!" I told Brisbee. "It's become international news—slander, sabotage, and all manner of skulduggery."

"I've never . . . ," Horner interjected.

"They've destroyed irreplaceable fossil evidence . . ."

"Technically, I only . . ."

"They even stooped to hurling rocks at each other across a quarry!"

"That was just the once," Horner admitted, "and their guys started it."

"You *knew* that this site had been promised to Mr. Lamb?" I asked.

"Well . . . yes. But you have to understand, Lamb is on the decline. He left the Institute of Sciences in shame. I, on the other hand, have just been offered the prestigious—"

"But science shouldn't be a competition!"

"Right! I couldn't agree with you more." Horner held up his hands in a show of defense. "The battle of the bones is over. That's why I'm here. No funny business. Just science. I've set up perimeters and gotten the dig site prepared. I've even made some solid progress—with Mr. Brisbee's invaluable help, of course. This is still Brisbee property, so I suppose the *final* decision on who takes the lead is still up to him—but I promise I can play nice however it pans out—especially now that I know what we're digging up. This site is like nothing I have ever worked on. The bones haven't spread at all, and I've found almost no fragmentation. It's unreal." Horner's defensive posturing melted away as genuine enthusiasm took hold. "We uncovered a portion of the rib cage during our preliminary work yesterday, and just this morning I've unearthed most of the midsection."

"You've done all that since yesterday?"

"That's precisely what I mean! I've never been a part of an excavation that went this smoothly. The terrain is marvelously amenable, and the bones are impeccable. Wait until you see it! I haven't even told you the most exciting bit!"

"What's the most exciting bit?"

"Wait and see!" If Horner had been trying to distract me from the Lewis Lamb powder keg, then he had succeeded—for the moment. My excitement and curiosity got the better of me, and I hurried up the rocky slope after the scientist.

I had spent months on my first and only real dig in the Ukraine, sifting through rocks on a fruitless search. If even a fraction of Horner's story was true . . . The ground began to level out, and ahead of us I could see where the soil had been churned. It was like seeing a sunrise for the first time. I glanced back eagerly at my employer, and my thudding heart sank. Jackaby had stopped some twenty feet behind us, his fingers gently testing the air around him. His attention began to drift away from the foothills and toward the bushy forest to his left. *You wouldn't*, I thought. *No, not now. You wouldn't do this to me.*

"Sir?" I managed as politely as humanly possible. "I'm sure you will want to see the site. It's only just ahead."

"Have you noticed anything in this general area during your excavation, Mr. Horner?" Jackaby asked. He turned on his heel and walked a few steps toward the greenery, his eyes dancing around the underbrush. "Something . . . tenebrous, perhaps? A dissolute anathema, of sorts?" He squinted, focusing hard.

"A dissolute what?" Horner looked back to where Jackaby was standing, and then glanced nervously at Brisbee. "Oh, Detective, wait. Maybe it's best if you don't—"

"That's where I found her," Brisbee interjected. His gaze was locked on the rocky terrain a few feet down the slope from where Jackaby was standing. Nobody spoke for several seconds, the wind having been knocked very suddenly out of the journey. "The doctor told her she shouldn't go out." The farmer's voice strained. "But my Maddie never liked being told what to do."

"Mr. Brisbee, I am so sorry," I said. My throat felt tight.

"And you saw nothing to indicate there had been an attack?" Jackaby asked.

"Sir!" I said.

Brisbee shook his head. "It's all right, young lady. I've been through all this with your man, Barker. My Maddie was a pistol. I should have known she wouldn't stay cooped up with everything going on. This place was never big enough to keep her satisfied. It was her idea to expand in the first place." He wiped his eyes. "I should've brought her up here, myself, so she could see it before . . ."

Charlie put a hand on the man's shoulder. Brisbee took a deep breath and continued. "It didn't look like an attack, Detective. She looked . . . peaceful. It was the fever that did her in—and the rocks."

Jackaby exchanged a somber glance with Charlie. Charlie's face was grim, and I could tell he was uncomfortable omitting the detail of the victim's mysterious bruise, but he kept to Marlowe's command and remained silent. Brisbee did not seem to notice the unspoken exchange. His eyes were wet, and he stood transfixed, staring at the rocky hill.

"And where are her remains interred?" Jackaby asked.

"Mr. Jackaby," I whispered, appalled.

"I should like to pay my respects before we proceed," Jackaby said.

"That's kind of you," Brisbee said hoarsely, "but we laid her to rest out behind Saint Izzy's."

"Saint Izzy's?"

"Saint Isidore's. She used to sing in the choir on Sundays. It's got a beautiful churchyard. It's all the way back up in Gadston proper, though, and you've only just arrived."

"I feel it would be of great value to my process to visit Saint Isidore's first. Come along, Miss Rook!" Jackaby began picking his way back across the uneven terrain.

Respect to the late Mrs. Brisbee notwithstanding, I still found it difficult to ignore the fact that there was a dinosaur waiting not twenty feet up the hill, and we were about to walk away. "That's very thoughtful, sir," I said. "But are you sure it wouldn't be better to begin our work on the site?" I prompted. "We are right here, after all, and we have the light. Perhaps we could visit the church in the morning?"

"I think this takes precedence, don't you? I'm sure we'll all be able to approach the case with clearer heads once we've taken a moment to honor the deceased."

I opened my mouth as Jackaby clambered back down the sloping hill, but words failed me.

"Mr. Jackaby," came Charlie's soft voice, "it might be more efficient to divide your efforts. As Miss Rook is most qualified to examine the fossils, perhaps it would be best to leave her behind to perform a preliminary sweep of the crime scene while you pay your respects with Mr. Brisbee. I would be happy to remain behind as Miss Rook's escort, if you like."

I nodded emphatically, still unable to vocalize my thoughts, and pointed at Charlie to indicate my firm agreement.

"The notion is not entirely without merit," Jackaby said. "All right. Make thorough records, Miss Rook. We shall compare notes upon our return."

I withdrew my notepad and held it up meaningfully. The farmer looked out of sorts, but he nodded and stepped back toward the path. "Do you mind giving this young lady few tour without me?" he called up the hill.

Owen Horner gave me a charming smile. "I should like nothing more."

"Well, okay, then," Brisbee said. "I guess we'll see you folks this afternoon." With that, the farmer led Jackaby back down toward the farmhouse. "Say, weren't you in the papers yourself, a few weeks back?" he was saying as they departed. "Something about an honest-to-goodness werewolf?"

"That article was painfully inaccurate," Jackaby said, his voice fading as they wound down the hill.

"Shall we?" Owen Horner gestured grandly when they had gone, inviting us toward the rough, dusty plateau. I had seen successful excavations in the past, but only in the pages of my father's field journals or as lithographs in a textbook. The scene that spread before me could not possibly have been confined within a printed page.

The entire Brisbee farmhouse could have fit easily into the wide grid the paleontologist had established atop the hill. The ground was uneven. To one side it had been broken roughly in thick, haphazard rows. I could see where the farmer's efforts to till the earth had ended and the methodical scientist's work had begun. Wooden marker spikes had been pounded into the soil along a perimeter of a few hundred feet, and a simple brown twine had been tied along them to define the site. Outside the string border sat piles of rocks and dirt. Within the boundary, the loose debris had been cleared away, and the first layers of soil had been removed. Peeking out from the red-brown earth were the bones of an impossible colossus.

Most of the prehistoric creature remained beneath the dirt, but a faint, incomplete outline had been revealed, and the figure it described nearly filled the site. Half a rib cage had been dusted clean, and several feet of vertebrae as thick as my waist curved above the surface before the earth swallowed them up again. Twenty feet away, a wide lower jaw with nasty-looking sharp teeth had been unburied. If the visible bones were an accurate indication, the entire specimen was taller than a house and just waiting to be exhumed.

My eyes could not grow wide enough to take it all in. My whole body tingled. This was completely unlike my only previous personal experience, a miserable expedition I had attended in the mountains of the Ukraine. All of those frozen months had yielded a handful of scattered bones—all of which had later been confirmed to come from common mammals. This was . . .

"Impossible," I breathed.

"Isn't it?" Horner's voice was hushed and close to my ear. I felt the gentle pressure of a hand on my lower back, and he held his other in front of me. "Let me show you."

I accepted the hand out of courtesy, and he escorted me down the uneven terrain toward the beastly bones. I peeked back to be sure that Charlie was coming, too. He was keeping just a few paces behind, although his attention seemed to be more focused on the scientist than the astounding discovery. The ground leveled out, and Horner stepped away to fetch a pair of gloves from a pile of tools.

We were at the creature's stomach, so close I could reach out and touch the pale ribs. The sheer size of the thing was dizzying. "There is no way that you did all of this alone in just a few days," I said. "This is at least a week's worth of labor for even a very large team."

Horner shrugged with a cocky grin.

"No, seriously—how did you manage it?"

"Well, I can't take all the credit. First of all, Mr. Brisbee has the fortitude of a workhorse. He was with me every morning for the first few days, hauling rocks and dirt. Second, the bones are scarcely beneath the surface." Horner spun to marvel at his find. "I thought, at first, that geological shifting might have pushed them to a higher strata. The same forces that made these foothills could have done that much—but the more we uncovered, the less that seemed to fit. If the ground had been churned up enough to expel the specimen from its grave, the bones would not have remained so neatly arranged. Aside from what we've done to uncover them, the whole skeleton looks entirely undisturbed. The soil is rocky, but it's relatively soft and easy to work with. I can hardly blow away a layer of dust without uncovering a new fossil. They're not encased in stone, yet they're preserved pristinely. It's astounding."

"It is, absolutely." I moved closer, inspecting the nearest bones. They were only partially exposed, but once freed, the ribs looked as if they would form a more spacious cavity than the trapper's carriage.

"So far as I've been able to tell, the basic anatomy is not unlike a *Dryptosaurus*—only easily twice as large." Horner pointed toward the head. "The jaw tells us that it was a carnivore, of course." Centuries of fossilization had dulled them, but from several yards away I could see that the long canines were still vicious. I could also see that one of them was missing. A row of distinct points was interrupted by a smooth, concave hole where a tooth should have been.

"I take it that's . . ."

"The reason you're here? Yes. We uncovered the lower jaw on the very first day I arrived. Tremendous initial find. You can bet those teeth held a keen edge when this brute was alive. Beautiful artifacts. Such a shame."

"When did it go missing?"

"They were all there when I wrapped up for the night, about three days ago. In the morning, we found Mrs. Brisbee's body. Then the doctor was called, that reporter kept asking questions, some neighbors came around, and the police. I didn't even make it up to the site again until

Brisbee had ridden off with the body and I was alone. Any one of them could have walked off with it."

Horner pulled on a pair of gloves. "Take a look in that midsection I just cleared. See anything interesting?"

I did not know where to begin.

"Are those flint rocks in its stomach?" asked Charlie. I hadn't even realized that he had come to stand beside me.

Horner jabbed a finger at the policeman, looking very pleased. "Gastroliths. Good eye. They're stones of any sort—flint, in this case—that animals swallow to help with digestion. It's common in birds."

"Except they're not common in dinosaurs—at least not in meat eaters," I said. "A few sauropods have been found with them, if I recall, but only ever herbivores."

Horner clapped his hands together. "You *do* know your stuff! Ready for another? Put these on and follow me." Horner handed me a spare pair of leather gloves. They were several sizes too large, but I pulled them on. He trotted a few yards down to the feet of the beast. Its claws were as vicious as its teeth. Horner stopped in front of a leg bone taller than he was. I followed, and he leaned down to the base of the massive fossil.

"I take it that's the femur Brisbee pulled out with his horses," I said.

Horner nodded. "Now watch this." He took hold of the tremendous bone with both hands and lifted it upright like a strong man at the circus. It was a rather shameless display, but his strength was impressive nonetheless. Upright, it looked like the great menhirs, massive standing stones that my father had once studied in France.

"Very impressive, Mr. Horner," I said.

He laughed and set down the specimen. "The fact is, either one of you could perform that stunt just as well. Would you care to give it a try, miss?"

The femur was half again my height and as wide across as my shoulders. Skeptically, I leaned down and positioned my fingers beneath it. As I pulled, to my own amazement, it tilted up, rising several feet off the ground. "My word," I exclaimed. My grip within the oversized gloves slipped, and the priceless artifact thudded gracelessly to the ground.

"Careful," Owen Horner and Charlie said at once. The scientist caught hold of the fossil, shifting it carefully back into place, and at the same moment Charlie caught hold of my arm to steady me, but he let go almost as quickly and stepped shyly aside.

"It's as though it's hollow," I said.

"The medullary cavity," Horner replied smartly. "It's a space in which bone marrow and adipose tissue were stored when the creature lived."

"No, that can't be it." I shook my head. "I watched my father and his team articulate a skeleton at the museum, and it took three grown men to support a bone smaller than this. Could it be structured more like a pterosaur's?"

"Possibly," he said. "Pterosaurs did have bones like birds,

sturdy and lightweight, but that's because they were designed for flight. I would wager what we're looking at here is an especially large relative of the *Allosaurus*."

My head swam as the reality of the discovery washed over me again. It was as if the childish dreams that had lured me away from home had all come true. "May I help?" I asked. "I do have some experience."

"So I gather. What about the missing piece?"

"The more thoroughly we understand what's missing, the more thorough our investigation will be. I could be an invaluable member of the team."

Horner leaned in close. "My dear, of that I have no doubt. So long as I'm running the show here, your assistance is more than welcome. You've already proven you're as clever as you are lovely." He gave me a wink.

The man was a ridiculous flatterer, but my heart leapt with excitement to be back on a real dig. It was almost enough to forget that he would be running the show only as long as it took Lewis Lamb to arrive, at which point he'd likely be run out of town. I took a deep breath, looking over the bones. I would enjoy it while I could.

Chapter Seventeen

The afternoon flashed past. Charlie paced about the perimeter, looking for anything he might have missed during his preliminary examination. He found frustratingly little, and eventually he came to assist Horner and me, carting wheelbarrows full of dirt down the hill while we dug and swept the site. I had only just started exposing the upper jawline, when the sun began to sink beneath the treetops on the far side of the valley. I strained my eyes, trying to brush out the contours of a few more mighty teeth before we lost our light completely. Horner had been right about the ideal conditions of the dig, but I felt like I had barely made any progress at all. It was maddening to think how much of the skeleton still lay waiting beneath the soil.

Only when Hugo Brisbee came to coax us from the site with the offer of a hearty meal did I realize that I had seen nothing of Jackaby all afternoon. Brisbee welcomed us into the farmhouse, and as we crossed through toward the kitchen, I spotted my employer in the parlor. He was holding a pair of slim glass tubes side by side, turning them in the light of the lamp. One was filled with something dark, the other with something pale that rattled about against the glass.

"Good evening, Mr. Jackaby," I said, stepping in to join him. "We were about to sit down to supper. What's that you're looking at?"

"Graveyard dirt," he answered without turning, "acquired from Mrs. Brisbee's plot."

"Can graveyard dirt tell you anything?"

"Not enough. The soil is unsatisfied," he said, "and so am I. Mr. Brisbee seemed to need a moment alone, so I paid a visit to the funeral parlor while we were on the grounds as well. I found the mortician away, so I let myself in. They were preparing another body. Denson. Male. Fifty-seven. I find two sudden and unexpected deaths by mysterious malady a mite suspicious, particularly in so small a town. From the look of things, the late Mr. Denson succumbed to his supposed illness the same night as our farmer's wife died. He lived alone, however, and was not discovered until more recently. He had traces of the same aura. It is becoming unmistakably familiar. He bore the same mark as well, just beneath his collar. Livor mortis has added a good deal of discoloration, so it seems the injury has once again been overlooked. The medical examiner in this little town is deeply disappointing. In the interest of giving the deceased some justice to take to the grave, I liberated a rear molar before he could be entombed." He gave the second vial a little shake, and it rattled.

"You stole a dead man's tooth?"

"He made no objection. It is my hope that I might glean something useful from a closer study. Much of the essence of a living thing is distilled in its teeth. Did you know that? It's why the tooth fairies are so fond of them." He held the vial up reverently. The thing was slightly yellowed, its root a dirty pink.

"Have you found anything distilled in Mr. Denson's molar?" I asked.

Jackaby scowled. "There is something infuriatingly familiar here, but identifying it is like trying to pick out the smell of a clover in a bouquet of roses."

"Well, perhaps you'll have better luck at the dig site tomorrow," I said. "Horner showed me what went missing, and it turns out it's a tooth we're after there as well. Not one you could fit in your little vial, either—the thing must be the length of my forearm."

Brisbee came to fetch us, and the vials disappeared into Jackaby's coat. We filed into the dining room, where Charlie and Mr. Horner were already sitting down to eat. As we helped ourselves to fresh greens and steaming cuts of pork, Brisbee leaned in toward Jackaby.

"So, Detective," he said, "you were explaining your special talent to me on the road earlier. Tell me, does it only work on spooky creatures, or can you read people, too?"

Jackaby raised an eyebrow. "The categories *spooky creatures* and *people* are not as separate as you might imagine. I can read people. The truth is I can't not. Your aura, for instance, is a burnt orange."

"Huh. How does that work, then?" Brisbee said. A spark of intrigue lit his eyes. "Can I change my own aura? Make it lighter or something?"

"Not exactly. Auras are complex manifestations of intangible factors. It's not something you can adjust like a knob on a gas lamp."

"All right. What else do you see?"

"I'm not sure that is a good idea," Charlie interjected. "Mr. Jackaby's ability is not a parlor trick."

"It's fine," said Jackaby. His eyes narrowed as he surveyed the farmer, taking a silent inventory. "You are tethered," he announced. "Bound from somewhere deep inside of you. You resent your bonds, and yet you cling to them. You are proud and you are willful, but most of all," he said, his head cocked to one side as he spoke, "you are profoundly and wretchedly lonely."

Brisbee's expression sank gradually and unevenly. "Huh," he said. "I suppose that's . . ." He cleared his throat. The eager light in his eyes had dimmed, and he suddenly looked tired and embarrassed. "That's true."

"Of course it is," my employer said, casually scooping a large helping of mashed potatoes onto his plate. His voice was still obliviously earnest.

"We built this farm from nothing," Brisbee continued. "Maddie drove more than a few of the nails in this very room. Our boys grew up here, too. There was a time you could barely take a step without one of them underfoot. This place was supposed to be their inheritance—it's all I have. I always thought that they would . . . but Johnny left for the city first chance he could, and then Percy made it into university. I don't blame them. We were both so proud, we didn't even mind when it was just the two of us again. But now . . ." He trailed off and pushed a bit of broccoli around with his fork.

"There's something I can see as well, Mr. Brisbee," I said.

"Hmm?" Brisbee looked up from his plate. Jackaby eyed me curiously.

"I can see that you're *not* alone. Not tonight," I said.

Brisbee glanced around the table at the four of us. Charlie looked reassuring and affable, but I believe it was Horner's broad, goofy grin that did the trick. The smile tiptoed back up into the farmer's cheeks.

"Ah, now I see it," said Jackaby. "Perhaps I was wrong, Mr. Brisbee. You do look a little brighter."

Silverware clinked, and the conversation around the

dinner table grew boisterous and optimistic as the night wore on. Horner ruminated dreamily about what he was going to name his dinosaur, and Brisbee could scarcely wait to hear back from the reporter at the *Chronicle*. Jackaby, Charlie, and I finally bade good night to the others and headed down the road to Charlie's cabin.

The night was cloudless, and the moon and stars cast more than enough light to illuminate the path. With murder and mystery still hanging in the air, I might have found the walk intolerably eerie—but the happy energy of the evening hung around us.

"You would have been very proud to see Miss Rook at the site today, sir," Charlie told Jackaby as we trod along. He gave me an admiring smile, and I felt the heady warmth of a day's successes spread through my chest.

"You were no slouch yourself," I said. "You were very clever to spot those flints so quickly."

"Charlie helped with the dig as well?" Jackaby said.

Charlie nodded.

"Surprising—I should think that *un*burying bones would go against generations of instinct to do just the opposite, wouldn't it? Ouch! Watch your step in the dark, Miss Rook—you just kicked my shin. Where was I? Right—I was saying that coming from a family of dogs—ouch! You've done it again, rather hard that time. Really, the path isn't even bumpy here."

"Mr. Jackaby, please try to be a little more sensitive," I said.

"What on earth are you talking about? I am quite sensitive enough, thank you—and getting downright tender in the vicinity of the legs, at the moment."

"It's all right, Miss Rook," Charlie said. "The hound is not everything I am, Mr. Jackaby. I am not controlled by his instincts, but I am not ashamed of them, either. In fact, I have enjoyed the freedom and privacy of the country more than I expected. It has been a great relief to let myself run on all fours from time to time, away from the prying eyes of civilization."

Jackaby spoke before I could voice the same caution. "That might not be wholly advisable. Your excursions into the wilderness may not have been as covert as you presume."

"Your friend, the trapper?" said Charlie. "I think he might find me a bit more difficult prey to track than his typical fare."

"I wouldn't be so confident," I said. "Hudson's typical fare includes a bird that can cut brass like butter. He's no stranger to impossible creatures, and he's eager for more of them. Too eager."

"So, I'm an *impossible creature*, now?" Charlie teased gently.

"She's right," Jackaby cut in. "He's already looking for you, Charlie. I'm fond of the fellow, but it would be wise to stay on two legs for a while."

We came through a copse of trees and reached our destination. Charlie's house was small, built into a mossy little clearing not far from the road. In the bright moonlight I could see that it had a rustic charm.

Charlie coaxed a fire to life in a short potbellied stove, and soon the cabin was pleasantly warm. It had only two beds, his own and one for a guest, but he offered them to Jackaby and to me, insisting he was more than comfortable enough on the floor. He gave me fresh linens and bade me good night, leaving me in his chamber while he set Jackaby up in the room adjacent. I thanked him and shut the door, playing over the impossible events of my day as I changed into my nightgown. With the excitement of the surprises waiting to be uncovered in the morning, I was sure I would not sleep a wink.

The room did not feel like Charlie's. He had not lived in the house for long and had not properly furnished it with any personal effects, but as I lay my head on his pillow, the scent of the policeman, like a gentle sandalwood, swept over me. The rest of the world melted away, and sleep came for me, after all.

In the morning, I awoke to the rays of sunlight cutting through the curtains and the sound of a teakettle whistling in the kitchen. I tucked my hair up into a loose bun and pulled on a shirtwaist and a sturdy skirt—another I had borrowed from Jenny. I slipped on my shoes and emerged to face the day.

Charlie greeted me with a smile and a cup of tea. I hated him just a little bit in that moment, pressed and shaved and lit from behind like some angel in a Renaissance painting.

An errant lock of hair flopped into my eyes, and I blew it to the side with a puff. It didn't matter, I reminded myself. This was my adventure. In short order I would be up to my waist in dirt and dinosaur bones, not drinking English tea with an insufferably perfect policeman.

"The tea is not very good, I'm afraid," he said as I accepted the cup and saucer. "It's the only tin I could find in the house. I have coffee if you prefer."

"No, no, this is lovely. Thank you." I took a sip. It was probably the worst tea ever brewed. I took another sip.

"Would you care for some breakfast?" Charlie asked. "Mr. Jackaby was content with just a bit of toast before he left, but I would be happy to make some eggs or–"

"Jackaby left without us?" I interrupted, shaking the last of the morning fog from my eyes and setting down my cup.

"Just a few minutes ago," Charlie said. "Although I gather he has been up since well before the sun."

"Does that man ever sleep? Would you mind terribly if we went after him right away? I'm keen on getting back to the dig site, myself, and I'd rather not leave those artifacts and my employer alone together."

"Of course." Charlie fumbled the teacup and saucer into the sink with a clatter as I fetched my coat. I was soon mounting a dappled brown-and-white horse that Charlie called Maryanne. I would have given anything for a pair of riding breeches in place of my skirt, but I had not packed any trousers. I nestled in a bit clumsily behind Charlie, feeling awkward and unsteady as I perched sidesaddle on the mare. As Maryanne hastened to a gentle trot, I held tightly to Charlie's waist. His uniform smelled faintly of starch and cedar, and the trip back to Brisbee's flew past in a warm blur.

In almost no time at all, the roof of the old farmhouse came into view beyond the trees. "It is a beautiful valley," Charlie was saying as we cantered up the last leg of the journey. "I've explored a great deal since moving here. Perhaps sometime you would let me show you the south hills. There are beautiful waterfalls down that way."

"Charlie," I said, "please remember Jackaby's warning. Mr. Hudson seems friendly, but . . ."

Charlie nodded, sinking into his shoulders a little. "No more transformations. I know. I will try."

"Is it so hard to give up?"

"It's difficult to explain," he said. "It tingles. You know that . . . that prickling sensation you feel when you sit too long and your foot falls asleep? It's like that, except that it runs through my core. I can contain it, but the longer I suppress the hound, the more my senses grow numb and restless. It has been a blessing to be out here, where I could occasionally . . . stretch." He sighed. "I do appreciate your concern, truly—but please don't worry about me, Miss Rook. I am used to being careful."

Chapter Eighteen

Charlie tethered Maryanne to Brisbee's hitching post, and I slid down to solid ground. As we rounded the side of the farmhouse, I could see that Jackaby was only halfway up the rugged hillside. He had paused, leaning against a rocky outcrop to watch an angry scene unfold before him. I could hear Owen Horner farther up the hill. "This is absurd," he was arguing. "You have no right—"

"Gentlemen, if you please," Hugo Brisbee's voice chimed in.

"On the contrary," came a third voice. "I have every right, and a legally binding contract as well."

Charlie and I hastened up the path and joined Jackaby on the hill. Brisbee and Horner were on their way down, keeping pace with a stuffy-looking middle-aged man in a slate-gray suit and a Panama hat. The stranger held a slim briefcase, waggling it meaningfully at Brisbee, but he did not slow his pace toward the house.

"That miscreant should never have been allowed near the discovery," groused the man. "It is sadly unsurprising that he has already absconded with priceless artifacts."

"How dare you—I was the one who reported the stolen fossil!" Horner threw up his hands in exasperation.

The man ignored him and went on. "I have communicated with the police in Gadston that Mr. Horner is not to be permitted within a hundred yards of my property. I've been assured I have the full support of the department—ah, and I see they've sent someone out already." The procession had come to us, and the gray man drew to a halt in front of Charlie.

Charlie stepped forward. "I'm afraid I've heard nothing of the order, Mr.—?"

"Lamb. Professor Lewis Lamb. I spoke with Commander Bell in person."

"I'm sure you did. It's possible that word from the commander has been delayed. In the meantime, I believe we can all behave ourselves."

"Behave? Have you met Mr. Horner? Should he trespass again, see that he is incarcerated immediately. From this point on, the site of this excavation is to be considered private property and kept free of any outside interference."

"Even if he's coming up there as my personal guest?" Brisbee asked.

"I don't think you understand, Mr. Brisbee." Lamb turned to face the farmer directly. "We appreciate your efforts thus far, but now that I have arrived, there is no need for you to be directly involved in the excavation. The site is to be restricted exclusively to my employees and to me."

"What? I don't understand."

"He's kicking you out, too," Horner informed the farmer with a grunt.

"You can't do that—this is still my land!"

"Actually I can, Mr. Brisbee, according to the very explicit parameters of the contract you signed. Amateurs will not jeopardize the integrity of this discovery. Speaking of which, who are all these people?" Lamb finally seemed to notice us, surveying Jackaby and me with suspicion.

"Oh, um, good morning, folks." Brisbee raised his battered old hat in a polite greeting. "This is Lewis Lamb. He's here to . . . um . . . He's here about the fossils. He arrived first thing this morning. Lamb, this is Mr. Jackaby and Miss Abigail Rook. They're the ones I mentioned earlier. You'll be interested to know Miss Rook is the daughter of another dinosaur fellow. Daniel Rook, was it?" I nodded. "She was a big help yesterday with the bones, and Mr. Jackaby is a first-rate private detective, too. He's been in the papers. I'm sure if you'd just rethink this nonsense, you'd find there are a great many people here ready to help."

I gave Lamb a smile and extended my hand. "Delighted to meet you, sir."

Lamb looked as though he had tasted something foul and was deciding whether to swallow and be done with it or spit it out. "This is precisely the sort of unprofessional mismanagement I am here to prevent," he said, and carried on walking past me.

I let my hand drop and exchanged a glance with Owen Horner. He rolled his eyes.

"The site is no longer open to every semiliterate rube with a shovel and every doe-eyed pair of pigtails that wanders up. Mr. Brisbee, in the interest of maintaining a professional working relationship, I will overlook the amount of time Mr. Horner and these amateur hobbyists have already been permitted to traipse about my excavation site—but I trust that, from this point onward, you will honor the agreement laid out between us to the letter. I have a team of exceptional lawyers. I should hate to see you lose this farm outright should they find you in breach of contract."

Brisbee's face fell, and his hands flopped to his sides. Lamb stalked toward a carriage parked in the shade of the barn and rapped sharply on the door. "Wake up, you laggards," he called. "It's time to start earning your keep!" The carriage rocked, and out climbed a pair of bleary-eyed men. The first was a tall, thin man with mahogany-brown skin and black hair, who yawned and stretched as he moved to the back of the cab. The second man was pink faced and pudgy, like an overripe peach, topped with a splash of beet-red freckles and a mess of orange hair. He rubbed his eyes and strapped a bulky burlap satchel to his back. Clambering to hold on to a bundle of long aluminum poles, he dropped several of them before finding his grip, and they clanged loudly against the cart.

Lamb groaned in annoyance and started off again up the hill without issuing any further instruction. The red-headed man collected his things and wordlessly shuffled past us, following Lamb back toward the foothills behind the farmhouse. The other man hefted a collection of pick-axes and hammers over his shoulder and moved to join his colleagues. He paused on his way and shrugged apologetically. "The professor doesn't make a great first impression, but you get used to him."

"Does he make a great second impression?" Horner asked skeptically.

"Mr. Bradley! Now!" Lamb yelled from halfway up the hill.

Mr. Bradley took a deep breath and shifted the tools on his shoulder. "You get used to him," he repeated, and hurried away.

Brisbee turned from the departing procession and back to us, his mouth opening and closing "What just–?" he managed at last.

"You backed the wrong horse," said Horner. "I told you you should've signed the site over to me."

The farmer looked as if he might cry.

"Well," I said, "nobody is bleeding or pressing charges—at least not yet—so I suppose that actually went better than I might have hoped. I noticed that you didn't throw rocks at anybody, Mr. Horner. I do appreciate your restraint."

"Least I could do, beautiful." Horner gave a halfhearted wink, and then looked back up at the foothills moodily. "But the day is still young."

Brisbee brewed a pot of bitter American coffee, and we watched from the back porch of the farmhouse as a wide canvas wall gradually rose to shroud the entire dig site. From a distance, all that was visible of our evening's hard work were a few piles of loose sod around the perimeter.

"I wish I hadn't sent that telegram yesterday," the farmer said glumly, taking a swig of the black brew. "Seems a shame to have that nice reporter come out all this way for nothing. Won't be much of a story for her to report now that Lamb's sealed everything up."

Horner was nursing his own mug, glaring moodily at the dirt. I knew how he felt. Brisbee took notice and looked more wretched still. "I'm sorry it turned out like this for you, Mr. Horner. You did so much good work. Will you be leaving right away?"

Horner breathed in deeply and straightened up. "I don't think so. As you say, it would be a shame to come all this way for nothing. I might just take in a bit of the countryside for a day or two, if you don't mind the company. After all, I would hate to repay your kindness by leaving you alone with that killjoy."

Brisbee nodded and looked slightly buoyed.

"Don't go doing anything foolish," I said. "Remember, you assured me you would play nice, however it turned out."

"Did I say that?" Horner chuckled. "That doesn't sound like me. All right, all right—you have my word. Nothing foolish. Don't count me out entirely, though. I am remarkably charming." He gave me a cheeky grin, as if to illustrate his point. "That stuffy old Lewis Lamb may warm up to me yet."

"Be careful," Charlie told him. "I would hate to be the one called to take you to lockup. Professor Lamb did not sound very open-minded."

"What about you, Miss Rook?" Horner said. "You've lost the site as much as I have."

"On the contrary," Jackaby answered for me, sounding jarringly cheerful. He leaned on the railing and looked genially out across the countryside. "We've lost nothing. Now that your little side-project up the hill is out of the question, we can focus our attention on the real reason we're out here."

"The real reason we're out here?" I said, glancing warily to my employer. With a reporter having been summoned just that morning, now was the wrong time for Jackaby to forget about his promise to keep our investigation of the murders discreet. "The real reason we are here is to investigate the bones behind that barrier, isn't it, sir?"

"In point of fact, Miss Rook, the reason we're here"—

Jackaby raised his eyebrows in my direction—"is to investigate the one that isn't."

"He's right," Charlie said. "There is still a fossil missing, even if its rightful owner has changed. It is time we directed our attention to pursuing the culprit."

"Maybe it was just a wolf or some other creature?" Brisbee suggested.

Jackaby scowled. "Yes. It is a distinct possibility that our perpetrator was not human at all. Trust me, we are considering that scenario very seriously."

"Your reporter will love that," Horner put in cynically. "The crime was plenty to spice up the story. She'll paper the Eastern Seaboard if you hand her a big bad wolf to go with it." Charlie kept his face stoically blank.

"I don't think it's worth bringing up wolves," I said. "The prospect is doubtful, anyway. Fossils wouldn't generally attract scavengers."

"Of course they would," Jackaby said. "Especially the sort of scavengers who read newspapers. I think it is high time we got to know the rest of the neighborhood."

Neighborhood was not the right word for the environs of Gad's Valley. Charlie, Jackaby, and I had to walk half a mile before we reached the nearest farm.

The front walk was unpaved and the house was modest, just a bit smaller than Brisbee's by the look of it, and its paint had faded to a peeling beige. Charlie and I stepped up to the door, but Jackaby sauntered around toward the back of the house.

"Sir? What are you doing?" I asked.

"Investigating," Jackaby replied flatly.

"Well, you can't just walk into someone's yard unannounced. Besides, doesn't investigating usually involve questioning people?"

"I've nothing against people as a general rule, but people don't tend to have the sort of answers I'm looking for." The fence post just above Jackaby's head exploded in a spray of splinters with a resonating *BLAM!* A woman stood in the open doorway across from him, a plain white apron tied around her waist and a fat-barreled rifle in her hands. "Of course, people do have a way of surprising you from time to time," my employer added.

The woman held her chin up high and stared down the barrel at Jackaby. It was not the most intimidating glare, but her rifle more than compensated. "You're on my property," she said.

"I am indeed," Jackaby replied. "And you noticed. Well done."

From inside the house came the sound of excited barking. The woman held the rifle steady as a black-and-white sheepdog bounded past her and into the yard, circling my employer repeatedly and sniffing him in all of the customary awkward places before rolling over and awaiting a scratch on the tummy.

The woman sighed and shook her head. "If you've come to steal the world's least intimidating guard dog, I'm real close to just letting you have him."

The dog flopped his head back to look at his mistress upside down.

"Nobody's impressed, Toby."

"Please lower your weapon, Mrs. Pendleton," said Charlie, hurrying forward and holding out his badge. "The gentleman is with me."

Mrs. Pendleton nodded to the policeman and let the rifle down gently.

"You know this woman?" Jackaby asked.

"We met recently," said Charlie.

"That's right," Mrs. Pendleton said. "Just last week. Mr. Barker here put my Abe in lockup overnight. My old man can get a little goofy when he's had a few too many."

Charlie nodded. "Mr. Pendleton was heavily intoxicated, singing loudly and brandishing a firearm in the middle of Gadston's Goods and Grocery."

"He was celebrating," she explained with a hint of a smile. "It was our anniversary."

"Which does account for his choice in love songs," Charlie said. "He has a fine tenor voice."

"Doesn't he just?" Mrs. Pendleton loosened and leaned on the door frame. "I know he can be a handful, but he's a good man underneath. Oh, did his pants ever turn up?"

"You will be the first to know. Mrs. Pendleton, please

allow me to introduce my associates, Detective Jackaby and his assistant, Miss Rook."

Mrs. Pendleton nodded toward Jackaby. "Detective, huh? What's that thing on his head?"

I suppressed a giggle. Jackaby's cap looked a bit like a child's wobbly sketch of a hat—the sort of sketch you might accidentally mistake for a lumpy elephant or perhaps a floret of broccoli, if you weren't holding it the right way up. At best, it was yarn trying very hard to be a hat.

"What?" Jackaby scowled. "Honestly, woman, this hat is a priceless rarity! It was knit from—"

"Not really the time for that, sir," I said. "Please, ma'am, we're in the middle of an investigation. I'm afraid that's why my employer—erm—inadvertently crossed your property line. He's looking for something unusual."

Mrs. Pendleton leaned toward me. "Has your employer looked in a mirror?" she said.

"There has been some criminal activity in the area," Charlie said, cutting in before Jackaby could object. "Thefts of valuable property and some suspicious persons lurking about. We are only trying to protect the valley, Mrs. Pendleton—including you and your husband."

"I look out for Abe, and Abe looks out for me." Mrs. Pendleton patted the butt of her rifle. "And we look out for our own. I appreciate your concern, but I think we'll be all right. You can have a peek out back if it makes you happy. Just don't touch anything."

Jackaby nodded eagerly. "Won't be a moment, madam. Just looking for residual traces of paranormal malignance, something indicative of heinous moral grotesquery."

"You're weird. Watch out for duck poop."

"I always do!"

Mrs. Pendleton turned her attention to me as Jackaby hurried around the corner, Toby bounding after him. "So, what'd they take?"

"A bone," I said. "A very old bone."

"What on earth would anyone want a bone for?" she asked.

"Your guess is as good as mine," I said. "Maybe better, in fact. Is there anything people do with bones out here in the valley? Some local custom or something?"

"Nope," she said with a shrug. "If they're big enough, we might toss them to the dogs to gnaw on, same as anyone. Keeps Toby out from underfoot for a while."

I nodded. "Thanks anyway."

Jackaby conducted his inspection quickly, looking un-impressed as he rejoined us. We thanked Mrs. Pendleton kindly and made our way back to the road.

"Any luck?" I asked.

"The farmstead was as disappointing as that woman's taste in fashion. My hat was the most interesting thing in the place."

The next farm yielded nothing more of consequence, nor the next, nor the next after that. We covered seven farms and several miles of Gad's Valley before we finally abandoned our efforts. The most interesting abnormalities we uncovered were a chicken that had flown the coop and a cow that had eaten a neighbor's flower garden.

"This may be the most exceptionally unexceptional countryside in the history of countrysides," Jackaby grumbled. "What about smells?"

"Sir?" I asked.

"Smells. Charlie's as good a bloodhound as any police force could hope for. Have you picked up a scent?"

Charlie looked at me and then back at Jackaby. "I'm afraid I can't, not without . . . changing."

"Out of the question," I said. "We'll find our clues with good old-fashioned, normal detective work."

"Ugh." Jackaby tossed back his head. "That sounds awful."

We plodded steadily back toward Brisbee's. After a long morning of disappointments, I entertained the quiet fancy that Professor Lamb might have become amenable in our absence. It was almost within the realm of the imagination, if only level heads prevailed. "What do you suppose are the chances," I mused aloud, "that tempers have died down and everyone's gotten along since we've been gone?"

Charlie shook his head bleakly as we came around the bend. From fifty yards away I could see Brisbee and Lamb having it out on the porch, Lamb's hands gesturing angrily as he spoke and punctuating exclamations I could not quite discern. Lumbering toward them was a heavy figure who looked at first glance like an impossibly broad giant, and then at second glance like a man wearing a coat made out of smaller men. Finally I realized I was witnessing Hank Hudson loping across the farmstead with Lamb's lackeys pulling him back, one on either arm. Their combined efforts appeared to have a minimal effect on the sturdy trapper.

"Slim," said Jackaby. "I would suppose the chances are slim."

Chapter Nineteen

Charlie rushed up the road ahead of us to break up the scuffle, and Lamb's employees dropped away as he approached. Lamb was growling about boundaries and preservation, adding several foul phrases in conjunction with the name Owen Horner. Brisbee leaned against the railing, looking unimpressed as Lamb rattled on. Hudson's cart had been parked beside the hitching post, and tethered side by side, the trapper's brawny steeds made Charlie's Maryanne look tiny.

"Will somebody please tell me what's going on here?" Charlie demanded. Five voices immediately erupted into fervent explanations, and Charlie had to wave them silent. "One at a time! One at a time. Mr. Hudson, if you please?"

"Well, let's see. These two clowns are angry 'cause I tried

to take a look at them big bones up on the hill without asking their permission. Didn't know I needed to buy a dang ticket. I guess I missed my chance for the free show yesterday. That Lamb fella's mad 'cause apparently he fuddled the wording on some contract of his, and Brisbee found a loophole. Didn't catch all the details, but from what I gather, Lamb's got rights ta keep the bones hidden away, but he still needs Brisbee's permission if he wants ta pack 'em up and ship 'em off to his fancy university. Brisbee's makin' him keep 'em here, instead. Lamb ain't thrilled, but he can't do much about it without breaking his end of the deal and losing his rights to the dig. That's about the long and short of it. Oh—I get the feeling there's something else Brisbee's happy about, too. He said he was planning on showin' that gal from the *Chronicle* something—but he wouldn't say what. Didn't get much time ta ask before Chuckles here came down to start yelling at him."

"Aside from the editorializing, would you say that's accurate?" Charlie turned to Professor Lamb.

"It's not the half of it," Lamb spat.

Charlie sighed. "Please, Professor—tell me what you are upset about."

"Horner! Horner is obviously up to something! And Mr. Brisbee has been allowing, if not abetting, his mischief! This sudden decision to argue semantics over our contract, which is needlessly delaying my research, is clearly a ploy manufactured by Horner to distract me! Brisbee knows as well as I do that Horner is up to no good, and I do not appreciate his cavalier attitude about it!"

Brisbee tossed up his hands. "You don't like it when he's here; you don't like it when he's gone. I'm not worried about Horner, and to be honest, I'm not worried about the bones you say he stole. I'm sure they'll turn up." He brushed Lamb aside and stepped off the porch. "This whole thing's just a big tantrum, Officer. Professor Lamb wants to take his toys and go home, and he's just mad that he can't. He'll get over it."

"I'm sure you're right. All the same, where is Mr. Horner?"

"He should be back any minute now. That reporter sent a telegram that she'd be in Gadston on the three o'clock, and Mr. Horner volunteered to pick her up. He said he had some things to do in town, anyway."

"And you didn't find that the least bit suspicious?" mumbled Lamb moodily from behind him.

Brisbee ignored him and continued. "She won't be disappointed, either. I found something that's sure to make for a good story for the *Chronicle*, whether or not this curmudgeon opens up the dig site."

Jackaby raised his eyebrows. "Hudson mentioned something about that. I don't suppose you care to elucidate?"

"Well . . . I was going to hold off until they got back—but one of the kids has gone missing."

"A child has gone missing?" Jackaby said. "When?"

"No, no—a *kid*," said Brisbee. "One of my baby goats."

Jackaby had already turned to walk away, mumbling. "This valley and its infernally insignificant . . ."

"That isn't the good part," Brisbee continued. "I just hope Miss Fuller brings her camera this time, because the tracks around the goat pen are something to see. We were just talking about how maybe some scary creature was involved, and there they are."

Jackaby turned back. All eyes were on Brisbee. Hudson broke the silence. "Tracks?"

"That's right." The farmer rocked back and forth on his heels. "Footprints. Not from my livestock or from some old boot, either—they're huge with sharp claws."

Not one of us was braced for the farmer's announcement. I might have suspected Charlie of breaking his promise, but he looked as stunned as the rest of us.

"This is ludicrous," said Lamb. "Although—if there is a wild animal on the loose, then that is all the more reason to relocate to my secure facility at Glanville University."

"Show me," said Hudson.

Jackaby did not wait to be escorted, stepping between Lamb and Brisbee and hurrying around the house toward the barn. Hudson was on his heels, and Brisbee kept up. I began to follow but paused as I noticed that Lamb was not moving. His eyes were on the road. I turned and spied a cart bumping toward us in a little cloud of dust. Horner was returning with Brisbee's reporter.

"Mr. Jackaby," I called, but he had already trotted out of

sight around the building, Hudson and Brisbee close behind. I caught Charlie's arm before he could dash away after them. "I don't think Professor Lamb should be the only one here to welcome Mr. Horner back, do you?" I said. Charlie shook his head, watching the approaching carriage.

Lewis Lamb took a few steps toward the foothills and bellowed, "August! August Murphy. Get down here! Now!" A mop of red hair poked out of the canvas enclosure. Murphy hurried down the rolling hills and was out of breath and panting when he reached his employer. "Well," Lamb told him, "you know what to do."

The carriage, a weathered two-seater pulled by one of Brisbee's workhorses, ambled up to the farm. Horner was at the reins with a woman in a stylish striped coat beside him. Before the wheels stopped rolling, Murphy leapt up onto the side of the car and began to grapple with Horner. Horner let out a startled yelp, apparently as surprised to find himself in the scuffle as we were to witness it.

Charlie ran forward to break up the commotion, but Murphy had already leapt back to the ground. He brandished a slip of paper over his head, marching proudly back toward Lamb. Horner swung himself out of the cart and stalked after him, his usual confident swagger reduced to weary frustration.

"Here it is, Mr. Lamb!" Murphy called. "It was in his waistcoat, right where you said it would be!"

Horner snatched the paper back out of his hands from

behind, and the man spun around, trying to grab it back. "Enough!" Charlie barked, pulling the men apart. "Let's have it, Mr. Horner," he said with a sigh.

Horner passed the slip to Charlie reluctantly.

"Would either of you care to explain?" the policeman asked.

"It's a receipt from the post office," the redheaded man declared triumphantly. He looked smug and out of breath.

"I can see that." Charlie looked at the paper, turning it over.

"Does Lamb own the postal service now, too?" Horner glared at Murphy, who retreated a little nervously. "I can't even send a letter without your permission?"

"But you didn't send a letter, did you?" said Lamb coldly from behind Charlie. "You sent a package, and you sent it to yourself. Am I wrong, Inspector?"

Charlie looked up. "The receipt confirms it."

"Well of course it does!" Horner exclaimed. "I'm not here on holiday. I've been doing legitimate, hard work. Not that it is any of Lamb's business, but I was shipping off my collected notes and rubbings before his thugs could steal those away from me, too. That crook has some nerve accusing me of being a thief!"

"No one is calling you a thief, Mr. Horner," said Charlie.

"I most certainly am!" Lamb declared. "Even if all you sent were rubbings and notes—which I doubt—that would be confession enough! The discoveries at that site, both physical and intellectual, are my property, and not to be disseminated. My contract with Mr. Brisbee is very clear on that point."

"This is what I've been telling you about," Horner said to the reporter, who was watching the dispute with the detached interest one might reserve for an unexceptional tennis match.

"Officer, arrest that reprobate!" Lamb roared. Charlie took a deep breath.

"You crazy old man," Horner countered. "I had the whole dinosaur to myself before you plowed in here! Why would I have taken a single tooth?"

"We both know that this is about more than a tooth! I want those fossils you pilfered today, before you conveniently ran off to Gadston, and I want you locked up in a cell where you belong!"

"He's stolen something new from the dig site?" Charlie asked.

Horner threw up his arms in exasperation. "I haven't stolen anything!"

I turned to Lamb. "If you would just allow us to visit the dig site . . ."

"Young woman," he said, cutting me off, "I don't care who your father is. You're not welcome on that dig site, and neither are any of your friends—so you really have no reason to keep hanging around."

The woman in the striped coat stepped out of the

carriage at last. "It's Lewis Lamb, isn't it?" she asked, not waiting for a reply. "Nellie Fuller with the *Chronicle. Enchanté.* May I be the first to say that fetching dust-gray suit really brings out the color of your personality. Now then, I'm a bit of a detail girl, so please humor me. What specifically are you accusing Mr. Horner of stealing?"

Lamb scowled. "I don't need to explain myself to you. If Horner wants to use paleontology to impress yet another vapid female in a pretty dress, then he can take you and your come-hither ringlets and go find his own dig site. He knows what he stole from mine."

"Why, Mr. Lamb, how kind of you to notice." Miss Fuller put a hand to the jet-black curls peeking out beneath her hat. "I was hoping for a *come-hither* look this morning. Of course, if my hair is preventing you from carrying out your work, I would be happy to stuff it up under my hat. Then again, if your opinions on women prevent *me* from carrying out *my* work, then I would be more than happy to suggest a place for you to stuff *them*." She gave the professor a saccharine smile and a polite nod.

Owen Horner looked at Nellie Fuller as if he might be in love. Lewis Lamb glowered. "How dare you!" he sputtered. "I am an institution in the scientific community . . ." His dark eyes bounced from person to person until they settled on Charlie. "Well? I have important work to do on that site. Are you going to do your job, or just let this criminal wander about freely while his associates harass me?"

"I would love to help you, Professor," Charlie said, "but if you want to formally accuse Mr. Horner, then you must accept that the site of the excavation is also a crime scene."

"Well of course it's a crime scene!"

Charlie continued evenly. "Which would mean that it is within the jurisdiction of the local police and our consulting detectives to investigate." I perked up.

The professor breathed in deeply and closed his eyes, rubbing the back of his neck angrily. "Fine."

I could feel the smile spreading across my face. It had been a long day of false starts, but the evening was suddenly jumping forward. The unusual dinosaur, the stolen fossils, the unsolved murders, even the ominous pale man—they were all tied to those rocky foothills like frayed threads from the same cord. There were secrets buried behind that canvas wall, and I was resolved to unearth them.

Chapter Twenty

"Look but do *not* touch," Lamb repeated for a third time as Charlie and I followed him to the entrance in the canvas. "And let me remind you that everything you observe is completely and utterly confidential."

"Your secrets are safe with us, Professor," Charlie assured him.

Lamb's eye narrowed, but he pulled back the canvas flap and we stepped inside. The enclosure was not a tent, but more of a wide privacy fence. Each wall angled inward toward the top, which provided a bit more shade, but left the top wide-open for sunlight. The tools had been laid out neatly, and here and there smaller drop cloths and tarpaulins had been draped over sections of the skeleton. The widest of these covered a broad stretch of earth toward the creature's back. Whether these were in place to protect the fossils from the elements or because of Lamb's paranoia about privacy, I could only guess. Lamb and his crew had made considerable progress. The contours of the head were fully visible now, and although the midsection had been partially shrouded under the tarpaulin, it was clear that Lamb's team had uncovered the full curve of the gigantic beast's spine.

Mr. Bradley, the slender dark-skinned man, was working his way down the creature's neck with a brush and fine chisel. He smiled at our approach until he caught Lamb's glare, and then hastily returned to his work.

"You say you're Daniel Rook's daughter?" Lamb asked as he walked us down the length of the creature.

"That's right," I said.

"Well, let's see if you actually picked up anything useful from your father's not entirely negligible career. To what bones do the tibia and fibula attach?"

If he had asked me to thread a needle or play the harpsichord, I might have balked, but I had assembled model skeletons as a child the way most little girls assembled jigsaw puzzles. "To the femur at one end—that's the knee joint—and to the tarsals on the other—the ankle."

Mr. Bradley kept his head down while Lamb was looking, but he snuck me a supportive nod as we passed. I wondered how someone so pleasant had come to work for a walking scowl like Lewis Lamb. "And what is after the ankle?" my inquisitor continued drily.

"The same as it is with humans, the foot and the toes. Metatarsals and phalanges, if you prefer. With most dinosaurs, as with modern birds, the metatarsals are actually clear off the ground, with the weight of the thing on its—"

"Wrong," Lamb interrupted.

"Wrong? No, I'm quite certain—"

"You're wrong, Miss Rook. As you can plainly see, after the ankle joint there is . . . nothing at all. That is the point. My dinosaur's entire foot has been stolen."

I looked down. The massive femur was still there. Beneath it lay the long tibia and fibula, but then there sat a series of hollows in the earth, outlining where the creature's long talons should have been. The bones of the foot were gone.

"These were definitely here last night," Charlie said, stepping carefully around the hollows. I nodded.

"I tried to stop her, boss!" wheezed August Murphy suddenly from the entryway. His freckles were lost in a mask of beet red.

Nellie Fuller was stepping over a pile of freshly turned soil. Her slick, striped dress looked as sharp as her tongue, cut expertly to complement her full figure. It was out of place in the dirty mess, but she strode across the uneven terrain with confidence.

"Just what do you think you're doing?" Lamb snarled.

"Journalism," she said. "It's a terrible habit, I know, but I can't seem to kick it. Hello! Isn't this a handsome fellow?"

Mr. Bradley fumbled with his chisel.

"I mean that strapping brute you're digging up." Miss Fuller said. "But what's your name, mister?"

"Bradley. Bill Bradley, miss."

"Good name, Bill. Alliteration always looks sharp in typeset. What species would you say you're uncovering?"

"Shall I bodily remove her, sir?" Mr. Murphy asked.

"Aw, Guster, if you wanted to dance, you really should have asked," Nellie called over her shoulder. "My card's all full up, now."

"Just go and look after Horner, you incompetent cretin," Lamb said to Murphy, stomping across the dig site to intercept the reporter. "You know very well that you are not permitted to be on the premises!"

"Do I? Honest misunderstanding, I'm sure. You should be more clear in the future."

"*More cl–?* Miss Fuller, I addressed you by name, looked you squarely in the eyes, and told you to *stay out!*"

"Then we're agreed that it was poor communication all around. No hard feelings, though, sunshine. I forgive you. Goodness, just look at the ribs on this behemoth! That first bone was impressive and all, but this is really a sight to see."

"I think you've all seen quite enough," snapped Lamb.

"But, sir, we've only just begun," I said meekly. "In fact, Mr. Jackaby really ought to be here as well. Do you think you could send one of your men to fetch him? He might be able to see . . ."

"Out! I'm done with all of you!"

"Professor Lamb," Charlie began.

"Don't you *Professor Lamb* me, Officer Barker! I am in direct communication with your supervisor, and Commander Bell has promised me your full cooperation. I played your game. I gave you your look. Now go get me my property—and take these . . . these . . . *women* with you."

"You're the boss," Nellie said, making no rush to leave and turning to me. "But *you* seem to be the brains. It's Abigail Rook, yes? Mind if I call you Abbie? Lovely. Before we go, do you happen to know the word for that bone that birds have right here?" She pointed along her sternum.

"It's called the keel," I said.

"That's the one. Is it just me, or is that a big fat keel?" She pointed toward a wide stretch at the creature's front, which I had missed entirely, having simply taken it for a flat stretch of earth. "Is that normal on a dinosaur?"

Mr. Bradley looked up from the creature's neck. His eyes were twinkling. "You think that's crazy? You ladies should see this." He stepped away and began to lift the tarpaulin shrouding the creature's back.

"That's quite enough!" yelled Lamb, vibrating furiously. Bradley dropped the canvas and froze.

He had not been quick enough. Miss Fuller and I turned to each other, and I saw reflected in the reporter's face the same impossible thrill that was dancing through me. Wings. The colossus had wings.

Lamb ushered us brusquely through the canvas flap, all but literally kicking us off the site. He gave Mr. Bradley an acid glare on the way, and I did not envy the lecture the poor man was likely to endure later. My mind was reeling at the implications of what he had revealed to us.

"What do you make of it, Miss Rook?" Charlie asked.

"It's impossible!" I said as we trod back down the sloping foothills toward the farm.

"This is front-page material, without a doubt." Nellie grinned.

"It's like some amazing amalgam of a theropod and a pterosaur! The scientific community will be absolutely astir!" I said.

"Abbie, darling, you're cute, but the scientific community won't be the half of it when I'm through writing the story," said Nellie.

"Your story will have to wait until I've finished my examination and am fully ready to release a formal report on the specimen." Lamb was keeping pace behind us, unwilling to trust that we could find our way unescorted.

"Surely it won't take long to finish a report," I said. "The figure is almost entirely intact, and the fossils are unbelievably well preserved."

"They *are* unbelievable, Miss Rook, which gives me

all the more reason for pause. I do not know how Owen Horner feels about the integrity of the scientific process, but I for one am not eager to be made a fool."

"You think they've been tampered with?" Charlie asked.

"Horner had his hands all over this site before we arrived. It would not be the first time he intentionally sabotaged a dig site."

Lamb's own record was far from spotless, but he was not entirely wrong. From what I had read in the journals, Owen Horner might have been more likable, but he was no more scrupulous. "Professor, is it really as bad as all that between the two of you?"

"Worse," Lamb said. "But it is not my fault! That brat hadn't even finished his schooling when we met. He had assembled a sizable theropod as the focus of his thesis, but the amateur had obviously attached the head of one specimen to the body of another. Naturally, I was obliged to report his error, and the disgrace set back Horner's thesis a year. His pride has been fueling this one-upmanship ever since. Whenever he can't outdo me—which is most of the time—he settles for obstructing me. Why do you think he keeps appearing every time I take on a new project? I can think of nothing Horner would like more than to push me into putting wings on a flightless body, or giving a pterosaur the wrong legs. It is not the sort of oversight I tolerate, so you will understand my reluctance to rush."

I did understand. Field research was exhausting enough without extra hurdles and misdirection, and Lamb's story had the unfortunate ring of truth. "That's fair," I said.

"There are other facets of the excavation worthy of skepticism as well," Lamb continued. "The site is notably shallow. Layers of ash in the soil suggest the area suffered a series of fires, which could potentially have affected plant growth and subsequent soil settlement. However, if one were to age the fossils purely on the visible strata, estimates would fall in the mere thousands of years."

"That's obviously wrong," I said. "Even the most recent Cretaceous dinosaurs died off–"

"Exactly! What's more, aside from the wings, this one appears most like an *Allosaurus*, which suggests Jurassic!"

"Pardon me, kids," Nellie chimed in. "A little translation for those of us who don't speak dino? You said it looks thousands of years old–how old *should* it look?"

"Somewhere in the area of one hundred fifty *million*," I said. She whistled. I turned back to Lamb. "You really think Owen Horner parted with a complete, pristine specimen? Just to make you look foolish?"

"I can't imagine that snake parting with so much as a toenail if he didn't have to." Lamb scowled. "But something about this dig is dodgy."

We had reached the farmhouse. Horner was just coming out from the back of the building toward us. Murphy had made himself Horner's shadow.

"I was just on my way to fetch you, Miss Rook," Horner called as we neared. "You really ought to see the tracks your boss has been examining. Come on. I'll show you around back."

"I'm sure we can manage to find a big red barn without you," Lamb said flatly.

"Oh, you're good at finding things," Horner said. "I'm just good at finding them first—like this dig site. I'm not sure Miss Rook has a week to wait for you to get there your way."

"Gentlemen, please." I shot them each an imploring look. Lamb rolled his eyes but bit his tongue, and Horner just chuckled and led the way.

The barn was a wide, red building, bordered with a chicken coop to one side and a collection of barrels and wheelbarrows to the other. On the path between the barn and the farmhouse, we found Jackaby and Hudson hunched over the dirt. Brisbee stood, watching. Jackaby held a disc of colored glass with symbols etched around the outer edge. He was peering through it intently, tilting his head this way and that as we approached.

"Sir?" I said.

"Peculiar." I could not tell if Jackaby had actually recognized our arrival, or if he was merely talking to himself. He tucked the lens into his bulky coat.

"Miss Fuller!" Brisbee said cheerfully. "Welcome! Wonderful to see you again!" Then, taking in the whole group of us, he added, "Oh good! So glad you folks are getting along. I've just made a fresh pot of coffee. Why don't I just bring everyone some refreshments?"

"That's really not necessary," said Lamb.

"No, no trouble at all." With a wave of his hand, Brisbee was already away, bustling off into the farmhouse.

"What exactly are you looking at, gentlemen?" Nellie Fuller asked.

Hudson leaned on one knee. "These tracks ain't like nothin' we got around here—least nothin' I ever hunted." He thought for a moment, and then added with a grin, "Yet."

My heart, which had been up in my throat since the revelation at the dig site, dropped suddenly to the pit of my stomach. I slipped back and slid toward Charlie while the others were crowding around to gaze at the footprints.

Charlie read my intentions and met me halfway. "In case you were wondering," he whispered in my ear, "I have never visited the farm in my other form. Whatever Mr. Hudson is tracking right now, it isn't me."

"Good," I said. "That's good."

Charlie's eyebrows knit, and his expression was torn. "If I *did*, however," he continued, "I might be able to put this whole business to rest a lot sooner. *Someone* stole those bones, and we've yet to uncover any obvious leads. Jackaby's right. If I could just pick up a scent before it has time to fade . . ."

"You know that's a bad idea," I whispered. "Mr. Hudson is already on the hunt for *something*, and even if it isn't you, you're still–"

"Rook!" Jackaby's voice broke me away from my thoughts. "What do you make of these tracks?"

"Me, sir? Wouldn't Mr. Hudson be a better judge?"

"Of course he would," said Jackaby curtly, "which is why I asked Mr. Hudson first. Now I am asking you."

"Looks like a bird," Hudson said as I shuffled past Lamb and moved to join my employer in the soft dirt. "Three big old toes and just a hint of a back one. They're real thin, but those talons are long and nasty. I thought Rosie was big. Whatever left this makes her look like a chickadee."

I finally focused in on the tracks and gaped. The footprints were very familiar. I had seen similar marks cast in plaster at the museum and sketched in my father's field journals, but more than that, I had seen imprints like these only minutes ago at the top of the hill. The markings were the precise size and shape of the enormous dinosaur's missing toes.

"Oh good grief," said Lamb. "This is getting ridiculous."

"Well, it has to be a hoax," said Horner.

"Oh, drop the act! Of course it's a hoax, but you would know all about it, wouldn't you?" Lamb waved a hand at the footprints. "The specimen's foot is missing! Horner has obviously used my fossils to stamp these impressions."

"What? Why would I do that?" Horner demanded.

"I don't know how your mind works. To distract me from my legitimate work, I imagine."

"He's right," Hank announced. "They're all pressed from the same foot. They go back an' forth like it's two, but they're all the left. Explains them being so thin, too."

"There's more to it than that," Jackaby mumbled, his brow still knit in concentration.

"Sir?" I asked. "Can you see something . . . special?"

Jackaby's eyes narrowed. "Fake or not, these prints were not made with simple fossils. Fossils are no longer living; they've been reduced to a mineral state, even less vital than dry bone. As I said before, studying fossils is no different than studying rocks." Lamb and Horner both bristled, but Jackaby ignored them and continued. "These prints have traces of something far more potent. It's not like the others, but there is a residual tincture here—an aura I cannot quite place."

"An aura?" Lamb asked. "What kind of detective are you?"

"I am an investigator of unexplained phenomena. My domain is the eldritch and the extraordinary." Jackaby stood. His expression bespoke a building enthusiasm. "Your missing foot is most peculiar indeed, Mr. Lamb—or else there is something even more peculiar afoot. Tell me about this dinosaur of yours."

"I'll tell you nothing, thanks—not around *him*." Lamb looked down his nose meaningfully at Horner, who rolled his eyes and threw up his hands.

"Oh for goodness' sake," I said. "Just a moment ago, Mr. Lamb, you were convinced that Mr. Horner planted the whole skeleton as a ruse. If he's the mastermind behind all this, then what harm is there in telling him what he already knows?"

"Wait, what?" Horner said, facing Lamb. "Now you're accusing me of putting the bones there in the first place? I thought you were accusing me of *taking* them!"

"Don't pretend to be–," Lamb began.

"It's got wings," said Nellie, loudly. "Oops. I guess it's out now, and you boys can stop quibbling about it. That thing on the hill has wings, Mr. Jackaby. Really big ones." Lamb glared daggers at the reporter, but she just shrugged innocently.

"That's impossible," said Horner.

"We've reached that point already," I said.

"It couldn't . . . It isn't . . . It can't possibly–," he said.

"Yes, we've done that bit already, too," I said. "But it does, and it is, and it can."

"It's easily fifty feet long!" said Horner.

Jackaby had been watching the exchange with interest. "I suspect the remains are not so deeply buried as your typical dinosaur?" he asked.

"Remarkably near the surface, actually," I said. "How did you–"

"Any signs of wildfires around the skeleton?"

"Ash in the surrounding sediment," I confirmed.

"Mr. Barker, didn't you say something about flint in the area of its stomach? Of course—it makes perfect sense. I must be dense for missing it earlier."

Lamb was scowling. "What do you know about my dinosaur?"

Jackaby smiled. "I know you haven't got one."

"Excuse me?" Lamb said.

"You've got something worlds more exciting," Jackaby said. His eyes flashed with a dangerous zeal. "You've got a dragon."

Chapter Twenty-One

Hudson's bristly beard split into a wide grin. Lamb looked incredulous. Nellie opened her mouth as if to speak, but then closed it again. "A dragon?" said Charlie.

"All of the evidence fits. Dragons were known to swallow flint to generate the spark they needed to breathe fire. The beast's presence in Gad's Valley is somewhat surprising, as most dragons of the size you're describing are reported to have lived around Great Britain and Germany—but migratory cryptozoology is an imprecise science. One thing is clear: their kind went extinct centuries ago. Far more recently than dinosaurs, of course, which accounts for its being nearer the surface. A few endangered Chinese breeds still exist today. The living Eastern varieties are much smaller, of course. More like snakes. Beautiful scales."

"Do you think this is a joke?" Lamb spat.

"No," said Jackaby. "Although I did employ a rather droll play on words earlier. You may have missed it. You see, the word *afoot* and the—"

"You're either a madman or an idiot. You're not a detective, with your *auras* and *dragons*. Was that a crystal ball you were looking through when we arrived?"

"A scrying glass. I've never had much luck with crystal."

"Mr. Lamb." Owen Horner had allowed a little glint of wonder to creep into his eyes. "I know it sounds impossible, and maybe it is, but can you imagine being the first professional team in history to uncover bona fide scientific evidence of dragons on earth? What do you say we put the past behind us and work together to find out the truth for ourselves?"

"I say you're mad. All of you. This farce has gone on long enough." Lamb whipped around, nearly toppling over Murphy. "Out of my way, you oaf. I am getting back to work—real, objective, scientific work. If I see *any* of you within the boundaries of my excavation site, you will be arrested. Isn't that right, Officer?"

Charlie looked uncomfortable. "I really don't think that's necessary, sir. Mr. Jackaby is very good at what he does. If you would just give him a chance . . ."

"You, too? Good Lord, I would expect as much from that backwoods trapper, but . . . wait a moment. Where is he?"

Hank Hudson, hulking mountain of a man though he

was, had slipped quietly away. Jackaby raised his eyebrows. "Is that really a question, Mr. Lamb? Hank Hudson has always been a bit of an enthusiast when it comes to uncommon animals. He has just learned that the remains of one of the most legendary species in all of human history are sticking out of the dirt a few hundred yards away. Where would you expect to find an individual of his disposition?"

Lewis Lamb's eyes flashed, and then he hurried around the farmhouse and up the rocky foothills toward his prize. Mr. Murphy stumbled and panted, trying to keep up, and the rest of us followed close behind.

By the time we reached the opening in the canvas wall, there was already a noisy commotion coming from within. Charlie overtook Murphy and hurried in after Lamb, imploring the men to remain civil. The rest of us pushed through the flap just as Hank tossed aside the shroud that had concealed the beast's wings. The skeleton stood naked to the sunlight, Hank at its neck and Lamb cursing at him from across the ribs.

"Hah!" The trapper clapped his hands, beaming from ear to ear as he surveyed the whole creature.

Bradley picked up the discarded cloth and looked to Lamb for instructions. Lamb sighed and shook his head. "Oh, don't bother."

"This was one helluva big guy, wasn't he?" Hudson's voice broke through the moment. He gave an appreciative whistle. "I woulda loved to have a crack at him when he was alive.

Not much trouble to track a dragon, I imagine—but the real trick woulda been bringin' him down." He surveyed the figure with an impressed nod as he pondered the notion.

I tried to set aside my own disbelief as I looked at the complete form. Every scientific instinct in me resisted picturing the beast as a fire-breathing monster from mythology. Before I had met Jackaby, I might have been as leery as Professor Lamb—history and fairy tales lived in opposite ends of my mental library—but the longer I looked, the more the shelves slid into one another, and the more possible the impossible became.

The figure was built a bit like a pterosaur or a modern bat, with wide wings in place of arms. The dragons in my storybooks had always had both, like angry lizards with wings tacked on for show. The bones before me were more biologically believable. The creature lay on its side with one wing spread out above its back, three long, thin arcs of bone reaching nearly to the tip of its tail. If the beast was fifty feet from end to end, it would have been at least a hundred from wingtip to wingtip. Given its sturdy hind legs and wicked talons, it was not hard to imagine the living creature scooping sheep from farms and doing battle with intrepid armor-clad knights.

"Yes, that looks about right," said Jackaby, casually. "And it looks as though your missing bones have found their way home as well, Mr. Lamb. Nice to have this whole business sorted out so promptly, isn't it?"

Lamb's head whipped around, and I followed his eyes to a clumsy pile by the figure's femur. "They're back?" He hurried to the formerly missing fossils and began to meticulously lay them out again.

"I was just going to tell you," said Mr. Bradley, stepping out from behind Hank. "The canvas was pulled up over on that end while I was working. Someone tossed them in and then ran off. Never saw who it was. Nobody was there when I peeked under. I was heading out the front when this . . . um . . . gentleman came rushing in." He nodded toward Hank Hudson. Next to the trapper, the slim fellow looked like a sapling beside a redwood.

"The return of the bones changes nothing," Lamb spat. "That degenerate Horner is obviously still to blame. He must have panicked once he saw that the police were sticking around. Not that you've been any help at all. If that criminal is not locked away by the morning, you'd better believe your superiors will be hearing from me."

"Mr. Lamb," Charlie said evenly. "You know there is no proof . . ."

"You have *two* damned detectives!" Lamb waved an arm in our general direction, faltering somewhat as he glanced between my employer and me. "Or what apparently pass for detectives in this backwater valley. *Find* some proof before he makes off with anything else. And while you're at it, an invaluable artifact remains missing." He was right. The dragon's wicked jawline was still broken by a distinct gap.

Chapter Twenty-Two

The theft of the bones from under all of our noses had been bad enough, but their return was all the more vexing—they added a baffling layer to the mystery without solving anything. Were they connected to the murders at all? What could be worth killing for, but not worth keeping?

Jackaby hiked back and forth between the footprints and the fossils, scowling at the earth and muttering to himself. With the last of the daylight fading, Nellie Fuller carried her camera up the rocky hill, and was already loading a plate into the slot before Lamb sent his goons to stop her. Mr. Murphy snatched up the tripod and tromped righteously down the slope with Nellie on his heels, while Mr. Bradley stood guard resolutely in the entrance.

Charlie asked both paleontologists to consent to a search

of their belongings, which nearly set Lamb off again, and which Horner simply refused out of spite. By dusk, nothing had been accomplished and everyone was exhausted.

Hudson had quickly tired of all the drama, turning his attention to the surrounding wilderness instead. The massive prints might have been fakes, but he was not ready to rule out a real wild creature making off with the tooth. He had not returned by the time the sun began to dip low in the sky.

Lamb's crew set up cots directly on the dig site, and Brisbee invited Miss Fuller to stay the night in the spare room of the farmhouse.

"When you promised me an unbelievable story," she said, "I didn't realize you meant it literally. I'll be laughed out of the newsroom if I go back pitching 'Dragon in the Dirt' without the proof to back it up. This may be the scoop of the century, but I'll sleep a lot easier once I've got a clean photograph to bring back with me."

"I'm sure you'll get some good pictures tomorrow," he assured her. "Once everyone's had a little time to sleep on it."

"I'm sure that I will, Mr. Brisbee," she said. "I've been to the Arctic and the Orient and back again, and I never missed a deadline. Don't think for a moment that a dirty tarp and a grumpy old man will stop me from snatching my story from the top of that hill."

"That's the spirit." He punctuated his enthusiasm with a

clap. "I'll go set you up some blankets and get your room all sorted. You come on up when you're ready."

Owen Horner sidled up as Brisbee was bustling off into the house. "Let me get that for you, beautiful," he said. Nellie allowed him to collect her suitcase and camera equipment.

"Be careful with that," she said as he scooped up a tall wooden box.

"Your valuables are safe with me," he promised.

"I'm more worried about you being safe with them. Those are my spare tubes of flash powder in there. They're basically explosives just waiting for a spark."

"Sounds downright romantic when you put it like that," Horner said with a wink. "I'll be careful, honey, don't you worry. Your room is right down the hall from mine. You're welcome to come visit if you get scared during the night."

"Oh, my dear Mr. Horner," she said, giving him the tender look a nanny might give to a proud toddler showing off on the playground. "Whatever might you do to make me feel safe in the middle of the night?"

"Try me. I think I could manage to put a smile on your face."

"You've got that going for you, I suppose—you do make a girl laugh."

"Aw, be honest now," he said. "You've been all over the world—did you ever meet a guy as cute as this?" He flashed his most winsome grin. It was hard not to smile back. If nothing else, the man had confidence.

She patted him on the cheek. "Just one, darling. I bought

a monkey when I was in Singapore. He makes me laugh, too, but he chatters less."

Horner took the rebuff in stride, chuckling loudly and carrying her belongings into the house.

"I do believe you've won the fellow's heart, Miss Fuller," I told her. We had found ourselves alone on the porch.

"Men's hearts are easy targets, Abbie. I'm much more interested in winning their respect."

"Oh, absolutely!" I found myself growing fonder of the brassy reporter by the moment. "Although, I must admit I wouldn't mind a bit of *both* from certain parties . . ."

"Like that policeman of yours?"

"I didn't say . . ."

"Give me some credit. You don't get far in my game with your eyes closed. I get it—who doesn't like a man in uniform? But trust me, men are never worth it. Behind every great man is a woman who gave up on greatness and tied herself into an apron. Romance is for saps, Abbie. You're sharp and you've got pluck. Don't waste it."

I swallowed, digesting her advice. "What about you?" I said. "On all your wild adventures, you've never fallen for anyone?"

She kept up a canny smile, but the ends of her mouth faltered. "The trick about falling is to catch yourself before you hit the dirt."

"You don't strike me as the sort of woman who's afraid of a little dirt."

She laughed. "Nor you. I dare say it might just be your element, from what I saw today. How's a good girl from England wind up in the bone business?"

"My father," I said. "He was the expert."

"No kidding? And he wanted you to join the family business?"

"Not exactly," I admitted. "It's a long story."

"Well then," she chimed. "Now we're into my element. I love a good story." She slipped into an old rocking chair on the farmer's porch and gestured to the one beside it. With a deep breath I settled in next to her.

"All right, then, let's see. My father's career has always been sort of charmed," I said. "Or at least I was charmed by it. I grew up wanting to strap on a pith helmet and follow him to adventures, but he never let me. I had to satisfy myself just reading about him or seeing his discoveries displayed in museums around Hampshire. Just before I left for university, he was appointed the head of what promised to be the most prestigious dig of his career. I begged him to bring me along, but he said it wasn't ladies' work."

"A familiar tune." Nellie nodded.

"That was bad enough, but the real blow came when I learned he had invited Tommy Bellows as a sort of intern."

"Tommy Bellows?"

"Yes. Ugh–Tommy Bellows! A boy who went to the school across the road from mine. He made school prefect and cricket captain, and he always smiled in that thoroughly unpleasant way—as though he smelled something wretched but liked it. Tommy Bellows! The boy who ignored every very clear rejection I ever threw at him since primary school. The boy who smelled like too much aftershave and flirted incessantly with every girl he ever met, always with the same cocky grin he must have thought was dashing. Tommy Bellows!"

"Sounds like a charmer."

"When I asked my father what possessed him to bring Tommy Bellows instead of his own daughter, he told me that the field was no place for a young lady. What I ought to do, he insisted, was finish my schooling and find a good husband with a reliable job. 'Speaking of which,' he added in his most knowing, fatherly voice, 'this internship could help give that young Bellows boy a real leg up. He could have quite the career ahead of him.'"

"He didn't." Nellie put a hand to her mouth.

"He did. So that was that. The next day I ran away and found my own adventure."

"I'll say you did! Good for you! My goodness, I knew I was going to like you, Abbie. I just didn't realize how much. Your daddy is going to have to read about *you* for once. See what I mean? Leaving the boys behind was the best move you ever made. Never look back, darling!"

"Thank you—that's very kind. Really, though, there are

some good men in the world, too. Charlie is nothing like Tommy Bellows."

She reached across to my chair and held my arm gently. "Don't get me wrong—I'm sure he's a sweetheart. He'd probably treat you real well and keep you safe and happy. But do you want to be *safe and happy*, or do you want to be *great?*"

I didn't know how to respond. She was affirming all the reasons I had freed myself of my old life and all that stifling stability, but her version didn't exactly feel like freedom, either.

"You could be really great, too," she said. "I can tell. I don't know if you noticed, but even that windbag, Lamb, started talking to you like a human being out there. He couldn't help himself. You've just got a special sort of something about you when you aren't busy giving Officer Cutiepie the doe eyes."

I smiled weakly, and Nellie gave my shoulder a squeeze and stood. "Just something to think about, Abbie, darling. Get some rest. I'll see you in the morning."

I did think about it. I wished I could stop thinking about it as the sun began to rest on the tops of the trees, and I was thinking about it when Charlie came to ask if I would like a ride back to the cabin while Jackaby was finishing up.

"It is a lovely time of night for a ride," he said. "Sunset in the valley is always striking."

"I . . . No," I said. "Thank you, but I really ought to stay and assist. I'll head back with Mr. Jackaby when he's ready."

"Of course. Would you like me to wait here with you?"

I swallowed. "That's all right. I think we'll be fine, but thank you."

Charlie looked ready to speak again, but then he just nodded. He bade me good night, and I could hear Maryanne's hooves clopping away as I walked around the farmhouse to find Jackaby examining the goat enclosure.

The remaining kids had nestled in to rest in a corner of the pen beside their mother. I had never been much for livestock, but these were darling little things, all downy soft with fluffy little ears. They nuzzled one another sleepily, lying in a heap all together like puppies.

"They look cozy, don't they?" I said, pulling my own coat a little tighter against the crisp breeze.

"Hmm?" Jackaby looked up. "Oh, they may seem like sweet siblings, but they're terrible witnesses. Whatever snatched their little brother didn't seem to faze them in the least. I've been unable to get anything useful out of them."

"Well, goats are known for their stubbornness," I said. "Anything you'd like me to take down?" I pulled the note-pad from my pocket.

"Let's see. What do we know . . . ?" Jackaby grimaced as he collected his thoughts. "Three victims with bruises on their necks, a pale man with a nasty aura, one stolen tooth, and one un-stolen foot."

"I've got all that already," I said, flipping through the pages.

"And something else. There's something familiar here, but I can't place it. There are just too many variables. For a countryside so seemingly devoid of productive peculiarities, there are a lot of traces of paranormal presences here—fading whispers of something sinister, and yet no solid leads. Everything is just out of reach. I imagine this is how Jenny feels all the time. It's intolerably frustrating."

"We'll make more progress in the daylight, sir, I'm sure. Come on, then. I'll walk you back to the cabin. If we're going to brood over fruitless frustrations and complicated casework, we might as well enjoy a sunset along the way. Charlie says they're quite nice out here in the country." I sighed. "Still—a dragon, Mr. Jackaby! I'm still having trouble believing it! A real dragon! That's something!"

"Electromagnetic radiation traveling through the atmosphere along an inconsistent wavelength," said Jackaby, standing up. "And also magic. There's a phoenix involved."

"Come again?"

"The sunset. Of course, it also has a traditionally romantic connotation. You aren't making any advances, are you, Miss Rook? I have strict parameters about that. Very unprofessional. It was never a problem with Douglas."

"What? Ugh! No! No, I most certainly am not making advances! For goodness' sake—*not* making advances is exactly what I'm doing, in fact."

"Ah." Jackaby nodded. We walked in silence for several seconds.

"It's just that Jenny told me I *should* . . ."

"I really don't need to know," Jackaby said.

"But then Miss Fuller said I *shouldn't* . . ."

"Please don't, Miss Rook."

"Oh, never mind." I felt hot and embarrassed, and I wanted to hide. "Forget I said anything."

"I assure you, I will ardently try." The black teeth of the tree line had swallowed the sun like a ripe grapefruit, and the seeping mess of red and orange had begun to spread across the sky. It might have been every bit as lovely as Charlie had said, but I was finding it difficult to appreciate.

The crimson-tinted countryside passed by us in silence for a dozen paces. "So often," Jackaby said, "people think that when we arrive at a crossroads, we can choose only one path, but—as I have often and articulately postulated—people are stupid. We're not walking the path. We *are* the path. We are all of the roads and all of the intersections. Of course you can choose both."

I blinked.

"Also, if I hear any more nonsense about your allowing other people to decide where you're going in your own life, I will seriously reconsider your employment. You were hired for your mind, Miss Rook. I won't have an assistant incapable of thinking for herself."

"Yes, sir," I said. "Thank you, sir." The sky reached its richest red, and then it slipped into a deep purple and finally the blackness of night just as we arrived. The stars blinked down on us, and the moon washed the cabin in gentle blues. It had, indeed, been a beautiful sunset.

Chapter Twenty-Three

I was awoken some hours later by the sound of the bedroom door. I gathered together my senses and tried to
remember my surroundings. The room smelled woody,
and only starlight filtered in through the soft white curtains. Charlie stepped in quietly, padding to the side of the
bed. He put a hand gently on my shoulder. "Miss Rook?"
he whispered.

He put a finger to his lips. "Shh. Stay quiet, but there is
something outside the cabin."

My thoughts tripped and tumbled, and then clumsily
righted themselves. I blinked and rubbed my eyes. Jackaby's
silhouette appeared in the doorway, pulling his bulky coat
over his pajamas. "You're certain it's still out there?" my
employer asked in a whisper.

"My hearing is still very good, Mr. Jackaby." Charlie peered out of the bedroom window into the blackness of the forest.

"*What* is out there?" I said.

"That is what we intend to find out." Jackaby pulled the knit cap over his mess of dark hair and stuffed his bare feet into his shoes. "Stay here until we return."

I shook the last of the fog from my brain. "Well, you already know that isn't going to happen." I was out of bed with my own coat wrapped over my nightgown before the men could leave without me.

The three of us tiptoed to the corner of the cabin. Charlie took the lead, silently peering into the darkness. The surrounding wilderness was louder than I would have imagined. I strained to hear anything out of the ordinary, but the clamor of chirping insects and rustling leaves made it hard to focus. The forest itself seemed to drone on in a perpetual low murmur. Charlie held a hand up, and my employer and I froze. Tentatively, he leaned his head around the corner. I could hear it now, just the faintest crackling of leaves. Footsteps. Something was around the corner. Impossibly close—impossibly large.

"Mr. Hudson?" said Charlie.

The trapper stomped into sight, the wide barrel of his rifle dipping to the ground. "Shh." He held a finger to his bristly mustache and glanced behind him into the woods.

"What in the Sam Hill are you folks doin' out here in the middle of the night?"

"This is my cabin," said Charlie. "What are *you* doing out here in the middle of the night?"

Hank looked left and right into the surrounding forest. "Trackin'. Been followin' trails all night. There's somethin' big in the valley for sure, and not just an old bony fake. The prints get pretty thick around here. I lost a good one just outside your place. You seen anything?"

I held my breath. Charlie shook his head. The trapper nodded slowly and shifted his rifle to his shoulder. "Well, sorry if I woke ya. Guess I'd best be headed back, anyway. Y'all be careful. No tellin' what's lurkin' in the deep dark woods."

"What sort of footprints have you been tracking, Hudson?" asked Jackaby. He was peering into the trees toward the road.

"Dunno. Sharp claws. Real big. Why? You spot somethin' with them fancy eyes of yours?"

"No. Possibly no. Although . . . Can any of you see a faint metaphysical incandescence radiating just beyond that maple tree?"

"Of course we can't, Mr. Jackaby," I said. "Could you describe it?"

"I would say it's fifty or sixty feet tall, stout trunk. Still largely bare, although I imagine the spring buds are probably beginning to . . ."

"Not the maple, sir."

"Ah, yes. The aura is faint—shrouded or possibly just residual. It's terribly familiar. Sort of a . . . how to explain the color . . . sort of a lumpy bluish with a hint of peril. No, that's not quite right. It isn't really blue at all, is it?"

Three sets of eyes blinked at my employer.

"Oh, never mind."

"I got my wagon over that way," offered Hank. "Yer probably just pickin' up on leftover Rosie feathers."

Jackaby looked his friend up and down in the dark. He picked a speck from the man's fur cuff and nodded. "Yes, you're probably right. You have something of the same color about you."

"Hah! Anyone else told me I was 'lumpy with a bit of peril,' I might take it as an insult," said Hudson. "Well, y'all have a good night. Sorry I woke you, but do watch yerselves out here."

We nodded and said our good-byes, and the trapper was on his way. When we were inside, I planted myself in front of Charlie. "You see? I should have expected he would find his way here. You really must be careful."

"I have been careful, Miss Rook. If the tracks he's following are mine, they're not recent. Besides, I'm sure you are worrying over nothing. Mr. Hudson is a personal friend of Mr. Jackaby's, is he not? If he were to uncover the truth of my . . . my *family history*, he seems like the sort of man that would remain discreet, don't you think, Detective?"

"Hmm? Oh, yes—Hudson can be quite circumspect."

Charlie looked back to me. "I appreciate your concern, and I would certainly prefer that my little secret remain a private one, but I don't think I need to be afraid of Mr. Hudson."

"I wouldn't go quite so far as that," Jackaby said, hanging his coat and hat by the door. "Hudson is a remarkable man, and a valued associate, but he and I don't exactly share the same philosophies on sentient freedoms."

"Come again?" I said.

"He had a fish for many years, lovely golden thing he called Jinny. It could speak, when it raised its head above water. It had a surprisingly deep voice for such a little thing, although it spoke only Mandarin Chinese. Hudson copied down the little creature's words phonetically and took his notes to a few shop owners in the Chinese district, claiming the words were from an old book or some such. He determined that the fish was called Jinyu—hence the name Jinny—and it was offering to grant him any wish he might desire. It could turn his hovel into a palace, or transform every brick into solid gold."

"I heard a story like that in Romania once," said Charlie, "only the fish offered the old man three wishes."

"Yes, the golden fish is a timeless folktale in many traditions. Invariably, the fisherman asks for too much and learns some trite lesson about greed or compassion."

"What did Mr. Hudson wish for?"

"Nothing. He just kept the thing in an oversized aquarium until the day it died."

"Oh."

"Yes. Not that he mistreated the creature. Scarcely any other fish in all the world could have claimed a better master—although I suppose scarcely any other fish in all the world could have claimed anything at all, which is why he wanted it in the first place. I cannot speak Chinese, but the thing looked content enough whenever I saw it. I did find it rather morbid when he had the body mounted after Jinny passed away, but I suppose the fish wasn't using it any longer, and we all deal with mortality in our own ways."

Charlie blanched. "He had it mounted?"

"He likes a rare breed," said Jackaby.

"It might not hurt to err on the side of caution," Charlie conceded. I nodded my agreement. "On the subject of keeping secrets," he continued, "have you made any progress on our ulterior investigation?"

Jackaby shook his head. "Mrs. Brisbee's killer seems to have left very little for us to find. The body in the morgue was several days cold—as is our trail."

"Body in the morgue?"

"Denson," said Jackaby. "I have his tooth."

"Oh," said Charlie. "Is that . . . helpful?"

"Not enough. I'm tired of chasing shadows. I would be back in New Fiddleham pursuing more prominent leads already, but there's something we're missing here—and not knowing what is driving me mad. Before we're through, I intend to know precisely what's really lurking in the deep dark woods."

Jackaby let the thought hang in the air for a moment before bidding us a curt good night and vanishing into his room.

For the rest of the night, my ears pricked at the slightest noises from the forest outside my window. I longed for the hum of city life, the occasional clatter of hooves on cobblestones or drunken singing as the pubs closed for the evening, but instead my mind made monsters out of every chirp and rustle. I had to keep telling myself that nothing nefarious was taking place in the shadows beyond my curtains—a deeply inaccurate sentiment, I would come to learn, but one that brought me what little rest I could find.

Chapter Twenty-Four

A knock on the door roused me from a fitful dream about claws and cages. "Time is wasting, Miss Rook," Jackaby announced as I pried open my eyes. The bright daylight was pressing unsympathetically into the bedroom. "There has been a disturbing new development. Charlie is already away."

I sat up abruptly, then swayed as the blood caught up to my head. "What sort of development—the bones? Have they found the missing tooth?"

"Better yet—they've found Brisbee's kid."

I rubbed my eyes. "With all due respect, sir, your priorities are a curious mess. Please tell me that Charlie Barker did not seriously rush off at the crack of dawn just to bring a lost goat back to Brisbee's farm."

"I'm not sure if he intends to bring it back, but I imagine he's rather interested in taking a look at what's left of it, and to see if he can find any useful clues amid the blood and debris."

I opened my mouth. I closed my mouth.

"I'm rather keen to have a look myself," continued Jackaby, "but I promised Mr. Barker not to leave you behind, what with the grisly nature of the mess. Come on, then. Bright new day and all that!"

I dressed quickly, and we reached the clearing in ten or fifteen minutes. It was back from the road by about half a mile, not far from the Brisbee farmhouse. How anyone could tell that the thing had ever been a baby goat was beyond me. Scraps of hide and hair were tossed all around the clearing, and the trees were splattered with dark droplets. Flies had begun to collect in busy swarms around the larger pieces. The image of a cozy huddle of cuddly kids hung in my mind, and the notion that this mess had once been one of them made my head swim.

"My word," I breathed. "What happened to the poor thing?"

Charlie was picking his way around the edges of the gore. He glanced up as we arrived, looking a bit chagrined to see me approach the morbid scene. I was half expecting him to insist that I wait by the road, but he said nothing of the sort. Instead, he just looked from one end of the carnage to the other and shook his head. "Mr. Brisbee found it this morning. He seemed pretty shaken up about it."

I couldn't blame Brisbee. I felt a little woozy myself.

"Reasonable enough. Find anything of interest so far?" Jackaby asked. The policeman nodded to a tree toward the middle of the mess.

"Whatever did this is strong. The marks are only a few feet off the ground, but they're half an inch deep in the tree bark. Could be teeth or talons. It's hard to tell." Jackaby knelt beside the tree and examined a series of gashes in the trunk. He snapped off a shredded piece of bark and tucked the splinter into the recesses of his coat.

"I can't say I love what you've done with the place, darlings," Nellie Fuller trilled as she trod into the bloody grove, her tripod swung over one shoulder of a slick checkered coat. "Far too much red for my taste—but I must applaud you for going bold. Oh Lord, there are even bits in the branches over there! Goodness! How marvelously grisly."

Jackaby and I exchanged glances. Charlie was watching the woman skeptically as she began to situate her camera. "Good morning, Miss Fuller," Charlie said. "You seem very . . . positive this morning."

"Sanguine, even," added Jackaby.

"Are you kidding?" She held out her hands, framing a rectangle with her fingers. "Giant bones in the hills, scary monsters in the woods"—she peered through her imaginary photograph directly at me—"and a beautiful young lady right in the middle of it all." She let her hands drop and looked at me earnestly. "Say, are you all right, sweetie?"

"Of course I'm all right," I said in what I hoped was a convincing tone. "I'm *great*, remember?"

"That's my girl. With your poise and my prose, we'll make every paper from here to Oregon!"

"I'm really not sure this is the sort of thing people will want to see . . . ," I began.

"Abbie, darling, do you have any idea how many newspapers Jack the Ripper has sold in the past five years? The masses love a gruesome mutilation. Don't get me wrong, I'll have nightmares for a week—ick—but this is gold! You don't mind a few quick photographs, do you?"

I glanced back to Jackaby. "It's fine," he answered, "as long as she keeps her distance and doesn't interfere. Make sure she doesn't go touching all the evidence."

"Make sure she doesn't go touching the scraps of blood and gore that used to be a sweet little baby goat?" I asked.

"Yes," said Jackaby frankly. "That."

"I think I can resist the temptation, Detective," Nellie called. "Is your boss always so sentimental when he's working?"

"Oh, he cares very much," I said. "He just doesn't show it with—you know—emotions."

"They're overrated, anyway." Nellie clicked open the legs of the tripod and nestled it into the mossy soil.

"What's that, Mr. Barker?" Jackaby was saying. I turned to look.

Charlie held out a little handful of what looked like

honey-colored hairs. "I'm not entirely sure. What do you make of them?" Jackaby took them and held them up to the light.

"Fur. Not goat. Not bear or wolf. Maybe wildcat?" Jackaby pinched them between his fingers and squinted at them. "Wait a moment," he said. "There are two different materials here. I would wager the first is from whatever beast took apart Brisbee's goat—but the other's not fur at all. Fibers of some sort."

I looked around where Charlie had found the samples. A shallow line had been rubbed near the base of the tree. "From a length of twine or rope?" I suggested.

Charlie followed my gaze and leaned closer to inspect it. "There are more fibers dug into the bark. She's right. Do you think the goat was tied here?"

"An offering?" Jackaby speculated.

Charlie shrugged.

"Very traditional choice, a goat," my employer mused. "Downright biblical. Wrong time of year for it, though. Historically the sacrifice of the scapegoat is a fall tradition."

"Is it possible," I suggested, "that the kid was less of a ritual sacrifice and more of a baited trap?" Charlie and Jackaby both looked up at me. "Because I happen to know a man who's pretty good at traps and who was definitely out and about in these woods last night." I could tell my theory was not a bit too wild for either of them.

"Smile for the camera!" Nellie sang out.

Charlie looked away as the grisly grove filled with a burst of white light. "Okay, give me a moment and we'll take another just to be sure." Nellie smiled blithely as she pulled the plate out of the camera, tucking it into a slim tin case and clicking it shut. She hummed to herself as she carefully popped the cork from a little silver tube of flash powder and began to reload the lamp.

Hank Hudson did not look the least bit put out by my suggestion that the baby goat had been part of a trap, when we intercepted his cart on the road a few minutes later. "I like the way you think, little lady!" he said. "Was it a real healthy tree, good bend to it?"

"I don't know—I suppose so." I hadn't been quite sure what to expect from the trapper, but he seemed oddly enthusiastic about the notion as he climbed down from the cart and trekked with us back to the site of the slaughter.

"How high up was the rope you found?"

"Not high at all," I replied. "Just off the ground."

"Hmm, well, that ain't no snare trap, then."

We reached the scene, and Hudson grimaced at the remains. "Somebody's a messy eater. Told y'all to watch yerselves out here."

He paused and regarded Charlie thoughtfully for just a moment, but then turned his attention to the claw marks.

"Let's see. Could be a young bear, markin' territory. They'll do that, tear the bark off a tree." He knelt by the gouges in the trunk. "Awfully low for a bear, though."

"What's that up there?" Charlie asked, pointing.

Hank glanced up the trunk. "Looks like a knothole. Maybe a bird's nest in there. Probably nothin'. I'll give ya a boost if ya wanna shimmy on up an' have a look, though." The policeman looked a little wary, but he accepted the trapper's help in reaching up to the first branch. He pulled himself up and scrabbled for a decent footing to inspect the hole.

Hank stooped down and rubbed a finger across the marks in the bark.

"What do you make of them?" Jackaby asked. "Have you seen anything like them before?"

"Three talons. Looks a lot like the marks Rosie leaves . . ." He trailed off.

"And like the tracks we saw up at the farmhouse," I added. I could tell the trapper had come to the same thought. "Smaller, but just like them."

"Them tracks up at Brisbee's were definitely fakes, though." Hudson turned to Jackaby. "Unless you know somethin' I don't know."

"The ones up at Brisbee's were," Jackaby said. He had a twinkle in his eye. "These ones, though . . ." He shook his head. "No. No, they can't be dragon tracks. That would be something to see, but dragons have been extinct for thousands of years. Even in biblical times they were highly endangered, which is why they are mentioned so infrequently in the scripture. Something living left these."

"There's dragons in the Bible?"

"Really, Hudson? Some of the best verses have dragons. Isaiah has a few particularly vivid passages about divine fury. Not just dragons, either. It goes on about unicorns and satyrs and something else . . . owls, I think."

"I shoulda gone ta Sunday school more when I was a kid," said Hudson.

"You said there were some smaller dragons alive today," I said.

"Yes, fine," Jackaby said. "A few rare Eastern varieties exist, but they're scarcely large enough to menace a muskrat. Certainly nothing big enough to do all this." The conviction drained out of his voice as he eyed the claw marks.

"You see something, don't you, sir?" I asked.

My employer only scowled. If he intended to answer, his response was cut off by a burst of motion above us, accompanied by the frantic flapping of wings and the snap of breaking branches. Charlie tumbled down, his fingers scrabbling to find purchase. On the last branch, his legs caught hold, and he swiveled abruptly, hanging upside down from the branch like a bat, his uniform flopping over his head. Above him, a brown-and-white owl gave out a shrill screech and fluttered off into the forest.

Charlie swayed back and forth slightly, sighing from

somewhere deep within his jacket. "You mentioned some-thin' about owls?" Hudson said with a sly grin.

Jackaby wore none of the same amusement. He contin-ued to regard the jagged marks with intensity, and a somber foreboding had rolled in like storm clouds to hang heavily over his face. His expression sent an icy shiver down my spine.

Again, the clearing erupted in a burst of white light. "Got it!" Nellie sang happily. "That one's the keeper!"

Chapter Twenty-Five

Nellie Fuller had brought with her a dozen spare photographic plates, and she was eager to capture as many photographs as possible for her article. Brisbee obligingly posed for a few when we returned to the farmhouse, but his enthusiasm had once again ebbed in the wake of the horrific slaughter.

Lewis Lamb was having none of it at first, sending Murphy after the reporter whenever she came too close to the barrier. Not to be daunted, she made a show of taking Owen Horner's picture instead, posing him directly in front of the canvas while he held up a trowel and smiled charismatically. The decision worked like a charm. Before long, Lamb had completely changed face, demanding that at least one photograph of him and his crew be taken from within the site, lest the public mistakenly attribute the find to his reprehensible rival.

Charlie made a point of finding himself out of the frame whenever the tripod went up, just in case he might be recognized by any of the *Chronicle*'s readers in New Fiddleham. By noon, Nellie had already gone through most of her photo plates and taken statements from everyone who would give her an interview. In her energetic presence, Owen Horner became even more resolved to stay near the discovery, which left Lewis Lamb perpetually on edge. The whole affair was beginning to feel like a carnival.

No progress had been made toward finding justice for the bloodless bodies, the missing tooth remained missing, and the horror in the forest was proving to be equally perplexing. For another day and a half, I worked closely with Jackaby, jotting details in my notebook as he scoured the forest and hunted for anything we'd missed. After one especially long afternoon of pushing through underbrush and hopping over trickling creeks, he finally caught a trail.

The tracks in the soft dirt had three sharp toes, but they were twice the size of the ones we'd seen in the bloody clearing. I lost sight of them as I tried to keep up with my employer, but Jackaby followed a trail of a different sort. He felt the air gently with his fingers, as if strumming an imaginary harp. When he caught on to whatever invisible thread he seemed to be looking for, he was off like a shot.

The trail wound through the woods for half a mile,

leading eventually to another farm. We emerged from the wilderness on the far side, but I recognized it as the drab beige building where we had met Mrs. Pendleton. I saw no clear footprints as we stepped out of the thick forest and into open land, but I noticed that the underbrush had been trampled and branches higher than my shoulder had been snapped back.

I knocked on the door while Jackaby hung back, scanning the property. I knocked again, but there were no signs of life within the house. Soon Jackaby grew impatient and gestured for me to follow. We slid around back to a field where half a dozen sheep were huddled close together near the barn. The creatures did not bleat or shuffle aimlessly about, but kept in a tight knot and trembled skittishly, even for sheep.

"What do you suppose . . . ?" I began, but Jackaby pointed to something out in the middle of the pasture. The space was flat, save for a lone elm tree in the center and a small heap of something in between. From where we were, it looked like a pile of laundry had fallen from the line–except there was no clothesline in the field. I swallowed. My veins turned to lead. "Is that Mrs. Pendleton?"

We stepped warily into the field. As we approached, Toby uncurled himself from the woman's side and paced between us and his fallen mistress, whimpering desperately. "Is she–?" I couldn't bring myself to finish the question. I already knew the answer.

"She's been dead for some time now," Jackaby confirmed with grim certainty. "Several hours, at least." Toby circled the body miserably, his big brown eyes pleading up at us.

I stood over the body. Her hair was tied back in a practical braid, and her skin was unnaturally wan. She wore a simple white dress marred by three broad, wet ribbons of red cutting diagonally from her neck down across her chest like a macabre sash. She was still clutching the wide-barreled rifle. Jackaby leaned down and closed the woman's eyes gently. Toby whined plaintively, and I knelt to comfort him.

"Someone should . . ." My voice failed me, and it took me a moment to find it again. "Someone should tell her husband."

"He knows," said Jackaby from behind me. He was walking toward the shade of the elm, where another figure lay in the shadows. "It appears Mr. Pendleton favored a pair of pistols. He met with the same end as his wife. They made their last stand together."

"She told us they looked out for each other," I said, although my words refused to rise above a whisper.

Jackaby straightened and continued toward the far end of the field. Blackbirds were circling overhead.

"Shouldn't we cover the bodies or something?" I managed.

"That sounds like a fine sentiment, Miss Rook. Please join me when you're through."

"What are you . . . ?"

He didn't turn back as he replied. "The Pendletons are not the reason we are here."

I found two clean woolen horse blankets in the barn, though only after dodging the sheep, which nearly trampled me as they crowded into the shelter of the building. Returning to the field, I shrouded the couple as best I could. The doleful dog whimpered and lay down with his head on his paws a short way off, watching me. As I knelt to cover the woman's face, something pressed sharply into my knee. It was mostly flat, a little larger than a half dollar, and blue green with a sheen of brilliant purple when it caught the light.

Toby growled quietly as I plucked it up. I composed myself, wiping my eyes as I crossed the pasture to find Jackaby near a broken gap in the fence. Broad planks of wood had been snapped in half, splinters spread out across the grass. I held my breath as I approached. The splinters, I realized, were not the only thing spread across the grass.

"Looks to have been a ram," Jackaby said, nudging something squishy with his foot. "And this bit is from a different sheep entirely. I would wager the farmers were just in the way. Livestock seems to have been the intended target. How many do you think it finished off—two or three all together?"

My insides churned. The air was thick and cloying. I stepped back from the massacre for some fresh air and found it in short supply. "Mm-hmm." I nodded. My eyes were welling up again, and I couldn't tell if it was because of the Pendletons, the smell, or both.

Jackaby picked something up out of the grass. "Buckshot," he said. "Whatever it was, it appears Mrs. Pendleton got a shot in, at least."

I looked at the gashes along the fallen fence post. They were twice as deep as the ones on the tree beside the goat, cleaving halfway through the thick board in a single stroke. "Does it look like dragon marks to you?"

"Wouldn't that be a marvelous peculiarity—but of course it's sadly impossible," said Jackaby.

"You're sure, sir?" I said. I tried to focus on the details of the case instead of on the horrors around me. "I'd be the first to say that dragons don't exist, but if those fossils are really mythological and not Mesozoic, is it such a leap to imagine one attacking local sheep? Do you see any . . . I don't know . . . magical aura or anything?"

"Yes, as a matter of fact." My employer's brow furrowed, and he traced a finger around the edges of one of the marks. "Now that you mention it, it is decidedly akin to the residual emanation from the fossils. Fascinating." He shook his head. "The fact remains, however, that we cannot possibly be facing a dragon. Those breeds went extinct thousands of years ago. You would be just as likely to see one of your lumbering dinosaurs roaming the plains today as you would a Western dragon. Besides, a dragon large enough to eat goats and sheep would leave a wake of fire wherever it went. There have been none reported, and Gad's Valley has been unseasonably dry this . . ." His sentence died off, and he cocked his head as he looked at me curiously. "What do you have there?"

I had been worrying the iridescent disc absently while he spoke. I looked down and handed it to him. "It . . . It's a scale, isn't it?" I said.

"Hmm." He nodded, turning the thing over in the light.

"That's a *dragon* scale, isn't it?"

"Miss Rook," Jackaby said, his eyes glinting, "I do believe it is."

Chapter Twenty-Six

It fell to Charlie to send word to the victims' families, and his face was stoic when he returned to the cabin that evening. Jackaby laid the strip of bark he had taken from the site of the slaughtered goat next to the scale I had found in the field. "Rook and I have found what we can, Mr. Barker. I think it's time."

Charlie looked at me, and I nodded. "Please give me a moment," he said.

Half of New Fiddleham had seen his accidental transformation during our first big case, but he was still deeply self-conscious about transforming in company. In truth, although I had been imploring him to avoid it, it was strangely heartening to see Charlie emerge from his room and pad across the cabin in canine form. His fur was patterned in caramel browns and dark blacks, and it looked softer than fleece. The last time I had seen Charlie as a hound, he had been pushed beyond exhaustion and badly injured. It was the hound who had saved my life when that first unruly caper reached its bloody end, and the sight of him in full health was a comfort.

He sidled up to the table to inspect the scales, sniffing each carefully before trotting back into the privacy of his chamber.

"They are definitely from the same beast," said Charlie when he emerged from his room, fastening the last button on his shirt and straightening his cuffs.

"There can be no doubt?" Jackaby asked.

"They are the same scent," Charlie confirmed, "or two beasts of the same family."

"If that's the case, then I hope the family is a small one," I said.

"Tell me everything you remember," said Charlie.

I told him about the farmhouse and the frightened sheep, the broad tracks and deep claw marks, the trampled brush and broken branches as high as my head. Jackaby, meanwhile, moved the scale from one hand to the other, holding it at odd angles and squinting at it through the little carved lens.

"The dragon from the grove . . . ," Charlie began.

"If it *was* a dragon," interjected Jackaby without looking up.

"The one from the grove was only a few feet tall, judging

by the marks in the forest," said Charlie. "Perhaps this latest is its mother?"

Jackaby shuddered. "Let's hope not," he said. "The most frightening monsters are monsters' mothers. Just ask Beowulf. I need to see the bones again." He held the scale in the lamplight and glared at it. "The evidence increasingly corroborates the improbable notion that dragons have returned, but there is something . . . *off.* It's not clean. Even with a scrying glass, the reading of auras is imprecise. I need to compare the artifacts directly. We will revisit the bones in the morning."

He retired to his guest room, still holding the scale and frowning in concentration. I found myself alone with Charlie in the warm front room of the cabin. He had shed the navy blue jacket of his uniform, but his clothes were as tidy and pressed as always. I wished I had not spent the day hiking through underbrush and traipsing through barns and pastures.

"I'm sorry that you had to see that," he said.

"See what?" I asked.

"The hound in me. I understand if it bothers you." He shrugged shyly, looking at the little tin stove.

"Oh no—not at all. I actually rather liked seeing . . . I mean, I wasn't gawking at you like some spectacle or . . . You . . . You make quite a handsome hound."

He looked up skeptically. "You are being very generous to say so."

"No, really. I think you have a very fine figure. Goodness, I meant as a hound . . . You look fine as a hound. Not that you don't have an excellent figure as a man. Oh Lord. I mean . . ." My cheeks were growing warm from ear to ear. "I mean that I don't mind at all, Mr. Barker."

We sat in silence while the little stove crackled quietly for what might have been only a few seconds and might have been an awkward eternity. "That is," he said at last, "very kind." He smiled and chuckled softly, regarding me with his deep brown eyes.

"What?" I said. "What is it?"

"Sometimes you remind me of someone I have not seen in a very long time," he said.

"Someone nice, I hope?"

He nodded. "You would like her. I love her—very much," said Charlie. "My sister, Alina. She and I were always very close. I miss her terribly sometimes, but she is still with the family."

"Oh," I said, struggling to concentrate as my mind weighed the information that I was like a sister to Charlie. "May I ask . . . why did you leave? If it's not too forward."

Charlie looked around his humble cabin while he considered. "The Om-Caini have no home," he said. "My people are nomads, always moving. We must, or we risk exposure. My grandfather has stories about . . ." His eyes caught mine in the firelight. "About dark times. With our family, though—away from outsiders—we can be safe. We can be ourselves."

He took a deep breath. "But then there was Bucharest. I liked Bucharest. In the middle of town, they used to have a busy market–they probably still do. I saw a crook cut a man's purse strings once and slip away between the stalls, and so on instinct I gave chase and I caught him. There could not have been much in the pouch, a handful of coins, but the stranger was so grateful when I returned it. His wife invited me to dine with them, but I declined. Already I had made a spectacle, drawn attention to myself. I knew I had to go . . . but something had changed. It felt right to run toward something for once, instead of always running away."

"And so you came to America?"

"The land of opportunity." He nodded. "Where I could be just another immigrant, starting over. I was not even twenty, and it was very hard, but it was right. My old life–the family life–gave me the freedom to be myself, but not on my own terms."

I nodded. "Which isn't really freedom at all." My family could not have been more different from Charlie's, but I knew that feeling very well. I wanted to remind Charlie that he could always be himself around me, in any form–but it felt like hypocrisy after days of reminding him that he should not. I reached my hand toward his, instead, while he sat gazing into the crackling fire–but I hesitated, and the moment slipped away.

"It's getting late. I shouldn't keep you up all night," he

said, rising to his feet. "I'm sure you need your rest after a day like today."

I bade Charlie good night and sank into my bed. In my mind I could see Jenny Cavanaugh shaking her head in disappointment at my shoddy display, and then Nellie Fuller rolling her eyes at my having tried at all. I buried my head in the soft pillow and willed the images away. I might be better prepared to slay dragons, I decided, than to flirt with boys.

We wasted no time the following morning. Jackaby took the lead, and Charlie and I kept close behind as we hastened up the road. The sun was just climbing over the wooded hills and we had nearly reached the Brisbee farm, when Lamb's carriage barreled down the road toward us, headed toward town. It teetered ominously on two wheels for just a moment as it rounded a bend, and then clattered down onto the packed earth, where it picked up still more speed. Mr. Murphy sat at the reins, his face so pale that even his freckles seemed to have been washed away. Mr. Bradley clung to the back, attempting to tether down a clumsy pile of tools as they hurtled away. He caught sight of us as his companion urged the horses on down the dusty path, and he shouted something that sounded very much like "Good luck!"

Lewis Lamb stood at the foot of the drive, hollering after

his associates. "You half-witted hayseeds! Can't you tell a hoax when you see one? Get back here this instant! Get back here!"

As the carriage whipped out of sight, he noticed us and made a beeline for Charlie. "You! You incompetent, incapable clod of a copper! I told you to have that delinquent locked up! Just look at what he's done! Look at it! He couldn't stand to let my team manage the excavation, and now he's ravaged the whole site with his underhanded skulduggery. This has gone too far!"

The complaints continued as we made our way back up the foothills. The closest wall of the canvas barrier hung loose and drooping, and as we neared, I could see why. The whole right side of the structure had been torn down roughly, shreds of fabric ground into the dirt. Lamb did not bother with the entrance flap. It still stood more or less intact, but it was superfluous now. He stepped over the battered canvas and fell silent, his rage overwhelming him beyond words. He just mutely waved both hands at the landscape before us and then threw his Panama hat into the dirt.

The dig site was a mess. In the past few days, Lamb's crew had dug a deep trench all the way around the figure and freed the skeleton almost completely from the earth. From what I had seen, their work had been conducted meticulously, but the bones before us were no longer laid out in neat, careful arrangements. Enormous fossils were scattered across the site, and the broad keel bone had been cracked in half. Atop a pile of battered ribs lay the tremendous femur I had lifted on my first visit, its surface raked with . . .

"Are those *tooth marks*?" I asked.

"I'm sure *he* would want you to think so," Lamb growled. "It does finally explain why he pilfered that tooth, which was bad enough. This, though . . ." He waved a shaking hand at the site again. "*This* is unconscionable."

"You still believe Owen Horner is behind this?" Charlie asked.

"Of course Owen Horner is behind this! His trick with the foot bones didn't fool anybody, so he had to step up his scheme. The staged bite marks and the false footprints—they're better this time, since at least he made them look a little more believable—but they're still so painfully obvious. I don't even know what nasty trick he managed to pull on my associates, but I'll see that he answers for that as well."

"Mr. Horner is a scientist, just like you," said Charlie. "I can understand why you might suspect him of stealing bones, but why would he vandalize them?"

"To conceal that he *has* stolen them," Lamb barked. "The left ulna, the clavicle, and several ribs, from what I've been able to inventory so far. I'm sure he was hoping I wouldn't notice amid all the devastation. I would say he was a fool for thinking he could get away with such a brazen offense, but with a lousy lawman like you patrolling the valley . . ."

"Hey! That's enough," I said. Lamb sneered and rolled his eyes.

"Come have a look at these," said Jackaby. He had wandered off while the scientist was raving, and now he stood over a deep imprint in the soil. Charlie and I joined him. Lamb just shook his head and sighed loudly.

"Waste your time if you like. They're fakes, just like the last ones," he grunted.

"They're not," my employer said when Charlie and I were close enough to make out the print clearly. It bore the same three wicked talons and single hind toe as the others. Although not quite as long as the fossil's, each of the front toes in the imprint was easily larger than my employer's entire foot.

"Sir," I said, swallowing hard, "do these tracks look even bigger than the last ones to you?"

Jackaby plucked the scale from his pocket and held it out in front of the damaged skeleton. He squinted and turned his head this way and that.

"Well, Mr. Jackaby?" Charlie prompted. "Unlikely as it sounds, this certainly looks like it could have been done by a creature a lot like this one." He gestured to the scattered dragon bones. "Are you satisfied?"

"Rarely." Jackaby finally looked up. "But they match too closely. As the saying goes, 'Here, there be dragons.'"

Even as the words left his mouth, the crunch of wood splintering and the terrified bleating of livestock erupted from the farm below. My employer and I exchanged a momentary glance—whether the look in his eyes was alarm or excitement, I could not say—and then we leapt into action.

Chapter Twenty-Seven

We had to weave around a tide of free and panicked goats as we made for the source of the clamor. Another terrific crunching sound issued from the direction of the barn, followed by the clatter of wood collapsing. As we reached the bottom of the hill, Horner burst out of the farmhouse and joined us. His hair was a mess, and his eyes were wild with confusion and concern. I could hear Lewis Lamb taking a deep breath to begin his customary accusations, but then we rounded the corner and it all left him in a whoosh. The wall of the barn was carved open as if it had been made of paper. The hole reached nearly to the roof, at least twenty feet high. On the far side of Brisbee's field, the trees shook as something massive vanished into the forest, leaving a ragged trench across the pasture in its wake.

We stared for several seconds. It was Lewis Lamb who finally broke the silence. His voice had lost all of its bluster and rage, and he might have been a child waking from a nightmare. "Wh-what is that?" I followed his shaking finger to yet another red, wet mess within the debris of the barn. The carnage was of the same sort as the prior sites, although the leftovers were larger.

"If I were to hazard a guess," Jackaby said, peering in, "I would say cows. Sadly, it seems Mr. Brisbee will need to buy his milk from town in the future."

"It's all my fault," said a voice from the back of the savaged barn, trembling and feeble. Charlie picked his way carefully into the building and Jackaby followed. They returned, supporting Hugo Brisbee between them. He seemed unhurt, but his knees had gone weak and he had trouble keeping himself upright.

"Help me get him up to the house," said Charlie.

"I made it angry," Brisbee half mumbled to himself. "I shouldn't have done it."

"What did you do?" Jackaby asked.

"I thought I was doing right by my Maddie. I thought . . . I thought maybe they would write about it all across the world. That maybe I could get her name in all the papers. She only ever wanted to get out of this valley . . ." He glanced around nervously. "It was me. I took the foot bones. I set them up, pressed them down with my boot. I–I thought it would make a bit of a mystery, get folks out, the way that first article brought you all out here. I put them back afterward . . . but it was too late." He shivered, turning his pale face apologetically toward Lamb, who had not taken his eyes off the forest. "It's all my fault. I woke the thing up, and it took my sweet Madeleine. N-now it's out to get me. It came and . . . and then the cows . . ." The farmer stopped speaking and began to whimper.

"Yes, I imagine that was a rather unpleasant spectacle," said Jackaby, glancing back over the sticky mess. "But I need to ask you a few questions, so please try to remain calm. If you do *not* remain calm, we may all be devoured in a horrifically violent manner by that very same medieval monster that consumed your cows—or possibly by one of the two similar monsters also presently at large. Are you calm? Mr. Brisbee?"

"He's fainted," said Charlie.

"Well that's not helpful in the least."

"Help me get him up the steps." They carried him up to the farmhouse and set him down on the sofa.

Nellie Fuller was racing down the stairs as we returned to the hallway, nearly tripping over her tripod in her haste. "I heard a noise," she said. "Have I already missed all of the excitement?"

"Nothing of consequence," answered Jackaby. "Stay indoors, however, unless you're enthusiastic about the prospect of being eviscerated. Now then, Miss Rook, Mr. Barker, we need to get to Hudson's."

"What?" I said.

"You want me to stay put?" Nellie asked, cocking an eyebrow at my employer. "Darling, have you met me?"

"You're both mad!" I said. "You really think it's safe to go out in the open right now? Remember the bit about being eviscerated?"

Jackaby shook his head. "Miss Fowler . . ."

"Fuller."

"Miss Fuller, the first eyewitness to this beast who hasn't been cut to ribbons is currently unconscious in the drawing room. You can go wherever you like, but your story lies with him." He turned to me. "As for us, we have two options at present. We can seek out the help of the one man we know who has experience hunting in these hills, pursuing big game, and containing dangerous supernatural creatures, or we can leave Mr. Hudson out of it and fend off a dragon on our own. It isn't that I don't think we're capable—I'm rather scrappy in a pinch—but I don't want to explain to the trapper that we went dragon hunting without him, do you? That just sounds like a poor choice. Come on, then."

We reached Hank Hudson's hut by midmorning, and my heart sank. The building didn't look like it had been especially robust to begin with, but now the western wall had been reduced to scrap, heavy oaken beams torn in half and bricks scattered into the yard. A thin trail of smoke crept from the crumbled remains of a fireplace, and the floor was dark with blood.

"Hudson?" Jackaby crossed the threshold carefully. The roof sagged as he did, and half a dozen wooden shingles slid off it, clattering into the rubble. He knelt and inspected the pool. "It's human," he said somberly.

Charlie nudged a brick aside with his foot and stooped to retrieve a blue-green disc from underneath. It was a match in tone to the one in Jackaby's pocket, but as wide as his entire outstretched hand.

"There's another in here," said Jackaby, moving deeper into the crumbling house. "And another. Varying sizes. And what's this?" He had reached a tight corner of the wreckage, where an upended table was the only thing keeping a heavy section of wall from collapsing farther into the room.

"Do be careful, sir," I called. He braced himself on the table leg and reached in to pluck something from the crevice beyond. As he straightened, the table slid and the wall groaned angrily. He was half a step ahead of the structure as the room folded in on itself like a house of cards. The back end of the roof slammed into the floor where he had just been standing, sending a cascade of tiles down into the blood and bricks. From somewhere deeper inside the cabin came a panicked screech.

"That wasn't the trapper," Charlie said.

"Rosie," I said. "That's his bird. She's still inside. Maybe Hudson is with her?"

Charlie did not meet my eyes. He was looking at the blood on the ground. There was an awful lot of it.

I swallowed hard. "Well, we can't just leave her. She's dangerous, but she doesn't deserve to be crushed and buried alive—and there's no telling when the dragons might return. By the look of all the scales around here, there may be more than three. Sir? Sir?"

Jackaby was staring at something in his open palm, a small handful of fluffy orange hairs. "One," he said. "There's only one. It isn't different dragons at all . . . It's one, and it's growing. Rapidly."

Rosie let out another screech, and my employer snapped into action. "You're absolutely right, Miss Rook. You should attend to the bird—it's the decent thing to do. I'll see if I can locate any of Mr. Hudson's more useful hunting supplies. We're going to need every possible advantage we can find. Charlie, I need you to return to Brisbee's farmhouse and tell everyone to run—to get as far away as possible. Then ride to every farm you can reach and tell them the same. We need to evacuate Gad's Valley. Go! Go!"

Chapter Twenty-Eight

From around the back of the trapper's cabin, I spotted a slim window I could just squeeze through into the back of the house. It was dark, but the light from behind me caught a bronze beak and glinted in Rosie's wide eyes. She hopped anxiously from one foot to another. The wall behind her cage had buckled, and the rafters were collapsing. One wide timber had landed against the cage, bending the cork-coated bars. I could see deep cuts along the beam where Rosie had sliced at it in vain.

"All right, girl," I said, taking a deep breath. "I'm going to pull you out of here, but nip even one of my fingers off, and I'll leave you to rot, understood?"

The rust-red head cocked to one side.

"I guess that will have to do." I took hold of the cage and

pulled as hard as I could, but it did not budge. The heavy timber had pinned it in place, and the metal was only bending farther as I tugged. Rosie's eyes bore into mine, but she made no move to strike at my hands.

I took hold of the golden pin in the cage door and pulled. "This is a terrible idea," I said. It stuck, but I could feel it shifting very slightly. "This is a terrible, terrible idea." I tried again. Rosie's head began to bob, and when the pin slid free at last, she exploded past me, screeching deafeningly. With the door unlatched, the cage bars crumpled under the weight of the girder. The whole room shook and then shrank with a loud, crackling roar. The bird and I both pressed back, away from the falling wood and masonry, into the far corner. When the rumbling stopped, I found myself in a dusty, oblong space no larger than a broom cupboard with an agitated wild animal who was, I realized in hindsight, too large to have fit easily through the window anyway, and far too excited to sit calmly while I figured things out.

Rosie screeched and flapped, and a metallic golden feather the size of a carving knife thudded into the wall beside my head. I caught a talon across my forearm, and another sharp blade grazed my cheek. I winced from the pain, shrinking away as far as I could, but there was nowhere to retreat. As the bird thrashed, a small hole opened in the roof above us. We both looked up at the sunlight in surprise, and then Rosie burst upward. Two quick strikes with her razor-sharp beak, and she was out, screeching into the cloudy sky. I stepped forward to climb after her before the whole place came down on my head, but something pulled me backward. I turned. The hem of my dress was pinned between the confounded timbers. I pulled and tugged, but the fabric was thick and sturdy, and the woodwork unyielding.

The ceiling above me creaked ominously, and my head swam. I tried to breathe slowly and not panic, but I was finding it hard to think. The air was clogged with dust, which spun like a dervish down the beam of sunlight, and the sting of the cut across my cheek throbbed. The ungrateful bird had left me with nothing but a painful reminder of just how dangerous a wild thing can be, which did not bode well for my upcoming dealing with a genuine dragon. I shook my head. With a sudden clarity I realized the bird had not left me with nothing. I reached behind me and felt the feather lodged in the wall. It was stuck deep, but with a little wiggling I had it free. In moments I had trimmed a rough edge off my skirt and clambered out onto the collapsed rooftop.

My eyes adjusted to the light, and I breathed clean air in gulps and gasps for several moments before making my way along sliding tiles back down to solid ground.

Jackaby poked his head out from a ramshackle shed and cocked an eyebrow up at me. "Where's the bird?"

I sighed heavily and pointed up at the sky. Rosie had long since vanished.

"You released a Stymphalian bird in the middle of Gad's Valley?"

"Technically," I said, "I released a Stymphalian bird in the middle of a collapsing hovel."

"Well." Jackaby nodded. "That would not have been my first choice, but good work not being dead, I suppose. See if you can keep it up. This whole ordeal is about to get quite a bit harder."

"Oh," I said, doing my best not to sway visibly. "That sounds grand."

Chapter Twenty-Nine

Hudson's horses had to be the most steadfast animals I have ever met. Jackaby fastened their harnesses to the trapper's cart, and the muscular animals only tossed their manes patiently in the breeze while they waited. Neither the dragon attack nor Rosie's screeching had spooked them. They were tall, healthy beasts, and the trapper clearly cared for them well. A hard lump caught in my throat as I wondered who would look after them now.

"The man he bought them from told Hudson they were descended from the battle stallions of the Trojan War," Jackaby said as he finished buckling the reins and patted the flank of one of the noble animals. "Even hinted at some local legend that their ancestry could be traced back to the mares of Diomedes, which would've made them the second addition to his menagerie with a Herculean history. A salesman's fib, I'm afraid, but I never had the heart to tell Mr. Hudson the truth."

"They certainly seem to be something special," I said, allowing Jackaby to help me up the step into the driver's box.

"Well, of course they are." Jackaby climbed in after me. "He expected nothing less of them, and treated them accordingly. They were never given the option to be anything but exceptional." His mouth turned up in a smile, and he gave me a meaningful glance, then clicked the reins and set the horses trotting off down the drive, leaving the remnants of their master's house behind.

Jackaby had tossed into the cart a motley assortment of sharp instruments and sturdy nets, but the collection did not look up to the challenge of subduing a twenty-foot dragon. "Is this everything you could find?" I said, peering back into the cart.

"I'm afraid so. Mr. Hudson's usual arsenal appears to be somewhat depleted. He must have moved some of his finer tools in anticipation of the hunt before he became the prey. We may never know, unfortunately. We will make do with what we have."

Jackaby had not yet expressed any sadness for the loss of his friend, but I could tell that it was weighing heavily on him. He had taken off his silly knit cap, and dark wisps of hair hung across his brow and framed his storm-gray eyes. Peculiar and harmless though he often seemed, there was an intensity to my employer that I never wanted to find myself up against. As I watched the shadows settle over his expression, I was silently glad that I was not the rogue dragon.

The cart rumbled up to the farmhouse by noon, and Jackaby pulled it into the shade of three broad pines. "What makes you believe the beast will return here?" I asked. "So far it's chosen a separate target for every attack."

"Because it must. This is where the bones were exhumed."

"Was Brisbee right, then? Is this some sort of spiritual revenge for disturbing the remains—like a curse or something?"

"Nothing like that." He stepped down from the cart.

"Then what?" I glanced at the thickly forested hills to the left and right before climbing down after him. Even with the sun high in the sky, the landscape seemed to afford far too many shadows in which a massive monster could hide.

"Shh." Jackaby put a finger to his lips, peering up toward the hillside. "Do you hear something?"

I strained my ears. "Voices," I said.

Jackaby nodded. He turned away from the hill and stalked up to the farmhouse, instead. Inside, he found Charlie Barker facing off against Lewis Lamb, Owen Horner, and Hugo Brisbee. Charlie turned as the detective approached. "Please, Mr. Jackaby, perhaps you can talk sense into them."

"What on earth are you still doing here?" Jackaby demanded. "There is an impossible predator of monumental proportions bound to descend upon this property at any moment!"

"I told them as much." Charlie sighed. "Mr. Horner refuses to leave. He says that the bones were his big discovery."

"You two can't possibly still be arguing about professional clout!" I said.

"It's not like that," Horner said. "I was here from the start, and I'll see it through to the end. Bones like those are the reason I got into this business, and you and I both know we'll never find anything like that specimen again, not if we dig till the day we die. I've already put up with this ornery bastard for the past week." He jabbed a thumb at Lamb. "A new monster should be a change of pace, at least."

"For once I must admit Horner has a point," Lamb said. "I haven't defended my dig site all this time just to watch it be obliterated by . . . by some wild animal." The paleontologist still could not bring himself to call the creature a *dragon*.

"What about you, Mr. Brisbee?" Jackaby turned to the farmer, who was sitting upright on the sofa but still looked a little wan. "You've seen firsthand the reason you should be running."

Brisbee nodded solemnly. "None of you would be out here if it weren't for my stupid pride. I lost my wife worrying about pictures on the front page." He sniffed. "Then I made it worse, disrespecting the dead. I brought this down on you folks, brought it down on myself, and on this farm.

We built that barn with our bare hands, and now it's torn up like a tin can. Maddie and I didn't raise our sons to let other folks clean up their messes, and I'll be damned if I leave anyone to clean up mine. If they aren't leaving, I'm not leaving."

Jackaby sighed. "You are all going to die. Miss Rook, shall we be off?"

"Wait, please," I said. "If anyone understands the significance of the site, it's me. I promise to look after your findings, gentlemen. Mr. Horner, if Professor Lamb survives but you're killed, do you really believe he will give you even a footnote in his lectures? And you, Professor—do you think Mr. Horner will hesitate a moment before taking full credit for this discovery the instant you're out of the way?"

The two men scowled at each other for a moment, and then Horner shrugged. "Well, she's not wrong," he admitted.

Lamb nodded. "If you head back to Gadston, I suppose I could be persuaded to come along—if only to keep an eye on you and ensure you don't go spreading more slander to the press about this disaster of a dig."

"Well, Mr. Brisbee?" I said. "I promise we will look after your farm as well. Your barn can be repaired, and your home can be protected—but your boys have already lost one parent this week. Please."

The farmer nodded slowly. "Thank you, Miss Rook.

I—I'll ride back with the scientists. Someone's got to keep those two from killing each other."

"Wonderful," said Charlie. "Now out! All of you!"

"Wait a moment," I said as the crowd filed out the door warily. "Where is Miss Fuller?"

Charlie frowned. "She wasn't here when I returned from Hudson's cabin. I suppose it's too much to hope that she headed for safety?"

"I certainly wouldn't count on it. Let's hope we can find her before she finds the dragon."

The men piled into Brisbee's wagon and pulled out onto the road. Horner leaned out the side as they picked up speed. "So long, beautiful," he called. "Steal me a good fossil if you get the chance!" He flashed a last grin and a shameless wink. Lamb cuffed him upside the back of the head, and he sat back down, laughing and rubbing the side of his head. A minute more and they were out of sight.

"Incorrigible," I said.

"Which one?" asked Charlie.

"That's a good point. At least they're on their way, finally."

"Are you two very certain you can't be persuaded to leave as well?" Charlie asked.

Jackaby shook his head. "No more than you could be persuaded to leave the good citizens of the valley in harm's way. We have work to do."

Charlie nodded. "I really should be going. There are at least half a dozen homes too close to this thing for comfort. I would be remiss, as you say, if I did not warn them. Good luck, Mr. Jackaby." He turned to me, and for a moment his chocolate-brown eyes locked tight on mine, unconcealed worry playing across his face. "Abigail," he said quietly, and then paused. "Be careful."

It was the first time I had ever heard him address me by my first name. I wanted to live long enough to hear him do it again.

Charlie climbed atop Maryanne, and the dappled mare raced off along the packed dirt road. I watched until he was out of sight, and all that remained was a settling cloud of dust. It was down to the two of us. Jackaby was at the trapper's cart, rummaging through the meager assortment of weapons and equipment in the back. He came up with a slightly dull machete, which he strapped to his hip like a broadsword.

"Well, sir?" I said. "Are you ready to slay a dragon?"

He pulled the ridiculous knit cap onto his head and smiled in a way he might have thought was reassuring. "No," he said. "No, I most decidedly am not."

Chapter Thirty

We climbed back up the hill. I had picked out a mountain-climbing axe, and held it to my chest with both hands as I walked. The tool had a sharp, if slightly chipped, edge on one side and a curved pick on the other. At the base of the short wooden handle was another steel point. I did not know what sort of confrontation to expect, or how well I would handle myself when the time came, but I was hoping the sheer number of sharp bits I wielded would increase my chances of success.

We neared the dig site, and my employer slowed. From the far side of the sagging canvas came the sound of labored breathing. Jackaby's hand caught me roughly by the shoulder, and I stopped midstride. He pointed downward. I was inches from planting my foot in a bear trap. A glimmer of hope played across Jackaby's eyes.

"Hudson?" he called.

A grunt came from within the site, and we picked our way quickly but cautiously over the barrier.

Hank Hudson was seated just inside the one remaining wall of the canvas. He was slumped forward, leaning his weight on his rifle for support. I understood why Jackaby had not found any more useful weapons at the trapper's cabin—the man had brought them all with him. A shotgun with a fat barrel lay beside him, and across his back was slung a bandolier loaded with rifle rounds and buckshot. His belt hung with glistening knives and wicked hooks, and over one shoulder was slung what looked to be a whaler's harpoon gun. He held his left arm against his chest, buried in the folds of his leathers, and he was pale and slick with sweat as he lifted his head to look at Jackaby.

"I'm real sorry, ol' buddy," he grunted, his deep, booming voice reduced to a gruff whisper. "I'm a damn fool."

"Good of you to realize it, old friend." said Jackaby. "A bit late, though."

"Hell of a way to go out, at least." Hank struggled to smile, and then coughed.

"If it was your intention to arrange your own funeral, you might have had the decency to avoid arranging ours in the process."

The man nodded solemnly and let his head sag. "That's

th' truth. I do feel right terrible about that, an' I aim to make it right or die tryin'."

"Mr. Hudson," I said. "You're injured—what happened?"

"Oh, hey there, little lady." He tilted his head toward me. "Yeah, he got me pretty good. I ain't done yet, though, and he'll have to come back around here soon enough."

I looked across at the scattered bones. "Will one of you please explain to me why you're so certain the dragon is going to come back for more bones? Isn't it more likely to pick off cows and horses and things that have"—I swallowed—"meat?"

"Would you like to tell her, or shall I?" asked Jackaby.

The trapper grunted. "Shoulda guessed you'd figger it out. Go right ahead."

Jackaby took a breath. "I told you I was not prepared to slay a dragon, Miss Rook, and I do not intend to. As I have insisted from the start, dragons have gone the way of *the dodo*."

Jackaby paused, watching my expression and waiting for me to catch up.

"No," I said as it sank in. "No, Mr. Hudson, you wouldn't . . ."

The trapper nodded, sadly. "'Fraid so."

"That beast is as much a dragon as the 'loathsome birds' in Darwin's dossier," Jackaby continued. "The creature is only a mimic realizing its full potential."

"You stole one of the kittens!" I said.

Hudson shrugged guiltily. "Couldn't let 'em *all* be skeeters."

"So," Jackaby went on, "after returning to the valley with his own chameleomorph—an orange tabby, judging by the molted fur in his cabin—Mr. Hudson couldn't resist trying a little experiment."

"In my defense," the trapper said, "I thought it was gonna be a dinosaur when I started."

"Wait," I interrupted. *"You* stole the first tooth? But that's impossible—you didn't even arrive in the valley until after it was in the newspapers!"

"I didn't steal it," Hudson said. "I wasn't in the valley when I . . . when I didn't steal it."

"Hudson . . . ," Jackaby prompted sternly.

"I did kinda bump into a fella who might have," he admitted. "I had just left your place up in New Fiddleham. I had the kitten with me and he saw it, only the guy seemed to know it wasn't no ordinary kitten. He said it was just a shame it wasn't *bigger.* He says it just like that, too, all meaningful like. *'Bigger.'* And then he shows me the tooth."

"Did you get a good look at him?" Jackaby asked. "Tell me, did he have a grim, mortiferous aura? Maybe accented by a faint lavender halo?"

"He was a funny-lookin' short guy," said Hudson. "Dark clothes. Real washed-out face. He gave me the creeps at first, but he said he was a friend of Coyote Bill's, and he thought a guy like me might be able to make use of a real old bone. I figured I already knew why he wanted to get rid of it, now that it was in the papers as stolen. Bill got all nervous when I asked him about the fella later. Downright spooked. Shoulda told y'all then . . . Stupid of me. I just got the idea in my head, and I had to know if it would work . . ."

The pale man I had seen in New Fiddleham at the train station—he had taken the bone. Jackaby and I exchanged a glance. If he had seen fit to murder Madeleine Brisbee to get the fossil—then why give it to Hudson so easily? None of it made sense. Who was he? Why had he come? Why did those people have to die?

"You've had the fossil since then?" Jackaby said. "The whole time we were looking?"

The trapper nodded sheepishly.

"Okay. I take it you reduced it to shavings, then?" Jackaby continued. "You must have laced the creature's food and kept the food sources varied to ensure only one single ingredient was consistent. Something like that?"

Hudson nodded again. "Ground it ta powder. He changed a lot quicker than I expected."

"'Much of the essence of a living thing is distilled in its teeth,'" I recalled.

Jackaby nodded. "Dragons—even dead ones, are powerful beasts. Dragon bones are potent, and a dragon's tooth doubly so—why do you think the remains are so rare? I can't imagine an alchemist or apothecary in all of antiquity who could resist adding some to his stores. Chameleomorphs alone are unpredictable—but you were mixing magics. You compounded the effects."

"He grew real fast." Hudson nodded. "Started sprouting little wings by the second day."

"And if you had just stopped then," said Jackaby, "he would not be growing larger still."

"He got all tetchy if I didn't add the powder," Hank said. "I was needin' bigger and bigger animals ta feed him. Like you said, I had to keep changin' it. He was my responsibility, an' I couldn't just let him go hungry, so I took him out a couple times to catch somethin' a little bigger. Heck of a thing to take a dragon for a walk. I didn't mean to let him eat Brisbee's kid, but it was just tied up in the woods, and once the dragon got close, he went nuts."

"The goat was tied up in the forest?" I said. Hudson nodded.

"Not far from Brisbee's," mused Jackaby. "I imagine the farmer had been hoping to add some authenticity to his claims about the footprints by *kid*napping one of his young goats. I doubt very much he had the stomach to kill the poor little thing, so he probably tried to just keep it safely out of the way instead. Bad luck for the kid."

Hudson hung his head. "I could tell it was gettin' outta hand, so I stopped givin' him the powder at all, no matter how grumpy he got. He was a good fifteen feet already, and I knew I was gettin' in over my head. I didn't give him any yesterday, but by this morning he just went berserk. Broke through his bars and made off into the valley."

"The Pendletons?" I asked.

Hudson nodded. "Got their blood on my hands. I was tracking him when I heard the gunshots. By the time I had gotten there, he had already stuffed himself on the sheep. I managed to drag him back to the cabin, but he snapped his chains and took off before I could get him penned."

"And you didn't stay with him?" Jackaby asked.

"Oh, I did my very best." The trapper groaned and straightened a bit, lifting his arm gingerly out of the folds of his leathers. "Stayed a little *too* much with him, so now there's a little bit of me left *inside* of him." I gasped. The end of his arm was wrapped tightly in bandages that formed a thick bundle, but it was clear that the trapper's left hand was gone completely. Dark red-brown blood had soaked his clothes from the hide of his jacket down to the dark lining of his boots.

"You need to get to a doctor!" I said.

Jackaby grimaced at the injury and surveyed the trapper properly for the first time since we had arrived. "You *are* in a remarkable amount of pain, aren't you?" he said, squinting at the trapper. "It's just rolling off you. In fact—I do believe you're dying. Hudson, are you dying?"

The trapper gave a noncommittal shrug.

"Miss Rook is right. At the very least we need to get you indoors."

Hudson gripped the rifle tightly with his remaining hand. "Not until I seen this through. I ain't so proud I won't welcome yer help, but I made this monster. One or the other of us is gonna see his end tonight. I set a few traps around the place, but I don't think they'll do more'n slow him down. Keep a weathered eye open. He's fifteen feet tall if he's an inch."

"That was before he got back to the site for more bones," said Jackaby heavily. "He was at least twenty by the time he went after the cows from Mr. Brisbee's barn. Let's just hope he needs another helping of dragon stock before he hits full size." Jackaby gestured at the fossils that lay before us. The bones had been roughly scattered, but they still described a creature fifty feet tall from head to tail, with a wingspan twice as wide.

Chapter Thirty-One

The sun was beginning to dip toward the tips of the pine trees that lined the valley, and still there had been no sign of the beast. I risked a run to the farmhouse and back to fetch some water, which the trapper accepted gratefully, although he was having difficulty keeping his head up to drink it. The air was growing crisp and cool, so Jackaby started a small campfire with a few dry logs and the wooden markers that had once surrounded the find.

"Which way do you think it'll approach?" I whispered to my employer over the crackle of the wood. He scanned the horizon with a frown.

"Mimic or not, a chameleomorph becomes a fully realized corporeal incarnation of its quarry, aesthetically, anatomically, and biologically. A dragon of that magnitude must be producing enough incendiary enzymes to exceed containment."

"What?"

"Smoke." Jackaby's eyes panned from one end of the valley to the other. "There should be smoke. This valley should be alight with all the wildfires a dragon that size would produce. We should see crackling flames and burning branches. At the very least we should see trails of smoke."

I glanced around us. The sky was beginning to redden as the evening grew older, but the only sign of any fire was our own.

"Do you think it's left the valley?" I whispered. It was difficult to decide if this was a dreadful notion or wishful thinking. I dared not imagine what destruction that beast's rampage could wreak on a populated city, but I was none too eager to see it for myself, either. I did not have long to ponder the possibility before my question was answered.

Jackaby froze, his eyes locked onto the forest across from Brisbee's field. I followed his gaze. Down the foothills, across the far side of the pasture, the tall trees shook and the earth trembled. A dark figure crested the treetops for just a moment and then thudded back to the ground. Jackaby drew his rusty machete, and I held tight to my climbing axe. The instrument grew smaller and feebler in my hands as I watched the shadowy form push through the wilderness. The valley fell silent for several impossibly long seconds, and then the dragon leapt into the sky.

There was no mistaking the figure as it lurched upward. The wings were enormous, leathery like a bat's and billowing slightly as they caught the wind. The hulking colossus caught the tops of a couple of pine trees roughly against its chest, and the crack of wood echoed across the valley like gunshots as the trees toppled. The blow cost the creature momentum, and it flapped awkwardly into the center of the field, kicking off into a shallow glide for a moment, and then landing again. It had more than doubled in size just since the attack on the barn, and as its feet touched the ground, I could see it was easily four stories tall. It loomed over the rooftop as it passed Brisbee's farmhouse.

Jackaby was muttering, mostly to himself. "The raw material from the latest bones seems to have accelerated the growth process. Fascinating, though—its instincts are clearly slower to manifest. See how it moves . . ." With another powerful leap, the dragon was suddenly airborne, the broad expanse of its wings blotting out the setting sun as it coasted directly toward us. Its movements may have been clumsy and imprecise, but it had enough control to direct its glide toward us, and Jackaby and I both leapt to the dirt as it dove, its talons clacking and whipping the air just over our heads.

The gargantuan beast was too slow to pull up before it hit the uneven terrain of the foothills, stumbling and slamming into the rocky ground. The earth shook, and I clambered to my feet, clutching my little axe as though it might have any effect at all against that mountain of teeth and claws.

The dragon righted itself and turned back toward us. I had seen artistic constructions of massive carnivores in the museum, big impressive dinosaurs with jaws stretched wide in predatory growls. They did not come close to the reality of this beautiful, hideous beast. The dragon was a lustrous blue green, but caked in dirt and mottled in pale yellows around its face. It had wide, wet, almost bovine nostrils, and a snout lined with bumps and ridges that grew thicker and sharper as they climbed up and over its brow, continuing down its back, like an alligator. Atop its head was a pair of horns, which curved backward like a ram's. Its scaly hide was stretched taut around its ribs.

The creature tilted its head and surveyed the three of us hungrily. Its stomach rumbled loudly, and it cringed, clenching its leathery eyelids shut. "I don't think a pile of dry bones will be enough to satisfy that thing," I said.

The creature's eyes darted open, golden yellow orbs with jagged black slits for pupils. It took one purposeful step toward us, and then another. I tensed to run, panic flooding my veins. Across the hilltop, dust and fossils shifted with each thudding footstep. Among them I caught sight of another motion. In the dim light, atop the bones, a figure stood. Before I understood what I was seeing, the dig site erupted in a flash of brilliant whiteness. "Smile for the camera, handsome," sang a familiar voice.

I blinked and the light was gone. The dragon shook its head and reeled on Nellie Fuller. She dropped the spent flash lamp and whipped the plate out of her camera, leaping aside as the dragon snapped its jaws. The camera and tripod splintered into scraps, and Nellie hit the ground in a hard roll. She was quick to recover, but the creature was quicker. In an instant it was looming over her again, those terrible teeth spreading wide.

"Peanut! No! Bad dragon!" Hudson's voice faltered on the last syllable, but he made up for it with the loud blast of a rifle shot. The heavy round glanced off the dragon's snout, and the creature furrowed its scaly brow.

"You named it?" Jackaby yelled.

"Told ya I was gonna," grunted Hank, and another shot rang out.

The second round caught the dragon squarely in the center of its neck, just under its chin. Neither blow pierced the scaly hide, but they were enough to draw the creature's attention from the reporter. Nellie scrambled across the hill and into the long trench that Lamb's men had dug around the site. The dragon narrowed a pair of angry golden eyes on the trapper.

Hudson tossed the rifle aside and plucked up his shotgun. He shoved himself up to standing and swayed immediately. The dragon's jaws spread wide, and the trapper let loose a barrel of buckshot into the soft pink of its throat. The creature bellowed in alarm and whipped its thick head back and forth, staggering away a few paces and pawing at its face with its wings. Hudson collapsed to his knees. The shotgun clattered to the dirt as he caught himself with his one good hand.

The dragon rose to its full height, rearing up with its wings spread wide. They shrouded half the sky in a blanket of dark emerald. The dragon's pupils were razor slits, and its nostrils chuffed angrily. It puffed out its chest, and it began to make a guttural grunting noise.

"Fire!" Jackaby yelled. "Fire! Get down—now!"

He wrenched me off my feet, and the world spun for a moment as the two of us tumbled into Lamb's trench. My axe bounced out of my hands, and the cold earth and smell of loose soil filled my senses for several seconds as Jackaby pressed me into the dirt. From above us came a rumbling, belching noise, and then a muffled hacking cough. Jackaby's hold on my back lightened as he rose to peer over the edge of the deep furrow. I slid up tentatively to join him.

The monstrous dragon was spluttering and twisting wretchedly. Beneath it, Hank Hudson lay crumpled on the ground. "It can't ignite," murmured Jackaby.

Nellie Fuller crept toward us through the trench with her head ducked low. "You're welcome," she said, sliding down to sit with her back against the earthen wall. "But I think you might owe me a new camera." In her hands was the slim tin case that housed her photographic plates. She clicked it shut and clutched it like a prize trophy.

"You shouldn't be here," said Jackaby, still peering tensely over the edge.

"I couldn't leave without my picture," she said, patting the little box triumphantly.

"We'll be lucky to leave with our lives," I said.

"That didn't keep *you* away. I knew you weren't the *safe and happy* type, Abbie." She gave me a wink. "So, what's our plan?"

"We need something more substantial than bullets and buckshot," Jackaby said. "There. Hudson's harpoon." The weapon lay beside the trapper, glinting in the soft light of the campfire. "I think that may be our best chance, but we'll need something to draw its attention before we can get—oh hell."

The dragon had regained its focus. It hunched over Hudson and bared its fangs with a deep, echoing growl. My stomach lurched with a primal dread. "We have to do something!" I whispered frantically. "It's going to kill him!"

"Keep this safe for me, would ya?" Nellie passed the tin photo case to Jackaby and pushed herself up. She slid a silver canister out of the pocket of her dress. The stubby tube of flash powder was capped with a simple cork. She stood and peered over the ledge.

Jackaby grabbed her jacket. "What are you doing?"

"I'm in the newspaper business, sweetheart." She pulled away and hopped out of the trench. "Drawing attention is what we do." The little cork dropped to the ground as Nellie launched into a run.

The dragon regarded her as she approached. Its lips pulled back in a terrible toothy grin, as though her charge amused it. She barreled forward undeterred and let the canister fly. It hit the campfire dead-on, and she threw an arm over her eyes as the whole world went white.

The brilliant burst remained painted across my eyes even when the flash had died away, and I strained to see through the afterimage. The blast had sent charred, glowing logs rolling along across the dirt, and gradually the outline of the hulking beast gained definition above them. Its head was turning this way and that as it tried to shake off its own blindness. It took me another moment to find Nellie. She was at Hudson's side, straightening with the harpoon gun in her grasp. The weapon's stock was broad, its barrel like a bulky cannon, but she held it firmly and spun toward the colossus.

Nellie Fuller was the very picture of greatness, brave and unstoppable—until the beast's jaws closed around her.

Chapter Thirty-Two

I watched in horror and disbelief. The creature's long, wicked fangs sank deep into Nellie's torso, and the harpoon gun dropped to the ground. With a toss of its head, the dragon whipped Nellie high into the air. She landed atop the fossils with a sickening thump, as lifeless as a rag doll.

I felt numb. The world was spinning. I was going to be sick.

The dragon did not pause for a moment, turning back to its prey almost before the woman's body was still. Hudson, who had seemed so massive and hardy, looked like a field mouse at the feet of a mountain lion. A vivid ruby stain spread from the dragon's lips and down its scaly chin. It spread its jaws wide, and the air was pierced by a screech.

The beast raised its head, and the shrill screech grew louder. It took me several seconds to realize that the sound was not coming from the dragon, but from somewhere far above us. I blinked into the amber sky, my mind still reeling. The grating shriek intensified, and before the creature could react, a red-bronze streak exploded out of the clouds.

"Rosie?" I breathed. The bird hammered into the dragon's head at full speed, spinning the colossus off balance and sending it tumbling sideways. Its leathery wings flapped once as it tried to steady itself, but before it could regain its senses, Rosie drove another blow into its chest, leading with her razor-sharp beak. By the time a handful of shimmering emerald scales had clattered to the rocky ground beneath the dragon, Rosie was already circling a hundred feet above, positioning herself for another dive. She could not possibly outmuscle the tremendous dragon, but still she cried out and struck at the beast, like a finch harassing a hawk. More scales dropped away from the beast's chest.

The dragon was catching on, ducking away from the worst of her attacks, and making lunges to snap the bird from the air when she flew in close. It was far too slow, though, and she wove around the beast, peppering it with aggravating jabs and screeching into the back of its head. Rosie baited it and dodged the monstrous jaws again and again, and the two gradually began to move away from the trapper.

From beside me came a voice, which at first swept past

my senses like a muffled echo. Jackaby shook my shoulder. "Now!" he was saying. "Quickly, Miss Rook!" He climbed out of the furrow, keeping his head low and his eyes on the battling beasts. I followed, scrambling to catch my footing as we hurried over to Hudson's motionless form.

"Is he . . . ?" I began.

"He's alive," Jackaby confirmed. "But only just. He should be dead, by all accounts, but he's stubborn like that. Help me lift him."

Jackaby stripped the trapper of his heavy bandolier and the belt of nasty hooks, and we pulled him onto his back. With Jackaby at the man's feet and me tugging at his arms, we managed to drag Hudson to the edge of the trench.

"In you go," my employer instructed. I slipped back into the furrow and tried in vain to get a good handle on the trapper's bulky shoulders from beneath.

"What now?" I called up.

"Catch!" Jackaby gave the body a shove, and I found myself suddenly buried under an enormous pile of Hank Hudson. I pushed and dragged my way out from under him, trying as hard as I could not to abuse the injured man any more than we already had. As I pulled myself free, I found the little climbing axe I had dropped lodged in the dirt beside me. I plucked it up and peeked over the edge of the embankment.

"Jackaby?" I called. "What are you doing?"

"We've been given our chance, at great cost," he said.

"Slim though it may be, I intend to take it before it is too late." He was making his way toward what was left of the little campfire and the pile of Hudson's weapons. "I hope my aim has improved since the last time I fired a harpoon. *That* was quite the soiree."

"Have you got a backup plan in case you miss?" I whispered urgently.

"Have you been paying attention?" he called back to me. "This *is* our backup plan—or perhaps it is the backup to our backup plan. That harpoon is still our best shot. If I can't land it, then I'm down to hoping I give the brute indigestion."

I swallowed, turning my attention back to the clashing creatures. The dragon was enraged and battered, with scoring along its rough hide and multiple patches of broken scales. Rosie had left several tattered rips in the giant's leathery wings as well. She was still circling and diving, but was not moving as nimbly as she had when the skirmish began.

As she swooped for another blow to the beast's head, the dragon lunged suddenly and viciously. Rosie ducked beneath the gnashing teeth, but the motion forced her into a shallow arc. The dragon's long, jagged tail whipped up and caught her as she passed. She was powerless to avoid it, pinwheeling out of control to land in a cloud of dust.

The dragon roared, deep and thundering, but its triumphant victory call was cut short. I did not hear the weapon discharge over the din of the creature's bellowing, but I saw, as if in slow motion, the harpoon sailing through the air. It struck the dragon solidly in the chest. A foot higher and it might have slipped through the broken scales to do some damage, but instead our best shot clanked off the dense hide and thudded into the dirt below.

The dragon swallowed its roar in surprise and turned its golden eyes to my employer. Jackaby tossed the spent harpoon gun aside and drew the dull machete from his belt. Silhouetted against the firelight, it was almost possible to imagine that he was some brave knight from the storybooks. My desperate mind could turn his ragged coat into a cape and the rusty blade into a sword—although it refused to let the atrocious knit cap become a shining helmet. Even delusions have their limits.

Jackaby stood alone against the looming dragon. "Well, Peanut?" he called out. "Shall we finish this?"

The dragon licked its chops. It stretched its sinewy muscles and advanced. The creature was fifty feet long, four stories tall, with teeth like longswords and talons that could tear through heavy timbers like toothpicks. Jackaby stood unwavering as it approached.

It was fifty yards away, then thirty, then ten, its limbs pumping rhythmically like massive pistons. Its wings scraped deep troughs in the dirt to either side as it came at him. Jackaby did not flinch. His eyes were focused on the few gaps in the towering monster's armor that Rosie had afforded us. He might as well have been gauging where to throw a pebble at an oncoming train. The dragon's golden eyes flashed with fury and hunger, and even from across the site I could hear its stomach rumbling in anticipation of its next meal.

A thought sparked in my brain. I took a deep breath as it built, held tightly to my axe, and vaulted out of the trench. The dragon's head reared back as it prepared to lunge at Jackaby, the scales along its muscular neck glistening blue green in the last of the flickering firelight.

I threw myself forward into a frantic dash over the uneven terrain. Ahead of me, a flaming, soot-black log had rolled from the little campfire. Without breaking stride, I skewered it on the point of my axe and leapt the last few feet to my employer's side. With a graceless heave, I lobbed the firewood, axe and all, into the dragon's mouth and slammed into Jackaby, allowing my momentum to knock us both beyond the path of the creature's snapping jaws.

Almost as soon as we had hit the ground, Jackaby was back on his feet, pulling me to mine. His urgent tug threw me back the way I had come. I careened forward, half stumbling, half racing, until I was close enough to dive back into the trench. I landed hard in the furrow and spun around. Jackaby was not far behind. Above him, the dragon seemed not to have noticed what had happened at first—but then the smoldering log slid down its gullet. I watched the creature's face contort. It craned its emerald neck and stared at its own distended belly. Jackaby leapt. He looked as though he might fall short—right up to the moment the dragon exploded.

It is odd to think back on it now, but in my memory there is no boom or bang to accompany the eruption—rather the sudden, deafening absence of sound. The blast knocked me flat against the ground and sent Jackaby flying over my head to slam into the opposite wall of the trench. He nearly tumbled beyond it, but managed to half fall, half pull himself down into the furrow beside Hank Hudson. Several seconds after the initial blast, in the deadened silence of the aftershock, we began to feel the heat.

I have never before, nor ever since, seen a fire like that dragon's flame. When I was young, I used to clamber into bed while the maid was laying out the linens. She would hold the ends of a bedsheet and toss it high in the air, letting it slowly drift down on top of me. The fire hung in the air like that sheet, rippling and billowing, and then settling gradually downward with surreal gentleness to blanket the landscape. It moved constantly, hypnotically, folding together ruby reds and brilliant oranges. Flickering white wisps shot past eddies of fluid gold as the undulating sheet descended.

I lay in the dust, stupefied as the bright, spreading expanse draped toward us. Whether from the pressing heat or the blinding light, my eyes snapped shut. I held my arms out in front of my face instinctively, waiting for the searing wave of flames to land. The heat intensified for what felt like an eternity, but then abated, easing into a dull warmth without the sting of a burn. I opened my eyes.

For a moment I could not understand what I was seeing. Above me hung a young woman with a golden complexion. Her long brown hair had slipped free from a loose bun, hanging disheveled about her temples. Her face was smudged with dirt, and a dark gash ran along one cheek. The image repeated in scores of long mirrors, like a shattered-looking glass. I blinked, realizing that the face was my own, and refocused my eyes. Rosie's golden wing stretched over me, sparkling in the dancing light of the flames.

To either side of us, the trench had become a wicked channel of fire, but already the flames were beginning to ebb. Whatever supernaturally volatile compound had fed the explosion, it was not eternal, and the licking tongues of flame found little purchase on the dusty earth. When they had died down to a shallow burn, Rosie pushed herself up and cocked her head at the crumpled body of Hank Hudson. He had been half buried in a cascade of dirt from the side of the furrow, but a faint wheeze escaped the trapper's lips.

Satisfied, the golden bird lifted herself up and shook a spray of sparkling embers from her back. She hobbled unsteadily as she stepped away. Her foot had been injured in the fight, but with two great sweeping wing strokes, she launched herself gracefully into the darkness. I could not see well enough to tell if the sun was still setting or if the stars had come out. A dark curtain of smoke hung heavily above the dig site, and in just a few moments Rosie had vanished into the black as well.

Jackaby was the next to recover. "That," he said sitting up, "was remarkably effective. Are you all right, Miss Rook?"

I nodded. "I think so, sir." I pulled one leg free of the loose dirt that had slid over it and quickly patted down the hem of my dress where an ember was threatening to scorch its way to my legs.

"Did you anticipate the full combustive potential of that maneuver?" he asked.

"Maybe not on that scale," I admitted, brushing off the dust and soot that had settled over my shirtwaist. "You said it was all dragon on the inside, but it didn't have any of the instincts . . . which means it didn't know about the flint. With all that natural fuel inside it, I figured it was like the flash powder—explosives just waiting for a spark."

"Right. Brilliant. It never swallowed the flint for ignition." Jackaby nodded. "And apparently it never learned to vent its reserves, either. Quick thinking, Miss Rook." He stood, running a hand through his dark, tangled mess of hair as he took in the sight. "Damn," he cursed. "I mean, I'm glad we're alive and all that—to be honest I wasn't sure how it might go for a bit, there. But still, it *was* one of a kind."

I swallowed, pushing myself up to standing as well.

"With all due respect, sir, I am perfectly all right with the notion of dragons remaining extinct."

"I'm not talking about that brute. That is a shame as well, I suppose—not his fault, really, but that's the nature of the beast. Chameleomorphs are rare, but they're hardly one of a kind. My hat, on the other hand, was made from the wool of one of the sole surviving yeti of the Swiss Alps, dyed in ink mixed by Baba Yaga herself, and painstakingly knit by a wood nymph named Agatha, expressly for me."

"You're bothered about your hat?"

"It was a birthday present. It had sentimental value."

I pulled myself out of the trench to survey the damage. At first I was not certain I had climbed up the correct side of the soot-blackened ditch, and when the reality of the scene washed over me, I blanched. The explosion had decimated the landscape. There was nothing left of the colossal dragon save a smoldering fire pit carved into the hilltop and the occasional scraps of ash that drifted to the earth like snowflakes. My eyes stung as I scanned the hill. I could find no trace of the indomitable Nellie Fuller.

Even the fossils she had fallen on had been obliterated. Only a few splinters of bone littered the hilltop. The most spectacular scientific discovery in modern history had been reduced to charred scraps no larger than my pinkie. Not even Horner and Lamb could be bothered to argue over these leftovers.

All across the blackened hilltop, pools of greasy fire

danced, and the destruction reached well beyond the dig site. A ring of charred earth half a mile wide bespoke the range of the explosion, and all around its perimeter trees and grass were crackling with orange flames. I cast my gaze down the hill. The field was ablaze. The already damaged barn had been leveled completely, and the Brisbee farmhouse had been ravaged by the blast. A broad section of the nearest wall had caved in, and what little had not been destroyed was now being eagerly consumed by a healthy fire. The farm was gone. The fossils were gone. Nellie Fuller was dead. I sat down on the edge of the trench and watched the ashes spin for a moment while I caught my breath.

Jackaby came over quietly and sat beside me. "There is a solemn dignity in a funeral by fire," he said softly. "It is an honorable tradition in many cultures."

I wiped a tear from my cheek with a soot-streaked hand and nodded. Nellie would certainly have preferred to leave this world in a glorious blaze than to remain left on the edges of it like a discarded rag. My throat felt tight.

Jackaby reached down and plucked from the ash a pale sliver. It might have been dragon bone, but it was no larger than a pine needle. He tucked it into his jacket anyway. "I must admit," he said. "I did not give paleontology enough credit. This pursuit of yours turned out to be of monumental importance after all—and your performance in it admirable."

"That is . . . generous, Mr. Jackaby," I said, "but we are

literally sitting in the ashes of a disaster we completely failed to prevent. What this pursuit of mine really turned out to be is an especially spectacular failure."

Jackaby shook his head. "Miss Rook," he said, "the greatest figures in history are never the ones who avoid failure, but those who march chin-up through countless failures, one after the next, until they come upon the occasional victory." He put a hand on my shoulder. "Failure is not the opposite of success—it's a part of it. And as failures go," he added with a lopsided grin, "this one was really spectacular, wasn't it?"

The firelight bobbed merrily in my employer's eyes, and behind him the roof of the farmhouse collapsed into a smoldering heap. I sighed, and in spite of myself I managed a weak smile. "It really was, sir."

Chapter Thirty-Three

It was not especially difficult to find spare lumber to construct a crude litter on which to carry Hank Hudson. Finding lumber that had not caught fire was slightly more difficult, but not impossible, and after some careful salvaging, we managed the task. Between the two of us, we hauled the burly, unconscious figure to his carriage at the bottom of the hill. The thick pine trees we had parked beside for shade had served the far nobler purpose of shielding the stalwart horses from the brunt of the firestorm. The heavy burlap of the cart's cover had been scorched in thick swatches where the flames had shot between the trees, but the animals were miraculously unhurt. The mighty steeds stamped their hooves as we came toward them in the semidarkness, but they did not bolt. We had just set Hudson down at the rear of the cart, when Charlie came racing up the road. He was not the Charlie I would have expected.

Having abandoned discretion, he was bounding hard and fast on all fours in full canine form. He held nothing back, raw strength pulsing just beneath his fur with the rhythm of each stride. He slowed as he caught sight of us, padding to a stop and panting heavily beside the cart. His deep brown eyes looked hastily from me to Jackaby. His eyes were the one part of Charlie that seemed constant, however the rest of him transformed.

"If you intend to make yourself useful," Jackaby said, "you would fare better with a pair of hands."

Charlie's furry head dipped down to glance at his own shaggy body. He looked up at me and then back to my employer sheepishly.

"Oh, of course," said Jackaby. He pulled off his bulky coat and laid it over the hound's back. Charlie trotted behind the carriage and emerged a moment later, buttoning the coat over his human body. The garment was long on him, but it did not hang as loosely over Charlie's broad shoulders as it did on Jackaby.

"Thank you, Detective. I apologize. I'm generally more careful to prepare. I just saw the fire, and I did not dare delay . . ." He caught my eye and stammered a little. "I–I am very relieved to find you in one piece."

"Not all of us, I'm afraid." Jackaby indicated Hudson.

"Oh no. He looks half-dead." Charlie's face paled as he eyed the trapper's wrist and the blood-soaked bandages.

"Indeed." Jackaby nodded. "And if we don't get him some proper attention soon, he'll be all dead."

The two of them maneuvered the litter into the back of the trapper's cart, while I moved aside the most violent instruments cluttering up the carriage. We draped the warm hide over the trapper, and Jackaby climbed back into the driver's box to take the reins. I agreed to remain in the rear to attend to the trapper, though I felt about as qualified playing nurse as I had felt playing knight.

Charlie opted to run ahead to fetch a change of attire from his cabin while we started the cart down the packed dirt road. He met us at the crossing a few minutes later, clad in a spare set of his policeman's blues. He climbed into the cart with me, taking a seat on the other side of Hudson. I filled him in on the details of the story he had missed, including Nellie Fuller's final moments, and he nodded somberly.

"I should have been there to help," he said when I had finished.

"I'm thankful you were not. The last monster we faced was nearly the end of you, if you recall. You may not remember it as well as I do, but it was *you* we had to carry through the night last time. I like it better when you're around at the end of my catastrophes."

The cart jostled as we crossed through the twin bluffs

and out of the valley, and the soft hide began to slide off the trapper. Charlie and I both grabbed for it, and in the darkness of the carriage my fingers caught hold of his, just for a moment. He smiled shyly and pulled back his hand, turning his attention to the trapper, but I saw his cheeks flush ever so slightly as we rattled onward.

We scarcely spoke again until the cart had rolled into Gadston, and then he hopped out and became a part of the busy rush to help Hudson into the small-town hospital. It was a meager facility, sharing a building with the barbershop, but it was better than the dirty trench or bumping carriage. The town physician was summoned, and lights began to glow up and down the street as curious neighbors awoke to the commotion. Once the trapper had been delivered into more capable hands, Charlie bid a hasty goodbye and rushed off to coordinate teams to combat the fires before they did too much damage in the valley.

When the commotion died down, I found myself standing beside my employer on the sidewalk. "Well," he said, "he has a strong heartbeat. That's a good sign."

"You think Mr. Hudson will be all right, then?" I asked.

"Oh, he'll survive. His aura is getting stronger already. You know, I think a good hook will suit him quite well, actually. He'll look a bit like Tyr, the old Norse god who lost his hand to a monstrous wolf—which, I think, will make Hudson happy in the end. He is a remarkable man . . . but it wasn't *his* heart I was talking about."

"No?"

"That Barker fellow," he said. "You mentioned botching things *romantically* earlier. I assume you meant with him. Your own heart nearly goes into palpitations in close proximity. Yes, I take it from your flushed complexion I've got it correctly. Good, I'm not always so keen when it comes to matters of affection."

"Mr. Jackaby, I hardly think . . ."

"I've no intention of discussing your amorous preoccupations at any length—believe me, it's no more pleasant for me than it is for you. I merely wish to remind you of what I said about failure. Chin up. March right through it. The only paths you can't travel are the ones you block yourself—so don't let the fear of failure stop you from trying in the first place. That boy has a good heart, and it was beating rather quickly back there, too."

"Mr. Jackaby, if I'm not mistaken, you're trying to be sweet."

"I'm being factual. I might also add that canine heart rates are nearly double the average human's, so my assessment may be moot. All the same"—he gave me a firm pat on the shoulder—"buck up. You're dreadful company when you're melancholy."

Chapter Thirty-Four

The Gadston locals did a commendable job suppressing the forest fire. The unruly blaze had already begun to spread, but the villagers formed a brigade. They rushed the valley with wide water barrels and carts laden with rakes, pitchforks, and tarpaulins. I don't know how they managed the feat, but somehow they kept the flames at bay during the night, and by morning the inferno had burned itself out. The sky was dark with heavy gray rain clouds that promised to open up at any moment and finish off the few errant embers.

I felt a little trepidation as I stepped out of my room at the inn. I had scarcely slept, and I was wearing a torn dress that smelled of smoke and earth—but I needn't have worried. The little restaurant next door was full of tired, happy men slapping one another on the backs with soot-black hands. The whole town seemed to be talking about the fire. The general belief, as I gleaned from the snippets I overheard, was that one of the big metal tent poles up at Brisbee's had probably attracted a lightning bolt. I could not bring myself to set the story straight. I had seen what really happened, and the lightning explanation sounded infinitely more plausible.

Jackaby came strolling across the street just as I emerged. He handed me a ticket. "We're on the morning train to New Fiddleham," he said. "Seven o'clock."

"So soon?" I glanced at the big clock above the town hall. It was a quarter past six already. "Can't we wait until this afternoon at least? All of my things are back at Charlie's cabin."

"Mr. Barker has very kindly seen to that already. He brought my satchel and your valise to the inn this morning."

"Wait, this morning? Isn't *this* this morning? When did you get up?"

"I never sleep more than a few hours at a time. Not since I inherited my particular gifts. One of the troubles that comes of seeing *beyond the pale* is that one also sees beyond the eyelids."

"You can see—I mean *see* see—even when you're sleeping?"

"I can never not see."

"Do you ever dream?"

"Vividly," said Jackaby. "Which makes discerning the

reality I am perceiving from the fiction of my imagination all the more troubling. It took me many years as a young man to become accustomed to the unnerving sensation. The nightmares were . . ." He stopped, his eyes as gray as the storm clouds above us. He seemed caught in a memory.

"Yes?"

"Nightmarish. We should be going. I'll fetch the bags and we can leave."

In a few minutes we were making our way down Gadston's quiet main street. The little hospital where we had deposited Hank Hudson was en route to the station house, and Jackaby and I stopped in to pay our respects. The big trapper looked pale and tired, but he lifted his head as we entered.

"Howdy, little lady," he managed in a hoarse whisper. "Hiya, Jackaby. Yer little police friend filled me in on what happened after I blacked out."

"You've spoken to Charlie already?" I said. "It's scarcely past dawn! Does anyone in America actually sleep?"

"Hah!" The trapper chuckled and then coughed, breathing heavily and letting his eyes close for a moment. "I owe you folks more'n I can ever–"

Jackaby cut in. "Yes, you do. That was stupid."

Hank nodded soberly.

"And reckless."

He nodded again.

"And also extraordinary. Did you notice the imbrication of the scales?"

"Layered like a boa's but tougher'n nails." Hank's eyes twinkled. "Real purdy, too."

Jackaby smiled and reached into his coat, and then he paused. "It will *never* happen again, yes?"

"You don't have ta tell me twice. I'd tie a lil' ribbon 'round my finger to remind myself, but"—the trapper held up his wrist, shrouded in fresh white bandages—"I think I learned me a lesson I ain't prone ta forget any time soon."

Jackaby nodded. He pulled out a blue-green scale and passed it to Hudson. "It was a catastrophic mistake, old friend, but as you say, it was a very pretty one."

Hudson took the scale in his good hand and flipped it over between his fingers, smiling weakly. He palmed it and turned to me. "How 'bout you, little lady?" he said. "I won't blame you if you hate me. I can't undo the damage I done."

Nellie Fuller's face hung in my mind, and I swallowed hard. Hudson looked no less tortured. It had been in his effort to keep her safe that he had nearly succumbed to the same fate. "I'm furious," I said, gently, "but I might have a soft spot for spectacular failures right now. Just try to get some rest."

"Thanks, kiddo."

"I'll ask Charlie to look in on you while you rest up," Jackaby said. "He's a good man."

Hudson nodded. "Wasn't sure about him at first, but he's more'n earned my respect. Wish I could say I'd done the same. Gonna take a while 'fore he has good reason to trust me." Apparently my expression revealed more than I had realized, because he looked at my face and chuckled. "You don't have to worry about me, though. I ain't gonna do no harm to a guy just 'cause he's a shape-shifter. Hell—I've known a few dogs I liked better'n folk."

I faltered. "You know?"

"Gimme some more credit than that, little lady. A set of footprints changes step-by-step from a big old hound into a man—it ain't exactly hard for an open-minded man of the woods ta put two an' two together. I can respect a fella's right to his own secrets, though—and I didn't wanna go makin' things uncomfortable for the poor guy—so I kept my yap shut. I sure wouldn't mind if he decided to let me in on it, though. I'd love ta go huntin' with a tracker like him someday. Ain't many bloodhounds you can take out for a brew with ya after the hunt. Hah!"

We bade the trapper good-bye, and I left the hospital with at least that weight lifted from my shoulders. "I'm glad he seems to be on the mend," I said. "I wasn't sure . . ."

"Hudson never ceases to surprise me," Jackaby said.

"You never did tell me. How did you come to be friends with a man like Hudson?" I asked.

"I'm a likable man," said Jackaby. "Lots of people are friends with me."

"Tell me," I said. "Please? Where did you two meet?"

"Where else?" he said. "On the hunt." The dusty road passed beneath us for a few steps while he reflected. "That may have been one of my own more spectacular failures, to tell the truth. A peculiar case had brought me up into the Appalachian Mountains in pursuit of a party of paranormal hunters. The Wild Hunt has a long tradition all across Scandinavia and England, down to Germany and France. European settlers brought the hunt here, and the hunt brought me to a snow-swept mountainside. Rather than trying in vain to keep up with the hunters, I had the foresight to position myself in the presence of their prey. As I predicted, the hunt came to me. I was admittedly less prepared for what that would entail."

"So, Hudson was part of the Wild Hunt?" I asked.

"No. Like me, he had tracked the quarry on his own. It was a beautiful animal. The white stag. I've never seen its equal. I was enamored with the beast. It was powerful and graceful, and faster than any living thing has any right to be. By the time the first arrows had landed, it was gone. I was not so quick. If it weren't for the trapper, I would not have survived the encounter. I thought he was a great bear at first—cloaked in a heavy hide and bounding out in front of me. He planted himself in front of the oncoming stampede like a living barricade and took the worst of the onslaught. By the time it was over, he had collapsed, exhausted. The hide looked like the world's largest porcupine, and more than a few barbed arrowheads had found their way through to his arm and side. He woke while I was treating him, and what do you think he said?"

"Ouch?" I guessed.

"He said, 'They didn't kill the stag, did they?' He didn't want the beautiful creature to die. Of course they hadn't killed it. The whole point of the white stag is to be pursued. It can never really be caught. It is the spirit of the hunt, the thrill of the chase. I think deep down Hudson respects that more than anyone."

"That's why you're letting him get away with all of this, aren't you?" I asked.

Jackaby looked back at me over his shoulder. "I think we can glaze over a few of the finer points of our report to Marlowe," he said. "Hudson may have carried the match for a while, but he didn't start this fire. He's a good man, and I think he's been punished enough."

The engine was already steaming when Jackaby and I reached the train station. A porter ushered us toward our car, and I passed my suitcase up to Jackaby. I had one foot aboard the train, when a familiar face sidled through the station house doors. Charlie Barker stepped onto the platform, a black-and-white sheepdog trotting obediently at his heels.

My heart leapt, and I tried not to smile too broadly as I hurried across the steamy walkway to meet him. "Shouldn't you be resting, Officer?"

"I've had a few matters to attend to," Charlie said. His eyes looked tired and his complexion ashen, but he seemed relieved to have made it on time.

"So I see." I reached down and petted Toby between the ears, and he leaned into my leg affectionately.

"He needed a home for the time being," Charlie said. "He's a good dog. He stayed with the Pendletons all the way to Saint Isidore's. I found him outside the door to the funeral home this morning. There will be a service in a few days." He spoke quietly, gently, as if nervous Toby might overhear him.

"And for Nellie Fuller?" I said.

"I've sent word to her family in New Fiddleham. There are no remains to send home, but a few of her effects survived the fire." He hung his head. "It does not feel right to diminish the valor of her actions, but her official cause of death is a lightning strike."

I sighed. Marlowe had made himself clear that it was in the public good to keep the case covert, and avoid stirring up panic with reports of dangerous creatures running amok. Blowing up a house with a fifty-foot mythical beast was the opposite of covert. However, I had to agree with Charlie that it did not feel right.

"Misters Horner and Lamb send their regards, by the way," he said.

"You've given them a visit as well? Is there anyone you've not spoken to since I saw you last?"

"It has been a busy night," he said. "I wanted to sort out the last of this mess before turning in. You'll be happy to hear those two are getting along. Well, they've stopped actively looking for rocks to hurl at each other, at least."

"I imagine not having any bones to bicker over may have helped," I said.

Charlie nodded. "It does simplify matters. Mr. Horner is bound for South Dakota this afternoon. He's already found another dig to attach himself to. Mr. Brisbee is making the most of the situation as well, it seems. I think it might be for the best."

"What might be for the best?"

"The farmer is settling his affairs in town, but he'll be accompanying Mr. Horner to the next excavation. I was not expecting Mr. Brisbee to take the news quite so well, but he seems more than ready to leave the valley behind and do some exploring of his own. He said it's what his late wife would have wanted, and I'm inclined to agree. He's given Lamb permission to root through whatever's left on the dig site and take it back to the university."

"You have had a full dance card, haven't you? I guess I should be proud to have made the list."

"I couldn't let you leave without saying good-bye." He looked into my eyes for several long seconds. I could have wrapped myself up in that gaze like a warm blanket. He opened his mouth as if to speak, but then paused and glanced bashfully away. He cleared his throat and straightened his uniform. "And thank you, of course, for all of your help," he said, "on behalf of the police department of Gad's Valley."

It began to rain gently. The little station's narrow awning did nothing, and the first drops chilled my neck and pattered against Charlie's uniform, darkening the blue in uneven speckles.

"Of course," I said, using every ounce of effort to will the disappointment out of my face. "We were only too happy to be of service, Mr. Barker."

He looked on the verge of speaking again, when the conductor bellowed, "All aboard!" and the whistle screeched.

"I suppose I had better . . ." I gestured toward the train.

Charlie nodded. "Good-bye, Miss Rook."

"Good-bye, Mr. Barker."

I turned and started for the car. This was the moment in the stories when the bold young man would come running after the lady. He would sweep her into a romantic embrace, and for one storybook moment everything would be safe and happy and perfect. In the wake of my grand disaster, with my dress still caked in blood and dust and soot, I really could have used a storybook moment. Just one.

I stepped aboard the train alone. Romance was for saps, I reminded myself. There was work to be done. Innocent victims had not yet been avenged, their killer still at large. I was not the *safe and happy* type. I stood at the end of the cramped hallway, feeling the opposite of great. Jackaby's head poked out of a cabin halfway down the car. "Miss Rook? Do you know which way you're going? We're over here."

"Yes," I said, but then I stopped and stood a little straighter. "Yes–I know precisely where I'm going." I turned on my heels and took a deep breath. "I'm choosing both paths." And I marched back out to the platform.

Charlie had not moved. His uniform had slowly grown darker as the specks of rain melted together. His eyebrows rose as he watched me cross the gap, and Toby stood at his side, wagging his tail in the drizzling rain. I kept my head high and did not stop until Charlie and I stood toe-to-toe.

"Miss Rook?"

"I'm going to kiss you now," I said. "That's going to happen."

Charlie swallowed, his eyes wide, and then he nodded quickly. I held on firmly to his starched lapel and leaned forward on the balls of my feet. His lips were warm in the chilly rain, and his fingers were gentle and delicate, if just a little tremulous, as he lifted a hand to my cheek. I dropped back to my heels. "I have work to do," I said. "I matter. What I do matters. But I look forward to hearing from you. Oh—and the next time you write," I said as he blinked his eyes open dreamily, "I do hope you will address me as Abigail."

The whistle blew again, and I hurried onto the train. The car rumbled to life as I dropped into my seat, and we gradually chugged forward. I slid myself close to the rain-spattered window and waved good-bye. Charlie stood on the wet platform just where I had left him. He looked tired and damp, but a smile was spreading from ear to ear. He waved back earnestly until the train sped up and the station slid out of view.

Jackaby had buried his nose in an old ragged book before Gadston was behind us. I sat back happily on my seat cushion, revisiting the moment in my mind. It was, with every reprise, an unquestionable victory—my first unadulterated success in weeks. I felt my cheeks dimpling in a sappy schoolgirl smile, and I could not even bother to bring myself to feign composure.

"Did you see . . . ?" I asked Jackaby.

He lowered the book just beneath his line of sight and eyed me inscrutably. "I see that you are . . ." He sighed gently. "Giddy."

"He kissed me."

"*You* kissed *him*—which I believe was rather the point. I'm sure Miss Cavanaugh will be very proud when you inform her. Please feel free to contain your enthusiasm until such time as you can share it with her."

"He kissed me *back*, though."

"Oh for Pete's sake. Melancholy might have been more palatable."

He ducked back behind his dusty book, and I contented myself with watching the rain stream gracefully across the window as the countryside rolled past.

Chapter Thirty-Five

Commissioner Marlowe stood on the platform with his arms crossed as we disembarked. He had the cheerful demeanor of someone who has been beaten about the face all night with a sock full of porridge—only even more so than usual.

"Marlowe," said Jackaby.

"Jackaby," said Marlowe.

"Commissioner," I said. "How kind of you to come to greet us. How did you even know that we would be on . . ."

"I make a habit of being well-informed," he said.

Jackaby nodded. "Then I take it you're already well-informed about the most recent developments in Gad's Valley? Well, that saves a great deal of paperwork on our end, doesn't it? Miss Rook, you should be pleased about that."

"I could use a few more details," Marlowe said.

"And you shall have them," Jackaby replied. "Rook is splendid with details—lots of descriptive adjectives. Maybe too many."

"We'll have a full report to you by tomorrow," I assured the commissioner.

"Good," Marlowe grunted. "In the meantime, I'll take the abridged version. Did you learn anything at all?"

I nodded. "There's someone in the center of all this," I said. A vision of the pale man hung in my mind. He had stolen the tooth. He had guided Hudson to breed the dragon. He had known about the chameleomorphs. I swallowed. He had killed all those people. "I don't know who he is or what he's up to—but he's the one to watch out for. I'll give you a full description in our report."

"Do," said Marlowe. He turned back to my employer. "And for future reference, *discretion* doesn't generally involve blowing a crime scene off the map with a fireball the size of an ocean liner."

"No?" said Jackaby. "Language can be such a nuanced art."

"The papers are calling it a lightning strike," I said. "So you needn't worry about your townspeople being gripped by any new monster panic."

Marlowe looked unsatisfied, but he nodded and we parted ways.

"Perhaps they should be," Jackaby murmured as we left the station.

Jackaby took a circuitous route back to his building, which led us past the New Fiddleham post office. He sidled up to the drop box and pulled a slim package wrapped in brown paper from his pocket. On the front, in his barely legible scrawl, I made out the word *Chronicle.*

"Sir?" I said.

"Miss Fuller asked me to keep this safe for her," he said. "I don't believe her final wish was that it gather dust on our shelves, do you?"

I stared. "Marlowe is not going to be happy about that," I said.

"That is a distinct possibility." He nodded thoughtfully. "I don't even know if the plates survived the heat. I guess we'll just have to see what develops, won't we?" The brown paper package made a tinny clank as it slid down the mail chute.

Jackaby's cheery red door was a welcome sight at the end of our journey. I had once been reluctant to step inside the unusual abode on Augur Lane, but now I could not have been happier to be home. Dropping my luggage in the foyer, I breezed through the zigzagging hallway and slowed only a little as I rounded the steps up the spiral staircase. I had so much to tell Jenny. I hoped that she would be proud of me, but I knew I still had to make amends for the way we had left things. I tiptoed to her door and knocked quietly.

"Jenny?" I said. When no one answered, I tried the

handle. It turned easily, and I pushed the door ajar just the barest sliver. "Jenny, it's Abigail. Are you still cross with me? It's all right if you are—I would be, too. I am sorry. Jenny?"

I was careful not to step over the threshold again without permission, but I let her door swing open and peered inside. The room was a portrait of destruction, and Jenny was nowhere to be seen. Bits of porcelain still lay scattered about the floor, a few shards embedded in the plaster of the walls. The armoire lay broken on its side, and the mattress and bed frame were on opposite sides of the room. Feathers littering the floor were the only signs that there had ever been a pillow. The windows had been stripped of their curtains, and in spite of the warmth of the noonday sun, I could see that the panes had frosted over. The only piece of furniture upright was the nightstand, which appeared to be unmolested by the spectral storm. A little sprig of bittersweets had been retrieved from the floor and placed daintily atop it, like a wreath atop a Roman pedestal. I stared at the scene for several seconds, and then shut the door quietly and went back down the steps.

Jackaby was in his laboratory when I reached the ground floor again. He was scowling and muttering to himself, drumming his fingers along the molten glass that had once been Jenny's amber vase. "What's on your mind, sir?"

"A catalyst."

"A what?"

"A catalyst. It's an agent that accelerates a chemical

reaction. It's not directly responsible for the results, just for how quickly they get out of hand."

"You mean like a mysterious pale man who nudges a few key elements into place until, before we know it, we've got a life-sized dragon blowing up over our heads?"

"You're becoming remarkably astute, Miss Rook. I do believe I've been a positive influence on you. The real question is *why?*"

"Well, it did destroy the crime scene, and any hopes we had of finding evidence."

"But he couldn't predict that it would end like that. So why give Hudson the bone in the first place?"

I froze. "Because he wasn't giving Hudson a bone. He was throwing one for us."

Jackaby raised his eyebrows curiously.

"Poor Mrs. Pendleton knew the answer ages ago. You don't throw a dog a bone because it's got any real meat left on it—you throw a dog a bone to keep it busy. The stranger knew about the chameleomorphs because he knew about Mrs. Beaumont, so he knew exactly what Hudson had in his hands when he gave him the bone. It didn't matter what happened then, because whatever it was, it was going to be bad, and we were sure to go investigate. The murders, the stolen fossils, the impossible beasts—can you think of a more perfect bone to keep us busy? And we've been biting from the start."

Jackaby considered this with a scowl. I waited for him to

tell me I was being foolish and explain it all away, but he only nodded solemnly. "Someone has gone to great lengths to cause this havoc."

"To what end?" I wondered aloud.

"And to what beginning?" Jackaby amended. "If our mysterious stranger engineered this dragon ordeal and the Campbell Street chameleomorphs, what else is he behind? Dangerous irregularities have been occurring with alarming . . . regularity. It is troubling to consider a criminal manufacturing paranormal mayhem. How long has he been at it? Did he orchestrate the reclusive redcap's rise to become a predator in public office? Plant the swarm of brownies on the mayor's lawn? Promote adoption of the Dewey decimal system in libraries across the continent? It's the not knowing I find most irksome."

"The Dewey decimal system?"

"It's gaining popularity. I don't trust it."

"We'll catch him, sir," I said. "I'm sure of it."

"I very much agree, Miss Rook. Now that we know whom we're looking for, we can do more than flounder in his wake. This spectacular failure of ours may prove to be just the catalyst *we* needed to propel ourselves toward the greater triumph." He nodded contentedly. "It makes sense, now. Oh, I feel much better knowing that there is a malevolent force out there, working directly against us at every turn, don't you?"

I smiled feebly. "It's a bright new world, sir."

"Indeed. Speaking of which, you should be happy to hear that Douglas has done a fine job of looking after our little transformative pests. They're all present and accounted for as slightly hairy Gerridae—and the house is still standing, which is nice."

I nodded. "Don't look in Miss Cavanaugh's room any time soon," I said. "Still a bit of progress to be made there. Although she did manage to pick up some of the flowers, so at least she's found her gloves, wherever you hid them," I said.

Jackaby paused with a hand on the door to his office. He scowled and reached into his satchel. "You mean these?" He pulled out a bundle of ladies' gloves. There were two or three pairs in varying states of wear.

"Oh—you kept them with you while we were away? Really? That's a little mean, isn't it?" I thought about the bedroom and the bittersweets. "But then, how . . ." Jackaby stepped into the office, and I followed. A prickly feeling rippled through me, like electricity in the air.

Jenny was perched in the chair behind Jackaby's desk. "Welcome home," she said. She gave our soot-caked clothes a glance. "Have you been cooking again, Jackaby?"

My employer did not answer her. He stared across the desk, and then a perplexed smile crept into the corners of his lips. "Miss Rook. You may want to fetch that little notebook from your valise."

"Sir?"

"Unless I am very much mistaken, we have another case."

The desk, I realized, had been cleared of its usual stacks of books and clutter, and a single file sat squarely in the center. Printed neatly on the front was the name *Jenny Cavanaugh*. The spectral figure reached out one bare, translucent hand and pushed the file firmly across the desk toward Jackaby. It slid without the slightest hesitation at her touch, coming to rest in front of my employer. A handful of notes and newspaper clippings slipped free from the bundle with words like *victim, murder* and *brutal* in bold type. Among them I saw a familiar image—an eerie man, pale and stout, and dressed in black. The hairs on the back of my neck pricked up.

"It's time." Jenny nodded. "I'm ready to know."

Supplemental Material

It was some time after the business of the bones that I remembered to ask Jackaby about his unlikely version of the voyage of the HMS *Beagle*. According to my employer, during his expedition in Mauritius, Darwin discovered and brought back to England a live specimen of a chameleomorph. Upon his return, he was given a private conference with King William IV, who marveled at the creature's ability to mimic its prey. The old monarch ordered Darwin to keep the existence of the creature an absolute secret.

The king feared he might die before his niece, Victoria, turned eighteen, since this would make the Duchess of Kent regent, ruling on behalf of Victoria until she came of age. The old monarch loathed the duchess. He made it quite clear that he hoped the power of the throne might never fall into the duchess's hands, but his health was failing fast, and Victoria's birthday was still months away. As a failsafe, the king ordered Darwin to feed the chameleomorph a steady diet of his own, royal blood. It was his hope that a facsimile king might rule just long enough for Victoria to come of age, if necessary.

Darwin, a loyal subject, reluctantly obeyed. Fortunately, William survived a full month beyond Victoria's birthday, and the bizarre project was aborted—but not before the beast had developed a nearly perfect resemblance to the old man.

With no human language or social cues, the doppelgänger was a grotesque caricature of the king. Most disturbing of all, the thing craved human blood, and it grew violent unless supplied with a meal laced with the stuff. When she learned of the secret, the newly crowned Queen Victoria was horrified and disgusted. She ordered the creature destroyed, along with all of Darwin's notes on the species, lest some immoral soul be tempted to recreate her uncle's abomination in a twisted effort to secure the crown.

Darwin again obliged his ruler, completely editing the monumental discovery out of his *Journal and Remarks* concerning the voyage of the HMS *Beagle*. The findings did fuel his interest in the abilities of organisms to adapt and change, and one can practically see the creature hiding just beneath the words in his subsequent publication of his work, *The Origin of Species.*

Ever the scientist, however, Darwin could not completely destroy such spectacular knowledge, and he created a secret dossier of the entire affair. These documents, never published, were kept in a location known only to Darwin himself.

At the time of his death in 1882, Darwin's dossier resurfaced. How Jackaby came to be in possession of such an impossible artifact I have never learned, but he allowed me to take a quick glimpse at its pages before returning it to the shady Dangerous Documents section of his private library. More than just chameleomorphs, the collection comprised accounts of dozens of unfathomable entities. In the few moments I had with the journal, I saw entries that I fear may never be cleansed from my memory. Strange and exotic grotesqueries seared themselves in my mind, but worse still were the ones all too familiar. It is a profoundly unsettling experience to see childhood nightmares—things recalled as horrid fantasies—laid plain, in perfect detail, upon the page. Jackaby had said not knowing was the worst, but I must confess, on many dark nights since then, I have found myself nostalgic for my ignorance.

Acknowledgments

There are several people I wish to recognize, without whom this series would not exist. Elise Howard has been Jackaby's fairy godmother in so many ways, using her magic to usher it through countless essential transformations. Thank you for helping get my ragged little manuscript all dressed up for the ball. Lucy Carson has stalwartly championed these books, pushing through hell and high water to help my stories weather the storm and see the light of day. Above all, Katrina Santoro has been Jackaby's guardian angel from the start. She has been a sounding board, an anchor to reality, and wings to greater heights. She has saved readers from some of my worst writing and helped bring out some of my best. At my most confident I consider myself her creative equal, and my efforts to earn the right to that claim have made Jackaby a better series and me a better writer. Thank you for everything. Thank you to my parents—Eleanor, Russ, Janice, Frank, Kacy, and Joe—and to all my friends and family. I am humbled to have received such supportive encouragement from so many people every step of the way.